AN AMERICAN GIRL

An American Girl

A NOVEL

RICHARD FELLINGER

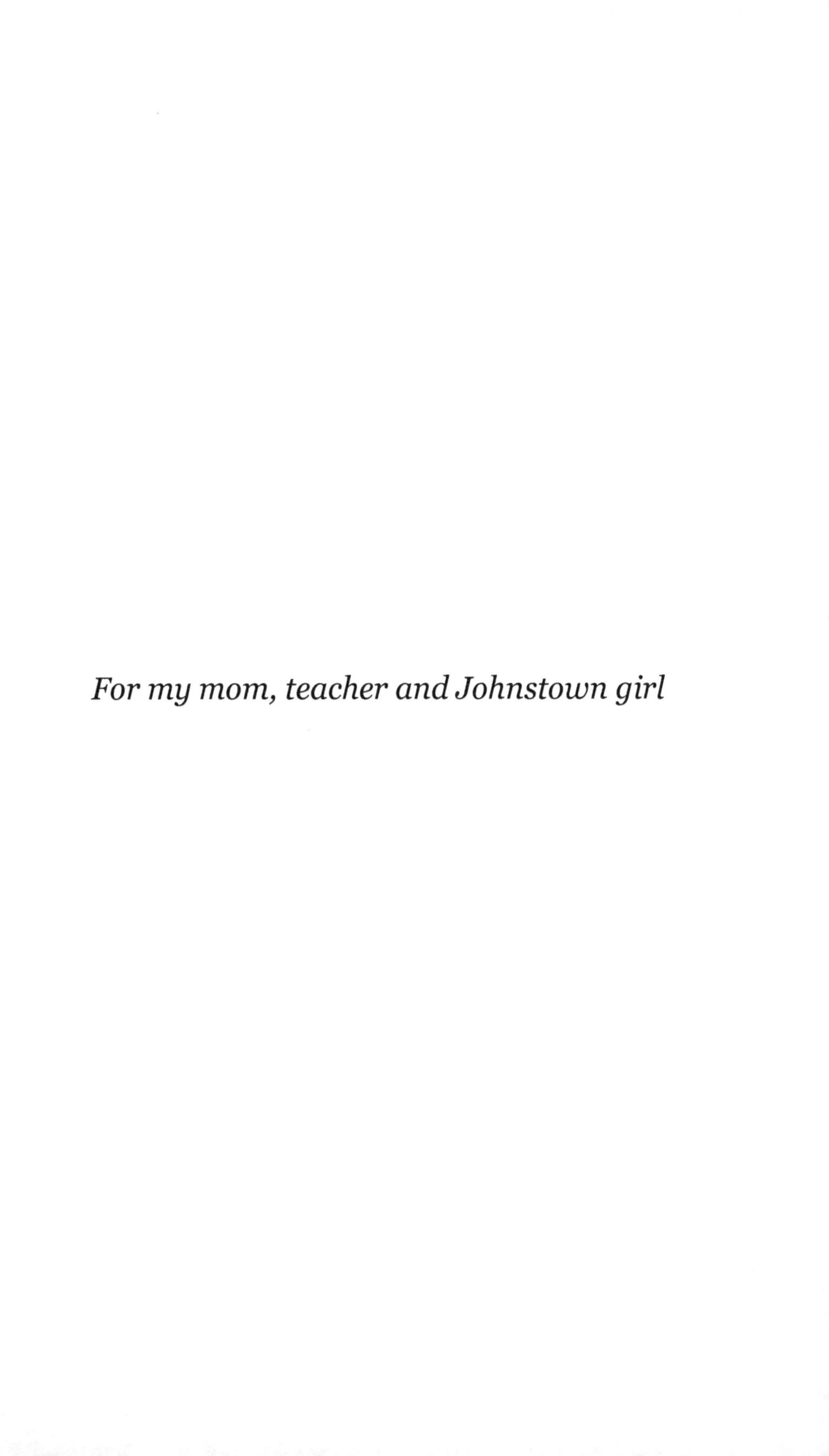

For my mom, teacher and Johnstown girl

ONE

IT HAPPENS EVERY TIME. Without fail, every single time. Every time Emma parks beside the encampment under the I-83 bridge, she gets choked up, has to pause and pull herself together before climbing out of her little blue Honda. And so it is today, a crisp Saturday morning in early spring, her son in the passenger seat, his mitt on his hand and orange Little League cap pulled low over his eyes. Usually she comes alone, but today she overslept and didn't want Thomas to be late for his game, so she figured she'd bring him along as she delivers her weekly care package.

Deep breath, and she calls him, hoping he has enough charge left on his phone this morning.

"Dad," she says. "I'm here."

"Where?"

"The usual spot. On the street."

A minute later she sees him, walking with a hitch toward the car, the hood of his camouflage sweatshirt over his head. She feels a knot tighten in her gut. This is never easy. It's why she waits on the street— the only time she went to the tent, saw his grimy sleeping bag, cardboard flooring, crushed cans of Coke and Bud Light, a milk crate full of his belongings, she broke into sobs.

She tells Thomas to wait, gets out, engine still running, and closes the door behind her—she doesn't want Thomas to hear anything her dad might say. She opens the trunk, lifts out four white plastic grocery bags. This week she's brought toothpaste, hand sanitizer, applesauce, pretzels, SpaghettiOs, bottled water. She drops the bags on the dirt curbside, then stretches out her back.

Her dad appears beside the car, eyeballs Thomas through the window.

"Who's the little terrorist?" her dad asks.

"Don't," she scolds. "He's your grandson, and I hate it when you say things like that."

"I didn't have no terrorist kids."

"Stop it. His name is Thomas, and his dad's parents came from Pakistan. Please call him Thomas." She slams the trunk. "I'm tired of asking you that—please call him Thomas."

He flips his hood off, rotates his head, squints eastward into the morning sun.

"Can you get the bags?" she asks. "My back is bothering me."

"Yeah," he says, and he bends down and gathers them, two in each hand.

"And what about your phone? Does it need charged?"

He gives her a befuddled look.

"Your phone," she says. "Is it in your pocket?"

He sets down two of the bags, pats the pocket of his baggy faded jeans.

"Yeah, I got it here."

"Give it to me," she says.

He hands her the phone, and she sees only six percent power remaining.

"Take those bags back to your tent, and I'll wait here and charge your phone," she says.

She opens her car door, reaches inside and plugs it into the dashboard charger. He lumbers off with the bags.

"How are you doing, buddy?" she asks Thomas.

"Okay."

"We'll go in about five minutes. Don't worry, you'll be there in time for warm-ups."

She pushes the door closed, crosses her arms and leans back against the car. She heaves a sigh. So much to deal with. The I-83 traffic pulsates up above, and a spring breeze carries the skanky smell of the nearby trash bags piled on the curb. The sun tries to slide underneath the bridge, just a sliver of it angling onto the pavement.

Emma Muller-Farooq has been back home for nine months, and this is her life. After her mom died, after her marriage blew up, after she realized that she couldn't afford to raise her son and work as an adjunct professor in New York, she decided to move back to Central Pennsylvania, look for an affordable apartment and a couple of new adjunct gigs, and make a go of it here. Closer to friends and relatives. Lower cost of living, and family friendly, supposedly. But really, what other choice did she have? Then she learned her dad, who'd always been hard-headed and insensitive, had descended into a mental abyss: He stopped going to work, quit paying his bills, lost touch with reality, and the house was gone to sheriff's sale.

He reappears, plodding down the hard-dirt path from the tents. Emma pokes her head inside the car, checks the progress on the phone. Only 55 percent.

"Let's give it a few more minutes to charge," she tells him.

"Give what a few more minutes?"

"Your phone. It's charging in my car."

He nods. Then there's silence between them. Emma crosses her arms again. He picks at his ear.

"I'd really like to make a doctor appointment for you this week," she says.

"I'm not going," he says.

"He won't bite." She immediately regrets her tone—too cutting— but sometimes she can't help herself.

"Don't matter."

"You're so stubborn," she huffs. "And you frustrate the hell out of me."

She lowers her chin, sees a soiled Q-Tip beside her feet, kicks it aside.

He sticks his hands in his pockets. More silence between them.

They never did have much to talk about. Emma was always closer to her mom, who died during the early days of the pandemic. A nursing supervisor at Harrisburg Suburban Hospital, she was short and plucky, a lot like Emma, and she contracted the virus a year before her planned retirement. She'd married young, worked hard her whole life, and sometimes Emma wondered why she stuck by her father, who drove a beer truck for the biggest distributor in the Harrisburg area and who never seemed to do anything to make her life easier.

Her dad, Joe Muller, is third-generation Pennsylvanian. Pre-World War I people, before the locals developed much animus toward the German immigrants in their midst. His great-grandfather brought his construction skills to this little corner of the world and became a home builder. Built several homes in Cumberland Borough, Emma's hometown, ten minutes west of Harrisburg, if you catch most of the lights, but that's all his descendants know these days. Which exact homes, they've forgotten.

Emma checks the phone again, and now it's at 85 percent, and she decides that's enough for now. She unplugs it and hands it to her dad without saying anything about it.

"We have to go," she says. "Don't forget the van from the mission will be here Monday morning, so be sure to come out for coffee and donuts and anything else they have."

"They're good people," he says.

"Yeah, they are," she says. "And remember, you have a grandson, and his name is Thomas, and he's a good kid, too, a really sweet kid."

***

Her back aches. She's sitting on those rickety bleachers watching the Astros rout the Cubs. This is the Cumberland Little League. Or, as far as Emma's concerned, the grass-and-dirt arena where grown men and even certain women spend their afternoons and weekends hoping their boys turn into gladiators—or at least find a path to a college baseball scholarship. With its proximity to Harrisburg, Cumberland is home to many of the average folks who make the state run—the secretaries and maintenance and highway workers, plus the folks who operate the feed plants and other industries that supply the fruit farms down in Adams County and the cornfields out in Lancaster County. Sitting just west of the affluent inner suburb of Camp Hill, which is home to a tidy sum of lawyers and lobbyists, Cumberland is a town with an inferiority complex.

The Astros usually win—they are one helluva a Little League team. Unfortunately, Thomas is the weak link—he'll never be a gladiator. He has two strikeouts again today, two innings in the outfield with no balls hit his way, which is a relief, in a way, because at least he didn't have the chance to commit any errors.

Thomas inherited Emma's athletic ability—meaning, none. And probably his father's too, though Emma doesn't know exactly what athletic talents he might have. Clearly, she doesn't know as much about him as she'd thought. She met Abid Farooq eleven years ago at the wedding of a college girlfriend. She was immediately smitten with his splendid green eyes and dark wavy hair. He was a digital marketing consultant from New York, smart and progressive, radiating self-confidence, a guy who knew the ways of the world and could navigate it with ease. But when it comes to judging guys, Emma tends to make some really bad errors.

Top of the sixth, last inning, and Thomas comes to bat once more, the Astros holding a 12-3 lead. Emma tries stretching her back, but it doesn't do much good. It's the curse of large breasts on a small frame: Double D, five-foot-three. If she could afford a reduction, or had time for one, she'd do it in a snap, but that's not happening anytime soon.

She pats the pocket of her jeans. In her pocket is a miniature, corked bottle with gold glitter inside. Her friend Tracey, a childhood friend she reconnected with when she moved back home, gave it to her for good luck this semester, called it magic dust, after Emma told her about her semester from hell in the fall: She taught four classes of freshman composition at two different colleges, which meant the usual headaches with two different commutes, two different sets of expectations and everything else, plus all the usual crap like skipped classes, late papers, texting in class, and the mind-numbing repercussions of grading so many crummy papers, and then on top of everything else one kid turned in a plagiarized paper that was available for sale online, then claimed he had no idea because his friend was supposed to write it for him, and when Emma filed a plagiarism case, the dean supported the student, thought he deserved another chance. So yeah, Emma's been carrying her magic dust in her pocket lately.

Contact, she thinks, hopes, pleads. Just make contact. Bat on ball. Is it really that hard? It might be—what does she know? Even a little dribbler to an infielder would be fine, because at least it wouldn't be a strikeout. And just then it happens: the ball dings off of Thomas's bat, rolls slowly to the first baseman, who jogs forward, scoops it up and tags Thomas out as he's sprinting for the bag.

"Yeah! Thomas!" Emma hollers, clapping above her head.

Confused looks come from the other moms in the stands.

After the game, Emma waits for Thomas at the car, her trusty little Honda, 160,000 miles and still going strong, the perfect car for an underemployed adjunct professor. The sun rests high in the sky, and the crispness in the air is gone. Emma feels warm in her gray Princeton sweatshirt. Thomas walks straight from the dugout to the car, black bat bag strapped across his back, his aluminum bat handle sticking out of the top. His jersey is untucked.

"Do you want something from the concession stand?" she asks.

"No." He's mopey.

"Good game," she says, her tone deliberately upbeat.

He shrugs, takes off his bag and shovels it into the back seat.

"You had a nice hit at the end," she says. Same upbeat tone.

"That wasn't a hit," he says. "That was an out. It's only a hit if you get on base."

"Oh."

They get in the car, but she waits to start the engine.

"Do you want to go out for lunch?" she asks, keys still cupped in her hand. "How about pizza?"

"I guess." Still mopey.

"What's wrong, honey?"

"Nothing."

"Something's wrong."

"I don't know. Maybe."

"The game?"

"No. Kind of. I don't know."

"Kind of?"

His shoulders droop, and he tilts his head toward the window, looking away from her. "What's a towelhead?" he asks.

"A what?"

"Justin called me a towelhead."

Emma's jaw drops, her mind buckles.

"He said towelheads can't play baseball," Thomas says.

Her mouth hangs open. She clamps her keys inside her fist. Her chest swells, outrage rising up in her like a mushroom cloud.

"Justin—the coach's son? He said that?"

He nods reluctantly, turns to look at her. "Don't do anything about it."

"Oh, believe me, I'm doing something about it."

She pops out of the car, strides across the parking lot to the Ford F-150, red with tinted windows, parked in the shade under the big tree in the back corner. Scott Bass, six-feet-tall and beer-bellied, is loading a bag of baseball gear into the pickup's bed.

"Excuse me," she says. "Coach?"

"Yeah?" He bangs the door of the bed shut with two beefy hands, turns her way. His orange cap is tilted upward on his large, sweaty forehead. "Uh, huh."

"I'm Emma Muller-Farooq, Thomas's mom." Her eyes burn into him. "We need to have a word."

"Why is that?"

She squares her shoulders, takes a collect-yourself breath. "I just heard something very disturbing. I mean, very disturbing."

"What might that be?" He wipes his brow with the back of his hand.

"Thomas just told me—" She pauses and gulps. "He just told me Justin called him a towelhead."

"Kids say things," he says.

"Yes, they do, and sometimes they say things they shouldn't say. That's my point here."

"I'll have a word with him. I'll tell him about being politically correct." He pulls his keys out of the pocket of his baggy cargo shorts.

"Um," she says, with a double blink of her eyes. "I think it's about more than being politically correct. That's a derogatory term, just like the N-word."

Maybe that caught his attention.

"Yeah, like I said, I'll talk to him." He steps past her, toward the front of the pickup.

"I'm just curious," she says. "Where does a boy that age learn a word like that?"

"I don't know."

"Do you use it at home?"

He stops, one hand on the door handle. With a half-turn of his head, he looks at her from the corner of his eye.

"Listen, I'm just coaching baseball here," he says. "I don't have to answer questions about our home life."

"In that case," she says, "is there a league president or someone I can talk to about this? Because I think it's pretty serious."

"Yeah," he says, opening the pickup door. "His name is on the Web site. Do whatever you want."

TWO

MONDAY MORNING, and the sun is warming the playground. Sweatshirts and windbreakers are strewn along the fence. It's the beginning of fourth-grade recess, and Buchanan Elementary's three fourth-grade classes have combined under the not-so-watchful eye of two teacher's aides. Some kids run and shriek, some climb onto the jungle gym, some form groups and start heated debates over who picks teams and who's it.

Thomas's group plays tag. Danielle Fossberger stands at the center of the group, about to take charge, but there's a dispute over whether it's her turn to pick who's it. Ryan Webster alleges that Danielle picked last week, so it's his turn today. Ashley Clay claims she didn't pick last week, either, so it's her turn today because Ryan picked after her the previous week. Thomas hasn't picked in weeks, but it doesn't matter to him, so he lets the other kids hash it out. Finally Danielle steps aside, concedes to Ashley, who tells Ryan he can pick tomorrow.

At the basketball hoop, a small faction of kids breaks away from the team-picking process. Justin Bass leads them, marching across the pavement after spotting Thomas Farooq.

Ashley points at Michael Baxter: He's it. The rest of the group scatters. Thomas turns and bumps smack into Justin.

"You're a snitch," Justin says.

"Nuh uh," Thomas says.

Michael Baxter notices that Thomas has stopped, an easy prey. He whacks Thomas on the shoulder. "You're it," Michael announces, and runs off.

Thomas rotates his head and watches Michael dash away, then turns back to Justin. His shoulders sag.

"I got in trouble because of you," Justin says, chest out.

Across the playground, the two aides, one middle-aged woman and another thirty-something woman, are engrossed in conversation.

"I told my mom not to say anything," Thomas says.

Ashley, Danielle, Michael, Ryan and the other kids playing tag slow to a jog, circle back toward Thomas. "You're it," Michael reminds him.

Thomas's eyes dart back and forth, between Justin and Michael.

"You're still a snitch," Justin says. He steps forward, into Thomas's face.

The other basketball players have abandoned team picking, have followed Justin, and they've formed a semi-circle behind him. The tag players start to rally behind Thomas. "Why aren't you playing?" Ashley asks.

Justin shoves Thomas, who staggers back two steps, then regains his balance. He feels a jolt of righteous anger, then lunges at Justin, fists flailing. Justin falls under his weight, and they collapse onto the pavement together as the boys and girls around them shout a medley of surprise, outrage, and encouragement.

The aides see the scrum. They run toward it, both of them yelling, "Stop it! Stop it!"

Thomas keeps swinging wildly, and Justin covers his face, blocking his punches with his forearms. One of Thomas's punches grazes Justin's arm and smacks into the pavement, and he stops, screams in pain, and Justin wraps his arms around him, wrestles him face-down into the ground.

The younger aide arrives, grabs Justin by the back of his collar with both hands, pulls at it, and he rolls off of Thomas. The middle-aged aide arrives next, clamps both hands onto Thomas's shoulders. She orders him to get up, and he slowly climbs to his feet, the fingers of his sore hand folded into his other hand.

Justin wiggles free from the younger aide's grasp, pops onto his feet, and the aide scoots between him and Thomas, hunched like a linebacker.

"I didn't do anything," Justin pleads. Snot is smeared across his mouth and chin.

"Yes, he did," Thomas says.

"We saw exactly what both of you were doing," the aide says.

***

Emma gets the call from the school secretary as she's sitting at a red light on Route 230, less than a mile from Penn State-Harrisburg. It's 10:40 a.m., and she has an 11 o'clock class, Rhetoric and Composition, her first of two Monday-Wednesday classes.

"I'll be there in twenty minutes," Emma says.

She pulls off the road, into a CVS parking lot, scrolls her contact list for the English Department secretary, Carole Brady. But before she taps the call button, she hesitates. How many times has she cancelled this class already? At least three times, maybe four—once when she was sick, and once when Thomas was sick, or was it twice when he was sick? And then once for a mental health day, of course. Surprising she hasn't taken more of those. But as it is, this could be the fifth. Not good.

But what choice does she have? Just cancel the damned class.

So she does, but not without asking Carole for a favor: "Do you have to mention this to anyone? I mean, anyone else in the department?"

"Technically, I'm supposed to," Carole says. "I'm supposed to notify the chair. But don't worry, I have a busy day, too, so she'll understand if I forget."

"Thank you *sooo* much," Emma says. "You have my vote for secretary of the year."

"Is that a thing?" Carole asks.

"I don't think so."

"What about your 12:30 class?" Carole asks.

"Oh, shit," Emma says. "I don't know."

"It's up to you."

"Yeah, cancel that, too."

Emma spins the car around, heads back to Buchanan Elementary.

***

This school always feels strange, foreign, like a spaceship that's landed in her backyard. It's a new school, built five years ago to consolidate three aging elementary buildings, which were squat, red-brick buildings with dark, narrow hallways and asbestos in the basement. This one also feels too big for an elementary school. It has an airy rotunda with a wrap-around staircase, tall windows that allow in natural light, a gym and performing arts center which are bigger than those at some high schools, and a long, covered driveway out front for bus drop-offs. Emma parks there, right out front.

She lugs her travel coffee mug with her, en route to the principal's office, even though there are only a couple of sips left in it. She didn't sleep well, so she needs every sip. She received a late-night email reply from the Little League president, who didn't seem to take her complaint very seriously. Though he promised to talk to the coach, he also seemed to downplay the slur: "I also realize that boys will be boys," he wrote.

Principal Eric Sounders is a tall, sandy-haired guy wearing a black tie loosely knotted under a baggy gray sweater. Fortyish, with lanky arms and a belly pouch his sweater doesn't quite cover. Emma's heard people talk about him, and she found it odd the way they refer to him only by his last name—not Eric Sounders, not Mr. Sounders, not Principal Sounders. Just Sounders. Now that she's met him, she gets it; his appearance doesn't command enough respect for anything else.

Sounders apologizes for keeping Emma waiting in a chair outside his office, even though she only had to wait a minute or two.

"I'm happy to meet with you in person," he says when he sits down behind his desk. "But we could have handled this over the phone."

"I'd rather discuss this in person," Emma says. She holds onto her coffee mug but drops her purse on the floor, settles into one of two seats across from his desk, and the empty chair beside her leaves her feeling inadequate. It's a chair meant for spouses, and she has none. Just her, here alone, handling this alone.

Sounders lays out the facts, as reported by the two aides and his follow-up interviews with each boy: Thomas and Justin were on the ground fighting during recess, Thomas claims Justin called him a snitch and pushed him, Justin denies it and claims Thomas started punching him over a team-picking dispute.

"Figures," Emma snorts.

"What figures?" Sounders asks.

"That he'd deny it. There's backstory here, you know."

He folds his hands on top of his desk pad. Long fingers, gnawed fingernails—and no wedding ring. That leaves Emma wondering, because he's rumored to have a high school boy who's often in trouble, has been expelled and is in cyber school. The Sounders rumor is one of the few hometown rumors Emma's heard since she moved back.

Maybe that also explains why his office feels so empty. No visible personal effects, none hanging on the walls, no degrees or awards or family portraits. There is one framed photo on the desk, but Emma can't see who's in it. On a bookshelf behind the desk is a plant that looks half-dead. Emma almost feels sorry for Sounders—a man with nothing to be proud of.

"Yes, backstory," he says. "There often is."

"Justin called Thomas a towelhead yesterday at a baseball game."

He winces. "Thomas didn't tell me that. Could that be why Justin called him a snitch?"

"No doubt. I reported it to the coach, who's Justin's dad."

"I see."

"So I'm dealing with a lot here," Emma says. The empty chair catches her attention again. It's burgundy leather, no armrests, matches the chair she's sitting in, looks like it's spent a few decades here in the principal's office. She feels like the chair is staring at her, judging her, and she resents that damned chair. She wishes she could pick it up and move it back against the wall, but that would be too weird at a time like this.

Sounders scratches behind his ear, with a look on his face that suggests he's thinking about something.

"I should mention something to you," he says. "It might be something you're interested in. Our district is working on a diversity plan. It's happening at the school board level, and I'm sitting on the committee, and you might want to be involved, provide some input. I think everyone welcomes parental input."

"Yes, um, yes," she says, surprised at the sudden turn in their conversation. Maybe she has an ally here? She takes a sip of cold coffee, her mind thrumming, and she doesn't know what else to say.

"Good," he says, picking up a pen. "I'll make a note of it."

"I'm an educator, too, you know. I teach English at Cumberland College and Penn State-Harrisburg."

"Perfect."

"Not so perfect," she says. "I'm an adjunct. But still, I just wanted to point out my qualifications."

"Certainly." He sets down the pen, a back-to-business look on his face. "As for today's incident, our policy calls for a suspension. But because this is Thomas's first, we can do an in-school suspension."

"But he didn't start it," Emma says, and she realizes she sounds like a schoolgirl, but there've been too many twists in her day and this conversation to control her tone any better. "And remember the backstory I just told you about."

Sounders scratches behind his ear again, this time looking flustered. "Yes, I understand, but he was still involved in the fight."

"What happens to Justin?"

"I talked to his parents by phone, and we're handling his situation according to policy."

"So you won't tell me."

He folds his hands again. "We're handling everything according to school policy."

"Where is Thomas now?"

"He's back in class. He seemed to have calmed down after I talked to him, so I think he's going to be fine. He also saw our school nurse, because he hit his hand on the ground during the incident, but his hand is fine, too."

She lifts her coffee mug to her lips, starts to take another sip, but decides against it—too cold, too yucky, and not doing her much good anyway. She looks at that damned empty chair again. Sounders looks at the round clock on the wall.

"He'll be going to lunch soon," Sounders says. "I'll check in and make sure everything's okay."

"Can I take him out to lunch? Or take him home?"

He gives a little nod. "You may take him home, but considering that he seemed fine, I really think reintegrating him in the school environment would be best. Kids are surprisingly resilient."

"Unlike adults, you mean?"

He lets out a chuckle. "Maybe so."

"Okay, then," Emma says, releasing a sigh, picking up her purse. "I guess my work here is done."

"I'll be in touch," Sounders says. "And I will get you the contact info for the diversity plan."

Emma stands up. "Goodbye," she says under her breath to the empty chair. "I hope we never meet again."

Sounders tilts his head, baffled. Apparently she didn't say it far enough under her breath.

"I was talking to the chair," Emma says. "I didn't mean you."

***

Maybe she should have listened to Thomas, Saturday in the car, when he pleaded with her not to tell anyone. He knew something like this would happen. He knew more than her about how kids treat each other, maybe even a little something about life, how the stakes are raised. But of course, he's a smart kid, from smart parents—Emma herself was valedictorian at Cumberland Area Senior High (or CASH, as the well-worn acronym goes) and earned a tuition-free ticket to Princeton. So much promise, and she always worked hard, too, did things the right way, but somehow the right things didn't happen to her. No, her life wasn't supposed to turn out like this, low on sleep, cancelling classes at her low-pay adjunct job to go sit in the principal's office, no man in her life, except her dad at the encampment, constantly worried about her only son's place in this world, and now, wondering what she's going to say to him when he comes home after a fight with a racist bully.

Should she apologize?

No, no, don't think like that. This isn't your fault. Don't blame yourself.

She tosses her purse into the passenger seat of her Honda, sits in the driver seat waiting to start the car, and she feels her shoulders wilt, the weight of those large breasts tugging on her back again, the weight of the world squashing her, and she breaks down and cries.

THREE

CUMBERLAND COLLEGE SITS on the southwestern edge of Cumberland Borough, a little college built by the Lutherans in the late 1700s before the town grew to support the state Capitol and the farms to the south and west. On mornings like this, a breezy Tuesday in spring, it smells bad. When the winds blow a certain way, they pick up the scents from the farms outside of town, and the place smells like cow manure.

Today, the winds blow that way. Even in class, the manure smell lingers in Emma's nostrils.

She has just returned graded papers to her 11 a.m. composition class, and thank God she was able to do that, with all the crap going on in her life right now. Her next class, her 2 p.m. class, will have to wait, because their papers are still jammed in her teaching bag, ungraded. As are two packs of papers from her Monday-Wednesday classes at Penn State-Harrisburg.

The room clears out, about half of the students paired up and chatting affably, the rest with heads down, checking their phones as they mosey out the door. Except Madeline Garvanitis. She's standing in front of the instructor's desk, both hands on her paper. She's a small, thin girl, about Emma's height, with pink streaks in her hair. She has a question.

"Yes, Madeline?" Emma says.

"Is this right?" Madeline asks, a quiver in her voice.

"Is what right?"

"The grade."

"Let me see it," Emma says.

Madeline hands her the paper, and Emma looks it over. On the back is written B+.

"Yeah, that's right," Emma says, and gives the paper back.

Madeline's eyes are wide, disbelieving. "I've never received a B before."

"It's not a B. It's a B-*plus*," Emma says.

"But I've never received a B before."

"You're forgetting the plus," Emma says. "Don't forget the plus part."

"I just don't understand," Madeline sputters.

"Let me see it," Emma says, sticking out her hand. Madeline hands the paper back, and Emma looks it over again.

It's a four-page paper, and Emma spots several grammar errors, plus a fragment and some clunky phrasing, all marked in Emma's purple pen.

"It's not a bad paper," Emma says. "But there are some grammar and phrasing issues that I noted for you. Did you see my notes?"

"Yeah, but I'm in the Honors Program." She twirls a strand of pink hair.

"One B-plus on one paper isn't going to jeopardize your Honors status."

"I guess."

Think like a mom, Emma tells herself. Moments like this, Emma tries to remember that every one of her students has parents—or at least one parent, like Thomas—who consider that student the most important being in the world. She wishes she could remember that more often, because when she stops to think about it, she's deeply aware of how special each of these kids are to someone back home. But in the midst of the daily grind, all of her responsibilities, the single-mom thing, worrying about Thomas, jobs at two colleges, paying the bills on that lousy adjunct pay, all those papers to grade, and all those little hassles, the constant need to remind those students to stay off their phones in class and keep their buds out of their ears, thinking like a mom for every kid is damned near impossible.

"Let me tell you something," Emma says, and she hopes her tone is soothing enough. "And I hope this is helpful, I really do—there are worse things in life than a B-plus. Much worse."

***

Lunch, the Hornet's Nest. It's the campus deli, named after the campus mascot, and Emma prefers it to the cafeteria, because the salad bar is better and she can grab her own small table without having to interact with any students. Who may or may not be conspiring to buy a paper or brooding over a B-plus.

Emma sits down with her small salad, just a dollop of ranch dressing, her usual, at a table along the wall. She knows it should be a working lunch, because she has all of those papers yet to grade, but she decides against it, leaves the papers in her bag. She just needs a breather.

At the table in front of her is a tall guy in a green pullover, with a hornet on the chest and Cumberland Baseball stitched underneath. He's sitting with a short, stocky guy, also in a green pullover, whose back is to Emma. The tall guy looks about forty, maybe mid-forties, has thick chestnut hair with gray streaks above the ears. Cleanly shaven, a nice face. He's attractive.

But more importantly, Cumberland Baseball.

"Excuse me," Emma says. "Do you mind if I join you?"

The tall guy is in mid-chew, a sandwich, and he shrugs and glances at his lunch partner for approval. "Sure," he says.

It's a four-seat table, and the short guy, whose pullover says Cumberland Wrestling, slides over so Emma can have the seat along the aisle.

"Thank you so much," Emma says, dumping her purse and teaching bag on the floor beside their table. She grabs her salad and slides into the aisle seat.

They do introductions: The tall guy is the head baseball coach, Myles Halprin, and the short guy is the head wrestling coach, Pat McKay.

"Look," Emma says, casting an apologetic look toward Pat, then zeroing in on Myles. "Here's my dilemma. It's this baseball thing."

"Yes, baseball certainly is a thing," Myles says. "Would you call it a thing, Pat?"

"It's a thing."

"Did you say you teach English?" Myles asks Emma. His face brightens: He's enjoying giving her a little teasing.

"Very funny, yes." She stabs a bite of salad with her fork.

"I'm sorry," Myles says, turning serious. "We shouldn't poke fun at the faculty. We need their support, especially when our athletes are in their class."

Pat nods agreeably.

"I do have two wrestlers in class," Emma says.

"How are they doing?" Pat asks, chomping on a chicken wing.

"Not well."

A knowing look crosses Pat's face, and he finishes his wing.

"What about baseball players?" Myles asks, lifting his sandwich.

Emma notices that he's not wearing a wedding ring. "I don't think I have any."

"So then," Myles says. "What about this whole baseball thing? Why is it such a dilemma?"

"My son loves it. He plays Little League, but he's not very good."

"How old is he?"

"Nine."

"What positions does he play?"

"Outfield, mostly."

"Right," Myles says knowingly, takes his last bite of sandwich.

Emma's phone buzzes. She reaches into her purse for it, recognizes the number. It's Buchanan Elementary.

"I better take this," she tells the coaches. She gets up from the table, finds a spot in the back by an empty table, covers her mouth with her free hand as she answers.

It's Eric Sounders.

"Is something wrong?" Emma asks.

"No, not that I'm aware of," Sounders says, yet he sounds nervous. "I'm calling with a little invitation, of sorts."

"Oh."

"I'm having coffee this weekend with Gayle Brungard. She's the board member who's chairing our Diversity Committee. Would you like to join us?"

"I think so, yes."

"It's just a casual little chat, touching base about things. No need to dress up or anything." The last line comes off as a clumsy attempt at humor.

"I haven't had the chance to put much thought into anything yet, to be honest."

"That's fine," Sounders says. "I'll introduce you to her, and you can get a sense of some of the things the committee is working on. She's easy to get along with."

"Okay, great."

"How's three o'clock Sunday at Java Hut?"

"It's a date," Emma says, and then cringes. She didn't say that, did she? Yep, face it, she did. "Sorry, that's not, um, not what I meant."

"It's okay," Sounders says. "I'll try to grab a booth when I get there, so you won't have to worry about any spats with any chairs."

"Very funny."

Dingbat. That's probably his opinion of her, she thinks as they say goodbye. Two conversations with him, two peculiar moments, and now he's started teasing her. But how does one advertise their academic credentials during the fickle developments of daily life? Not easy. Oh, well, he clearly has his own issues, so what's it matter, as long as he's nice about things. Mental note: Wear your Princeton sweatshirt on Sunday.

Back at the coaches' table, Myles and Pat have finished their lunches and pushed their plates aside. Pat yawns.

"Everything okay?" Myles asks.

"Yes, I think. I don't know, but probably. Or just maybe. Who knows, but probably."

"Glad to hear it," Myles says.

"I'm dealing with a lot crap these days," Emma says, digging back into her salad.

"Including this whole baseball thing," Myles says.

"Yes," Emma says, mid-chew. "Exactly."

"Bring your son to one of our games on Saturday," Myles says. "We have a double-header at home, and I'll show him around the dugout afterward, introduce him to some of the guys. He should like that, and maybe it will give him a little boost of confidence."

"Really?" Emma says. "Okay, yeah, sure. What time?"

"First game is at eleven o'clock, and the second game usually starts by two."

Not a date, Emma tells herself. Do not tell this guy it's a date. Do. Not.

"It's a, uh...it's a deal."

***

At home, Taco Tuesday. Thomas loves it. Emma, not so much, but she makes her tacos with ground chicken, so they're healthier that way. Then there's that heavy taco smell, which tends to hang in their apartment, so she burns sweet-scented candles in the kitchen.

They've rented one half of a green-sided twin home on the east side of town, 451 Cedar Street, half a block from the train tracks. It's okay. Could use some updates—newer carpet, nicer kitchen counters, a fresh coat of paint on the front porch—but it's big and spacey and has a fenced-in backyard. On Thomas's bedroom window, as well as the window to the extra bedroom, a faded sticker informs firefighters of decades past that there are children inside. Too bad, though, the landlord doesn't mow the yard regularly; the other half of the twin has been vacant since she moved in, so he clearly doesn't invest much money or effort in the property.

Thomas crunches on his first taco, spills shredded lettuce in front of him, leaves a saucy stain above his lip. Emma sits down at their little kitchen table with two tacos on her plate.

"I want to ask you something," she says. "It's about baseball."

"Yeah?"

She hands him a napkin, but he doesn't use it.

"After all of this stuff with Justin," Emma says, "do you want to ask for a trade?"

"No."

"Why not?"

"Trades don't happen in our league." He bites back into his taco, avoiding eye contact with his mom.

"I've heard of trades. They're a thing in baseball, right?"

He finishes his bite of taco, rolls his eyes. "Yeah, but not in our league."

Emma rubs her eyes with her fingertips. They've been irritated lately, her contacts bothering her more than usual. Seems like everything is bothering her more than usual. That little bottle of magic dust isn't helping anything.

"I think a trade might be a good idea," Emma says. "I could ask the league president about it, although he doesn't seem to take me very seriously."

"No, mom."

"Okay." That's it, she thinks. Don't push it. Remember what happened the last time she pushed someone's buttons against his will—the fight at school. So let it go; she asked, she tried. Maybe that's all you should do sometimes.

FOUR

THAT ADORABLE LITTLE BLOND English professor isn't in the stands for Game One. Myles must have scanned the stands a half-dozen times looking for her, and he would have seen her, because there's only the one set of stands, right behind home plate, and they're never packed because the games only attract a smattering of parents and girlfriends. The Hornets capture the first game, a 3-2 nailbiter over Elizabethtown College, and that leaves Myles satisfied, at least. He's a .500 coach, doesn't aspire to be anything more. Know your limits, he believes. Never aim too high or push too hard, because you'll only have to live with the bruising burden of disappointment.

That's exactly what happened to him, his own baseball career. He was a hard-throwing lefthander in the Phillies system, got his call-up to the majors at age 25, but never threw a single pitch in the big leagues. Because he didn't know his limits. In his very first practice after his late-August call-up, after a whole summer of throwing heaters in the minors, he pushed himself too hard, determined to prove himself and hit 100 mph on the radar gun, and felt a pop in his elbow. Then came surgery and another year in the minors, but he was never the same pitcher again. So he came home to his alma mater, Cumberland College, where Myles had once broken just about every pitching record in the books and been named back-to-back conference player of the year, and where the baseball coach was nearing retirement. One year as his assistant and Myles was hired as head coach. Ever since, his record has hovered barely above .500.

So for Game Two, his main goal is to spot that cute English professor in the stands.

Second inning, he sees her, top corner, on the home side, leaning back against the grandstand fence. Her hair is up in a clip and she's wearing jeans and a pink windbreaker, and the boy beside her is—her son? He doesn't look like her. Olive-skinned, dark hair poking out from underneath his orange baseball cap. Could he be adopted? Wait, no, her last name: What was it? An unusual name, hyphenated, but she wasn't wearing a ring. He's certain of that, even though he can't remember her name. Doesn't matter. The boy's her son; that's what she said—her son was struggling in Little League.

After the second inning, as the Cumberland fielders grab their hats and gloves and the click-clack sound of spikes fills the dugout, Myles strolls over to the stands, hands stuffed in the front pocket of his green Hornets hoodie. The sun is out, there's a slight chill in the air, and only the faint smell of manure wafts across campus.

"Glad you could make it," he says, looking up at them.

"We're glad you invited us," Emma says. "Sorry we're late."

"You're not late. Plenty of baseball left."

Emma introduces Thomas as her son.

"I hear you're a big baseball fan," Myles says.

Thomas smiles and nods.

"Stick around," Myles says. "And come down to the gate behind the dugout after the game. I'll show you around."

Another smile and nod from Thomas.

"Thank you *so* much," Emma says.

Cumberland loses Game Two 9-1, and the click-clack of spikes fills the dugout as Myles heads to the gate behind the dugout. Emma and Thomas are waiting there, and Myles opens the gate, offers a hand to Thomas, and they exchange a limp handshake. Myles turns back toward the dugout, and with a wave of his hand he encourages them to follow.

Emma pats Thomas on the back, says, "Go ahead." He follows Myles, she follows Thomas. Seeing the two of them in front of her like that, Emma realizes just how tall Myles is. Even taller than she thought. At least a foot taller than her.

"Guys, this is Thomas," Myles says to the dugout full of ballplayers. "He's a recruit, wants to play here someday."

"Actually, I was thinking Ivy League," Emma says to no one in particular. "But whatever."

A couple of ballplayers offer Thomas a fist bump. The rest finish packing their gear, and they trickle onto the field for cleanup duty. They grab rakes and pull tarps and scatter across the infield; some head out to the bullpen.

Emma recognizes one of the players, Shayne Kline, one of the last guys to zip up his gear. He was in her class in the fall, barely passed. He looks her way, sheepishly, and says, "Hey, professor."

"Hey, Shayne," she says.

"Hey, Lantini," Myles says to one of the ballplayers. "Why don't you take Thomas with you, show him how to put the bases away."

"Got it," Lantini says.

"I don't know who does it in your league," Myles tells Thomas, "but in college, the ballplayers have to take care of the field. It's one of their duties."

"Our coaches do it," Thomas says.

"Not here," Myles says.

"Let's go, buddy," Lantini says to Thomas, and they jog out to the infield together.

Myles plops himself onto the dugout bench, tells Emma to have a seat, too. She does, and they're alone in the dugout. She fiddles with the zipper on her windbreaker, slides it down, then back up.

"I wish I could get my students to work like this," she says. "You'll have to tell me what your secret is."

"Easy," Myles says as he leans back and crosses those long legs of his. "I control their playing time."

She chuckles. "I had Shayne in class last fall."

"And how did that go?"

"Not well. I'm a little surprised he's allowed to play."

"He's lucky," Myles says. "He avoided academic probation by the skin of his teeth, but he's doing better this semester."

"That's good."

"Overall, we have a good team G.P.A.," Myles says. "Nearly 3.0. Some of the guys make Dean's List every semester, like Lantini. He's an engineering major, really smart. But we always have a few guys that drag us down and need a kick in the ass."

"Next time I have a baseball player in class," Emma says, "I'm telling him I know his coach. And maybe I'll mention something about his coach's willingness to kick him in the ass."

"Go for it," he says. "Whatever it takes."

Emma watches as Thomas and Lantini each lug a base to a shed at the end of the dugout. Myles uncrosses his legs. She slides down the zipper on her windbreaker.

"And by the way," she says, "thank you for pairing Thomas up with the guy on the Dean's List."

"I always ask Lantini to show my best recruits around."

She grins, and she's surprised how comfortable and happy she feels here—in a freakin' baseball dugout. She leans against the backrest. Her back feels good today, thank God.

"Did you happen to hear what I said about the Ivy League, though?" she asks.

He takes off his green cap, forks his hand through his hair. "Let me guess," he says. "You're a product of an Ivy."

"That's right. Princeton."

"Ooh." He replaces his cap, pulls the bill down on his forehead.

"What about you?" she asks.

"I'm a Hornet. I grew up around here, went to high school at Camp Hill."

"Ooh, our rival."

"So you're a CASH grad?"

"That's right."

"My brother's the school board president. He moved over here about fifteen years ago. Cheaper taxes than Camp Hill. He has two girls at CASH."

"That's a coincidence," she says. "I'm having coffee tomorrow with one of the school board members. A woman named Gayle Brungard."

"I don't know her," Myles says, recrossing his legs. "I don't get involved in school board politics."

"Well, it looks like I am."

"Good luck to you." His sarcasm is laced with cynicism.

"Hah, it can't be that bad."

A few ballplayers lumber into the dugout.

Thomas hauls the last base to the shed. Myles shouts some instructions to the guys spreading a tarp over the pitcher's mound. More players arrive back in the dugout.

When Thomas and Lantini return, Myles stands up, pulls a green jersey off a peg on the dugout wall. It's an older version of a Hornets jersey, stitched with gold letters and the number 2, some fraying around the number. He tosses it to Thomas.

"This is for you," he says. "Thanks for coming to our game today. It might be big, but it's the smallest size we have."

Thomas holds up the jersey, wide-eyed.

"What do you say?" Emma instructs him.

"Thanks."

"That's so nice," Emma tells Myles, as she squeezes Thomas' shoulder. "This has all been so nice. Can I make you dinner or something?"

He doesn't skip a beat, because this sort of invitation has been his goal all along: "Sure."

FIVE

WHAT WOULD YOU CALL THIS—a dinner date? Just dinner with a guy? But what's the difference? Or should she downplay it even further—dinner with a colleague? It certainly is dinner, and he's certainly a guy, and they do work at the same college together, all true. But a date?

She calls Tracey, asks if she'll watch Thomas for the night. Tracey and her husband have two girls, one a year older than Thomas and one a year younger, they live only three blocks away, and Thomas gets along well with them.

"I'm having dinner with a guy," Emma says.

"Cool—so it's a date?" Tracey says.

"I didn't say that."

"It sounds like one."

"Call it what you want," Emma says. "He's a little older than me, I think."

"How much older?"

"I'd guess he's in his early forties. So five years, maybe. Could be six or seven."

"Guess what?" Tracey says. "That's no big deal at all. Five or six years was a big deal when we were in high school, but not anymore. If he's single and has a steady job, you go for it."

Tracey asks for more details—about him, about what she plans to cook and wear. Emma tries to stick to the facts: college baseball coach, very tall, angel hair aioli, and a champagne-colored V-neck sweater, just the right amount of cleavage.

After she drops Thomas off at Tracey's and makes a last-minute effort to clean up the place—Thomas's Nerf gun bullets are everywhere—she takes a quick shower and gives her hair a light curl.

And then doubt creeps up on her. Was this dinner invite too hasty? What does she really know about the guy? Why is he single at his age?

It's just dinner, she reminds herself. And he was so sweet to Thomas, who's wearing that baggy green jersey now, and who might wear it tomorrow and the next day, too. But still, Abid. A cautionary tale if there ever was one. Will she ever trust a guy again? She'll have to try. If she's ever going to meet someone, she'll have to take chances.

***

It was a June wedding. Becca Thompson, the bride, was Emma's roommate at Princeton, all four years. Emma drove to the wedding fighting mixed emotions, happy for her friend but dejected about her own prospects for finding a life partner. Becca was from Long Branch, New Jersey, and the wedding reception was at a supper club on the boardwalk in Asbury Park. Abid was a college friend of the groom from Syracuse.

She spotted him at the bar, ordering drinks. He carried himself well, with an easy poise; she saw it in the way he unfolded a couple of bills and flicked them on the bar for a tip. His hair was thick and wavy, his eyes bright and arresting. As he turned away from the bartender, a drink in each hand, their eyes met.

They chatted, they drank, they danced. Drank some more, danced some more. They even did the Chicken Dance together. When he suggested they check out the boardwalk together, she didn't hesitate to say yes, so he grabbed her hand and they weaved through the dance crowd, everyone shouting along with the throb of the music, *Don't Stop Believin'*, and headed out into the lush Asbury night.

A light breeze carried the sugary smell of crepes from a food stand. A bright, three-quarter moon hung high in the sky, the ocean glimmering underneath it. Hand in hand, they sauntered over to the boardwalk railing. Gaggles of people passed by, their voices cheery and muffled. A police siren wailed in the distance.

Abid leaned back against the railing, and Emma leaned into him, craned her neck and offered him a kiss. Nothing hot and heavy, just a peck. Then she bounced onto her tiptoes, wrapped her arm around his neck, planted a hot-and-heavy kiss on him. His lips tasted bourbon-sweet. The kiss lasted a full minute before she dropped onto her heels.

"Oh, God," she whispered, and she felt dizzy with delight. "Let's go somewhere alone."

They had a shotgun wedding, Emma six months pregnant, and it was a difficult pregnancy. The problem was HG, Hyperemesis Gravidarum, which her doctor described as morning sickness times one hundred. No known cause, but a small percentage of mothers suffer from it: constant nausea, often severe, regular vomiting. Which meant a steady diet of bland foods, lots of mashed potatoes and rice, and frequent prenatal visits. And water, water, water, as long as she could stomach it.

Thomas was born two weeks premature, five pounds and ten ounces, on the small side but not quite low birth weight, not officially. All in all, mother and baby both came out of it okay.

When Thomas was four, Abid told her he had to start traveling for work. Emma wondered if it was really necessary—shouldn't a digital marketing consultant be able to handle things remotely? But she wasn't overly suspicious, even though the travel didn't mesh with his increasing fondness for the screen. Be it his laptop or phone, he was always on one. She also began to suspect that he was real-life avoidant, didn't like to tackle problems head on, and she considered it an occupational hazard, and maybe he recognized that about himself, so he forced himself to go see people for important business matters. His consulting business was brisk.

He was away when Thomas caught a bad flu bug. A fever of one-hundred and four, nasty cough, green phlegm coming up in gobs, his thick black hair pasted to his little forehead. He was up in the middle of the night, sweating bullets after his second day of symptoms, when she texted Abid. "I'm really worried about him. Do you think I should take him to the hospital?"

"I can't be bothered with stuff like this," Abid texted back. "Can u handle it?"

"What the fuck?" she typed back.

No reply. She waited a few minutes and thumbed another message: "He's your responsibility too, you know."

Still no reply. She waited another minute and sent another message: "Are you there?"

This time he replied: "I told you, I can't deal with this right now."

"Can't, or don't want to?"

Again, no reply. She thought about it for a few minutes, stewing, imagining what the hell he was up to, and typed another question: "Who is she?"

The next morning, after Emma managed barely three hours sleep, she got her reply. "Okay, you must know," he wrote. "I suppose it's time I told you. I think it would be best for everyone if we divorced."

A digital divorce demand. That's what she got.

As it played out, with Emma starting the long and lonely process of tackling life as a single mom, she often wondered if she should have done something differently. But if so, what? Where was the different path she should have chosen? Did she miss it as a wife and mother, or did she choose the wrong course on that seductive night in Asbury Park? She could never settle on an answer. Because every time she recalled an interaction with Abid, she was reminded that without him, there would be no Thomas.

***

Myles stands on Emma's welcome mat in his scuffed penny loafers and tan chinos, and his insides suddenly skitter. Of course, he knew what he was doing all along when he invited her to a ballgame and accepted her invitation to dinner, but standing there on her welcome mat, seeing her green-sided twin home that needs some fresh paint, after pressing her doorbell, this feels real. He feels out of his league. An English professor—really, dude? Shouldn't you know your limits?

He massages his chest with his fingertips, steadying his emotions and preparing himself for...well, he doesn't really know what. What's the last good book he read—will he get quizzed on things like that? His back aches again. He jams his palms into his lower back and bows his upper half backwards, stretching. He has to stop sleeping on that damn couch, drag himself to bed at night rather than letting the drone of the television lull him to sleep. But hey, he has to stop doing a lot of things. Or at least cut back. Like drinking and gambling. He hears footsteps coming to the door, and he blows out a choppy breath, a last-ditch attempt at collecting himself.

And then the door opens wide, and Emma smiles warmly, looks even younger and prettier than she had in the other settings he's seen her. Her blonde hair is down and lightly curled, and she's wearing a sexy V-neck sweater. She put some real effort into this.

As he steps inside, Myles holds out the bottle of red wine he brought. She takes it and says, "Perfect, thanks. I hope you like pasta."

Her voice: low and throaty, very sexy. He's reminded that it's one of the first things that attracted him to her when they met over lunch the other day.

"Who doesn't like pasta?"

"Well, you know, the carbs and all. But I figured a big, athletic guy like you wouldn't mind some carbs."

He stretches his lower back again. "I'm not so athletic anymore."

"Really, back problems?"

"Being tall isn't all it's cracked up to be."

"I might not be tall, but I know what you mean," she says. "I have back problems, too." She throws her elbows back, stretching her upper back, not a trace of self-consciousness, showcasing her large breasts.

"I guess we have something in common," he says.

The place is sparsely furnished—a gray wraparound couch, a small side table, a large flat-screen on top of a walnut media cabinet, with a stereo, a box of CDs, and an Xbox. Only one picture on the wall, a framed 8x11 of Thomas as a toddler, wearing a white button-down shirt under a red sweater-vest. Sarah McLachlan plays on the stereo, soft and pure.

"So we're renting here for now," Emma says, a touch of embarrassment in her voice. "Eventually I'd like to find something more permanent, someplace where Thomas can really feel at home."

"Where is Thomas?"

"He's at my friend's house. She has two girls, and they get along wonderfully."

"Cool."

She waves him toward the kitchen. "I really like it," she says, "that my son hangs out with girls. Who cares what other people say. I feel like I'm raising a gentleman."

"I like to hang out with girls," Myles says in a deadpan voice, and Emma laughs.

The back kitchen door is open, a rip in the screen, and the breath of a warm spring evening blends with the smell of garlic and sweet candles—not enough of a breeze to carry that manure smell to this side of town. The kitchen walls are yellow, and there's a small window above the sink, framed in old varnished brown wood, various spices and a cup with pens and pencils on the ledge. The window's cracked open, too. Emma pulls two glasses from a cabinet, opens the wine.

Myles checks the round clock on the wall, even though he knows it's seven o'clock. He feels the need to confirm the time, because of a recent promise to himself—no more drinking before six.

"I'm making pasta with aioli sauce," Emma says, pouring the wine. "I make it the old-fashioned way. No cream or mayo. It's my mom's recipe. She was Italian, and I love anything that reminds me of her."

"Smells great," Myles says.

"That was a fun afternoon," Emma says. "I know Thomas really enjoyed it, and I can't believe how much I enjoyed it myself."

"I'm glad," he says, as she hands him a glass of wine.

She stirs the aioli sauce on the stovetop, then leans against the laminate countertop on one side of the sink, wine in hand. He leans against the other side, facing her. And there, he gets his first good look into her eyes: tired eyes, a grayish green. They clash with her spunky exterior.

"Even watching the game," she says before a quick sip. "Thomas explained some of the stuff to me that I don't know. Like when the one kid came into the game, he's called a relief pitcher. I love that name— we all could use some relief, right?"

"Absolutely," Myles says. "I was a relief pitcher, by the way."

"No kidding." She takes a bigger drink of wine. "Tell me more about yourself."

So he does, starting with his baseball biography, and she seems impressed, eyes popping when he mentions the Phillies (she knows that much about the game, at least). Then the brother, the school board president, his only sibling. Parents are retired, still living in Camp Hill half the year, Florida the other half. He pauses for a drink of wine before he brings up the topic of his only marriage, which ended eight years ago. How to tell a girl it ended when his wife caught him with a twenty-two-year-old grad student in a dark campus parking lot in the backseat of his Jeep?

"And I'm divorced," he says.

She holds her glass up in a toast. "Welcome to the club," she says.

He obliges, and they toast.

"So how did you end up back here?" he asks.

"And divorced?" She gives the sauce another quick stir.

"Well, yeah. I guess. It's your turn. Tell me more about yourself."

She sits down at the small kitchen table. He takes a seat, too. She scratches the back of her neck, breathes in, out. She's in no hurry. She wraps her hands around her wine glass. In the yellow light of the kitchen, she gets a better look at the gray in his chestnut hair—more gray than she realized. Light touches up front, thicker along the sides. A man who's been through things in life, but who seems to be wearing it well, and who wants to listen to her right now, wants to hear her story. Where to start?

She's an only child—seems a good place to start, right? Then, her mom, those hellish days early in the pandemic, how they had to say goodbye to each other on FaceTime. God, how she misses her mom; she stays in touch with some of the nurses who worked with her. Then onto her dad, and she blurts it right out: My dad is homeless. This morning she took him another care package, charged his phone, asked him yet again if he'd go to the doctor, but he won't even discuss it. Their old house is across town, a red-brick with good bones, recently sold at sheriff's sale, and she doesn't even have the nerve to drive by and see it. So she completely avoids that block.

"It's strange," she says. "My hometown doesn't feel like home anymore." She pauses, and her shoulders rise and fall with a heavy breath. She takes a drink of wine.

Myles takes a drink, too. He's waiting to hear about the men in her life, the boy and his father.

She feels a buzz coming on, and she tells him the whole story.

SIX

THEY POLISH OFF THE WINE with dinner. By now, Emma has a good buzz. Myles seems fine, steady; he holds his liquor well.

"I didn't get a chance to pick up any beer or wine today," she says apologetically, as she gets up from the table and opens a cabinet. "I don't drink much these days, but I think I have some vodka in here."

She finds a half-bottle of Smirnoff, left over from the holidays. "Yup, here it is, and I know we have orange juice. Make you an after-dinner drink?"

"You twisted my arm," he says, as he leans back in his chair and rubs his tummy.

Their aioli-stained dishes are still on the table. Emma clinks ice into two tall glasses, adds juice and a hefty portion of vodka to each. She hands a glass to Myles then plonks the juice down on the table.

"I'm not much of a bartender," she confesses as she sits down, her glass in hand. "But you can add more juice if you want."

Myles takes a cautious sip. "Whoa," he says. "I think a little more mixer might be a good idea."

He tops off both glasses with juice.

"Thank you," she says. "It's so good to do something adult for a change. And did I mention how cool today was?"

"You did, and I'm glad."

"But I should check on Thomas," she says, and pops up and glances around for her phone. She finds it on the far side of the counter and calls Tracey. He gets up and clears the dishes, leaves them in the sink.

"So how's it going?" Tracey asks.

"Good." She steps toward the next room, leans against the kitchen entryway, her back to Myles.

"How good?"

"Very good." She knows Myles is within earshot, so she doesn't want to say too much, doesn't want to admit she's seriously considering sleeping with this guy. "How's Thomas?"

"Great. They're watching a movie. Their bellies are full of pizza."

"When will the movie be over?"

"Don't worry about it," Tracey says. "He can spend the night. I'll bring him over in the morning, and you can tell me all the juicy details then. You enjoy yourself."

"Are you sure?"

"Absolutely."

"Can I talk to him?"

"Hang on. Let me pause the movie," Tracey says, then Thomas comes on the line. Emma says goodnight, tells him she loves him. He says he loves her, too.

"All good?" Tracey asks when she's back on the phone.

"All good."

When Emma ends the call and turns back toward Myles, he asks, "All good?" He must have heard the exchange, but that's okay.

"All good," Emma confirms.

"So where were we?" Myles asks.

"Doing something adult for a change," Emma says, and sits down and hoists her vodka. "Ooh, that is strong. Give me a little more juice."

He tops off her glass again. She feels a chill coming through the open door, gets up and pushes it closed, then suggests they move into the living room. As Myles settles into the couch, nipping on his screwdriver, she changes the music on the stereo to Nora Jones, lilting and seductive.

Dusky light filters into the room, and she feels him watching her. She takes a gulp of her drink. She feels light, dreamy, as she turns toward him. She feels all the worries of the outside world fading away. He's here, and she's here, and Thomas is safe, and there's nothing else right now. She feels like kissing him.

She puts her glass on the side table, climbs onto the couch, with her knees on the cushions, so she's facing him, eye to eye. "Adult stuff, huh?" she says, and leans in for a kiss. Just a peck at first, and then she leans in further, wraps her arms around his shoulders, and they kiss for a full minute. He's a good kisser.

She slides her knees out from under her, lies back on the couch, and with a fistful of his shirt, she pulls him on top of her.

***

"Is that what you call a doubleheader?" she asks.

He laughs out loud. "I guess so," he says.

It's almost midnight, and they're lying on their backs in her bed, where they came for the second round, which followed another round of screwdrivers. Their clothes are strewn across the floor. Through a crack in the blinds, a slant of streetlight cuts across the bed.

"I probably shouldn't tell you this," she says, looking up at the dark ceiling. "But that's the first time I've had sex since my divorce."

"Why shouldn't you tell me that?"

"I don't know. Maybe because I don't want to seem vulnerable."

"It's okay," he says.

She turns her head slightly, looking at him from the corner of her eye, waits to see if he says anything else, makes a similar confession, but he doesn't. She wants to ask—when was the last time for you, buddy? But she doesn't, doesn't want to press him, doesn't want to spoil this. There was a girl in his Jeep in a dark parking lot one time, and he confessed that to her during their last round of screwdrivers, but it was years ago, so take that for now, and just hope he's changed.

She feels nauseous, but also tired. A little too much to drink, but that's okay, nothing to feel guilty about, especially after all the troubles in her life lately, and she'll sleep it off. She turns her head away from him, allows her eyes to slip shut.

Middle of the night, her bedroom swathed in darkness, Myles sleeping soundly with his back turned, she wakes up feeling sick, her stomach roiling. She gags, covers her mouth, hops out of bed, darts to the bathroom. Vomits into the toilet.

She drops to her knees, tries to catch her breath. She runs her tongue across her teeth; her mouth tastes putrid, garlic and orange and bile. She feels dizzy. She vomits again.

There are footsteps behind her, onto the bathroom's linoleum floor, and then she feels Myles's large hands on her shoulders, gently massaging them.

"You okay?" he asks.

"I don't know," she says, twisting her head to look up at him. "But thank you for coming in to check on me."

"Of course," he says. "I'm not going anywhere."

"My relief pitcher," she says.

***

"The doorbell's ringing," Myles says, tapping Emma's shoulder to wake her up. "Someone's at the door."

Emma rubs her eyes, tries to blink the sleep out of them. A pale morning light fills the room, and her head hurts. Her stomach is twitchy, and her eyes are blurry. She feels her hair flat against her head. She sits up, checks the red digits on the bedside alarm clock: 10:01 a.m. "It's Tracey," she says. "And Thomas. I can't believe I slept this late."

"How do you feel?" Myles asks.

"Like crap."

"Adult stuff has consequences," Myles says. He pats at his own bed-head.

"Maybe we shouldn't have had that last round of screwdrivers."

"It seemed like a good idea at the time."

"Yeah, well," she says. "So do a lot of things."

The doorbell dings again. "I'll get it," she says, rolling out of bed. She pulls on gray sweatpants and a T-shirt.

"I have to hit the bathroom," Myles says, as he picks up his underwear and chinos.

"I hope we cleaned up well enough down there. Wait—what should we tell Thomas?"

"About what?"

"Why you're here."

"Oh, right."

Another ding.

"Oh, forget it," she says. "We'll just have to deal with it. I better let them in."

She blows out of the bedroom and down the stairs.

As she opens the front door, the kids dash inside—all three of them, Thomas and both of Tracey's girls. They slip past Emma and plunk down in front of the television. Thomas, still wearing his green Hornets jersey, which clashes with his orange cap, turns on the Xbox. Tracey steps inside, looking chipper in new sneakers and a pink North Face pullover. "You look rough," she says.

"I feel rough," Emma says.

"Is that good rough, or bad rough?"

"Huh?" She rubs a chunk of sleep-film out of her eye.

"You know, rough for a good reason, or for a bad reason?"

"Oh, I get it." She fluffs her flat hair with her fingertips.

Myles appears at the top of the stairs, tucking in his shirt as he descends. His hair is wet from sink-styling, and he smiles at the strangers in Emma's living room.

"Well, hello," Tracey says, smiling back at him.

"Hello," Myles says shyly.

Thomas's head spins around, eyeballing Myles, and then his eyes dart back and forth between Myles and his mom.

"This," Thomas says, "is kinda weird."

SEVEN

GAYLE BRUNGARD is a plumpish woman with blonde highlights in her hair, still with a soft, pretty face, must have been very pretty when she was younger. She has a light tan, so she must have recently been to Florida or some other Sun Belt spot. She's sitting with Eric Sounders at a corner booth at Java Hut, a mug in front of each of them. Sounders looks awkward in a khaki baseball cap which doesn't sit straight on his head. Emma spots them right away when she steps inside, and Sounders throws up a wave. She's five minutes late.

And she's hungover. But at least she remembered to wear her Princeton sweatshirt.

"I think I'm going to skip the coffee," Emma says as she slides into the booth beside Sounders. He inches to his right to give her space.

"There's always decaf," Sounders says, lifting his own mug.

Emma shakes him off, and she and Gayle do introductions, while Sounders offers nothing about himself. Emma keeps hers brief, emphasis on her Princeton degree and her CASH valedictorian status. Gayle's been a school board member for ten years, and her husband is a lawyer and county commissioner. He grew up in Cumberland, but she grew up in a little town called Boyertown in the eastern part of the state. They met at Penn State, the main campus in State College, married soon after graduation, and they've lived in Cumberland ever since, and now they have two kids in the district, a boy and a girl. She seems connected.

Emma's mouth is dry. She needs something to drink, so she excuses herself, goes up to the counter for a glass of water.

"Where were we?" Emma asks, back at the booth.

"Eric tells me you teach," Gayle says.

Emma's reminded: A pile of ungraded papers at home, and they're not getting graded today, not with this hangover. "Yes," she says. "English classes at Cumberland College and Penn State-Harrisburg. I'm an adjunct, though."

"It's a start," Gayle says. "I know the pay isn't great, but it'll lead to something."

"Will it?" Emma says, sipping her water. "I hope so."

Emma's stomach rumbles. Though she had a light lunch, a small bowl of chicken soup, it didn't settle well. The heavy smell of roasting coffee isn't helping.

"I'm so glad you're interested in our Diversity Committee, so let me tell you about it," Gayle says. She lays out the details: It was formed after the latest killing of an unarmed black teenager by a white cop and all the usual news coverage and street protests that ensued. Gayle has volunteered to chair it; Sounders is vice chair. Their goal is to promote the value of diversity in the Cumberland Area School District, which has slowly seen an increase in its minority population over the years, more minority families moving from Harrisburg into the suburbs. Another parent has suggested they create a resource guide, a list of books and movies and Web links, which teachers and students can rely on for instruction or awareness. Or just to cope, if need be. Gayle would like that to be the committee's first priority.

"I love it," Emma says. "Really, I just love that idea."

"Any ideas?" Gayle asks.

"Oh, my God, so many. I don't know if Eric told you, but my son is Pakistani. He's a really sweet kid, by the way."

Why does she always feel the need to say that?

"Anyway," Emma says. "We've read some great books. His favorite was *Freedom River*. And then there's *I Am Enough*, too. That was probably my favorite."

"It sounds like you know your stuff," Gayle says.

"She sure does," Sounders says.

Emma's stomach quivers, but she tries to ignore it.

"I could get a zillion more, no problem," Emma says. "I could enlist my students, offer them extra credit for recommendations."

Gayle sends Sounders a look, eyebrows raised.

Sounders, raising his coffee mug to his lips, nods back at her.

"In that case," Gayle asks, "would you like to head up our resource guide? Be in charge of compiling the list for us?"

"Yes, sure, absolutely," Emma says, no hesitation.

"Sounds like she's interested," Sounders says.

Emma hiccups, and her stomach quakes. Can't ignore it any longer. Something rises up in the back of her throat—something chicken soupish—and she throws her hand over her mouth.

"Excuse me," she says. "Where's the bathroom?"

Sounders points across the room, past the counter, and Emma bolts that way.

Inside the stall, she throws up again. Not a lot—there isn't much left in her stomach. Just a little chicken-soup glop. Afterward she wipes the corners of her mouth, lowers the seat on the toilet, and sits down for a spell. She runs her tongue across her teeth. Yuck, her mouth tastes so bad. She holds her head in her hands. This is so embarrassing. She should feel flattered by Gayle's offer right now, but this clouds it. Even worse, it's ruining her day-after with Myles, her chance to bask in the glow of a new relationship, if that's in fact where this is headed, and there's no indication it's not. She really likes him. He's an attractive guy, seems like a decent guy, and he really seems to like her, too. She should feel a glow today. But she doesn't. How to feel a glow when she's sitting on a toilet in a public restroom after vomiting for the third time in twelve hours and humiliating herself in front of her son's principal and a school board member? So, no glow.

She tries to gather herself at the bathroom mirror, re-fastens the clip in her hair, smooths out her sweatshirt, spits some of that yuck into the sink. She washes her hands, looks into the mirror. Her skin is sallow, dark circles under her eyes. She looks awful. She splashes some water on her face, dries it with a paper towel. Still looks awful. Can't stay in here forever, though, so she blinks a couple of times, tries to blink away the awfulness, even though she knows you can't just blink away the awfulness, decides to head back out there.

Back at the booth, she tries to downplay it. "Sorry about that," she says. "I must have eaten something that didn't agree with me today."

"It happens," Sounders says.

"Are you okay?" Gayle asks. Her tone is genuine.

"Yes, thank you. No big deal." She's touched by Gayle's concern.

"Excuse me, too," Gayle says. "I'm going to freshen up. Coffee runs right through me."

As Gayle leaves for the bathroom, Emma tries a sip of water, swirls it in her mouth, anything to dilute that bad taste in her mouth, lets it go down cautiously.

"You must think I'm a hot mess," she tells Sounders, setting her glass on the table.

"Why?"

"You know, just everything."

"Like?"

"My son gets in fights, I talk to chairs, I throw up in coffee shops."

He shakes his head. "We're all dealing with things, some more than others. I try not to be judgmental."

She's impressed—compassion, so rare from a guy. And she's reminded that his own son is rumored to be a serious discipline problem, and his own marriage is apparently in pieces. So yes, he's dealing with things, too.

"Gayle is really nice," she says. "Thanks for including me in this."

"I'm glad you're interested." He takes a healthy drink of decaf.

When Gayle returns, they revisit the guide. They work out a plan for connecting with other members by email and a timeline for Emma to present a draft of the list to the full committee, which also includes two teachers, one guidance counselor, and two parents.

"Let's have coffee again soon," Gayle suggests, "and we can talk about your progress. How's next Sunday, same time same place? I hope you're feeling better by then."

"I'm sure I will be," Emma says.

Gayle says goodbye, explains that she has to pick up her son after a drum lesson, but before she leaves, Emma hops out of the booth, gives her a hug. Gayle doesn't hesitate, hugs her back. Emma doesn't want to let go. Something about this woman arouses feelings of comfort and well-being, feelings that Emma doesn't experience much these days, but she knows she should let go, so she does, before the moment turns into another embarrassment.

"It was so nice to meet you," Emma says.

"Yes, yes," Gayle says. "I know you'll do a great job with this. Next week, right?"

"Yes, right."

Emma slips back into the booth with Sounders. "It's good to know there are still good people like that in Cumberland," she says. "It's my hometown, after all."

"Mine, too," Sounders says.

She studies his face, fights back the urge to reach out and straighten the hat on his head. How old, exactly? Should she remember him from high school? Early to mid-forties, forty-three if she had to guess, and about the same age as Myles, so no, she wouldn't remember him.

He finishes his decaf, but she doesn't touch her water, and they get up to leave. He holds the front door open for her, and they walk to their cars together.

"This was fun," Sounders says, jamming his hands in his pockets, as they stroll across the parking lot. "And productive."

Emma does a double-take. Did he say fun? "Yes, very productive," she says, and reaches into her purse for her keys.

"They have an acoustic guitarist on Friday nights," Sounders says. "He's very good. In case you'd like to come back."

"Um—" Her mind freezes. What is this? Did he just ask her out? She can't find her keys, so she digs deeper, underneath her purse clutter, the pens and hand creams and sanitizers and her wallet. All the while, she's racking her brain, can't find a thing to say to him in response. She stops, spits out the words, "My keys."

"Did you leave them inside?"

"I don't know." Still digging. "Oh, here they are. Whew."

"So as I was saying," Sounders says.

"Right," Emma interrupts, before he pushes this matter too far. How to process this—is her son's oafish principal really asking her out? Or is this about something else, something platonic, just a lonely man looking for some companionship? What to say? Can't say she's in a relationship, can she? One night with a guy, and she hasn't even heard back from him yet, though she figures she will. She will, right?

"Friday," she says, averting his eyes. "Fridays are tough. Thomas has a lot of things going on—you know, kid stuff."

"I understand," Sounders says. "Just let me know if you're ever free. He's a great guitarist."

"I'm sure he is." She hurries into her car, starts the engine, and backs out of her space quickly, so quickly she almost hits another car. The driver lays on the horn. Emma throws up an apologetic wave and takes off for home.

EIGHT

MYLES CAN'T DECIDE whether to call Emma or text her, nor can he decide when to place the call or send the text. What's the protocol these days? He's not good at these things. But he knows this much: He's smitten with her, wants to see her again, badly. He also knows she's busy this afternoon, meeting some folks from the school, so now isn't the time to reach out. As it is, he's contemplating an afternoon of Black Jack at the casino when his brother Ron calls, says he's taking down a half-dead tree in his backyard, could use some help.

"I'll be over," Myles says. "But my back's not in great shape."

"It's a small tree," Ron says. "If I can handle it, you can handle it."

No rush, Myles decides. He takes a long, hot shower, extra heat on his back, has another cup of coffee, watches an inning of the Phillies game. When he gets there, Ron has made progress—the tree is down, a pile of branches sits off to the side, sawdust spattered across the lawn. Ron has started cutting the trunk into logs.

"About time," Ron says, lifting his plastic goggles, wiping his brow with the back of his hand. "I could use a break."

He hands Myles his chainsaw.

"I thought you said you could handle it," Myles says.

"Not *all* of it."

Ron Halprin makes a comfortable living—he owns a company that sells firefighting equipment, and fire departments across Pennsylvania rely on him for their gear, radios, and rescue saws. Still, he refuses to pay for any service if he can do it himself; he's very conservative with his money. He often tells people he got the brains in the family. He didn't get the height or the good hair, like Myles. Ron is average height, receding hairline. Small eyes and a fleshy face. But perfect teeth—he takes good care of his teeth.

"You should have goggles," Ron says, wiggling his goggles off his head. "Here, take mine."

"What kind of tree was this?" Myles asks, straightening the goggles over his eyes.

"Hell if I know. A tree. Want any more info, ask my wife."

As Myles lines up his first log, he stops and sets down the chainsaw, readjusts the goggles. "These are tight," he says.

"You must have a fat head," Ron says.

"I always thought you had the biggest head in the family."

For the next hour, they take turns cutting logs, then stack them in a corner of the yard. In between each haul, Myles stops to stretch his back. When they plop down in patio chairs, Myles's sister-in-law Jen brings them each a bottle of Miller Lite.

"Nice work," Jen says. "But what about that pile of branches?"

"I'll get them next weekend," Ron says. "I think we're whooped for today."

Myles checks the time on his phone: 4:55 pm. He doesn't want to start drinking this early, hates to violate his new six o'clock rule, but then he figures it's only one light beer, so it's not like serious drinking.

Jen walks to the edge of the patio, surveys the yard. She's a square-figured woman with heavy breasts, never dropped her maternity weight, but has good skin and full red hair. "Just don't forget those branches next weekend," she says, and turns back inside.

Ron nods dutifully as she slides the screen door closed.

"So how are things at the college?" Ron asks, leaning back in his patio chair, taking a healthy swig of beer.

"Good. Status quo," Myles says.

"Really? I hear weird shit's going on over there."

"Such as?" He sips his beer.

"I heard they put tampons in the men's bathrooms now, to keep the trans kids happy. That's crazy."

"It doesn't bother me," Myles says with a shrug.

"It bothers me," Ron says. "Those liberal loonies are out of control. It's going to filter down to the school district soon, I just know it. Pretty soon, someone's going to want tampons in the boy's bathroom, but that shit's not gonna fly in this district. Believe me."

"I feel like I have more to worry about," Myles says. "I'm just trying to keep my ballplayers out of trouble, and out of the dean's office."

"Do you?" Ron says. "That reminds me—how's your love life?"

Myles smiles knowingly, nips at his beer. "Good, actually."

"Really, is it?"

"Yeah, I met someone."

"Who is she?"

"An English professor at the college."

"Nuh, uh."

"Yeah, seriously."

"You're shitting me."

"I'm not."

Ron lifts himself out of his chair, yells inside through the screen door: "Hey, Jen, get out here. You gotta hear this."

"I'm glad you find my love life so interesting," Myles deadpans.

"Jen thought we should sign you up for one of those online dating sites," Ron says, settling back into his patio chair. "So she'll be glad to hear this."

Myles shakes his head, and Jen appears at the screen door. "What is it?" she asks.

"Myles is dating someone—an English professor."

Jen's eyes pop. "Wow, good for you."

"I can't say we're dating," Myles clarifies. "I said I met someone, and she made me dinner last night. It was a really nice night."

"Still, that's great," Jen says.

"Unless," Ron says, "he's becoming one of them, one of those latte-sipping lefties."

"Stop it," Jen says.

"She's actually really down to earth," Myles says.

Jen invites Myles to stay for dinner, has a roast in the oven, plenty for everyone. He does, and it's a pleasant dinner. Ron and Jen have nice kids, so it's good to catch up with them, too. Maddie's a junior at CASH, and she's starting to look at colleges, really likes Penn State, main campus, says there's no way she's going to Cumberland College. Her younger sister Hailey is a sophomore, plays on the tennis team, but her season's off to a rough start. Myles tries to offer Hailey some encouraging words: "Hang in there. You're young. Keep developing your fundamentals. They can do a lot for you."

"How's your baseball team looking?" Ron asks.

"Pretty good," Myles says. "One game above .500 right now."

"When are you going to start bringing back some trophies?" Ron asks. "You were a professional ballplayer. Most of those other little colleges don't have that kind of coaching. You guys should have so much potential."

"We'll see," Myles says evasively. He sips his water—he never asked for another beer, and he's proud of himself for that.

After he drives home, dusk settling over the town, he texts Emma. He spent a good deal of time thinking about what to say while he filled up on Jen's roast, so it doesn't take him long to compose it: "Had a great time last night, hope u did 2, sorry it was awkward this morning."

She responds five minutes later: "I did, too. It's nice to hear from you."

His reply: "How bout dinner soon, my treat this time."

"I would love it."

NINE

A TWO-DAY HANGOVER—is that even a thing? Is it possible? If so, Emma has one on Monday morning. Her stomach is still queasy, her head still hazy and pulsing. She brews a pot of coffee, makes more than usual, hoping it will help, pours juice and plates a blueberry Pop-Tart for Thomas, then gets him off to school. One small motherly victory, though: Thomas is wearing a Phillies T-shirt, because she convinced him to throw his Hornets jersey in the laundry basket. Which is overflowing, as usual.

And now that she knows Myles's background, it's especially nice to see Thomas wearing a Phillies T-shirt.

When she fell asleep last night, which was earlier than usual, just after she tucked Thomas in and said his prayers with him, she was lulled by a sense of comfort. A new relationship and a sense of purpose, thanks to Myles and Gayle. She reviewed the words in Myles's text, and comma splices and textspeak notwithstanding, she was relieved to see it, glad he realized the significance of a day-after connection and that graceless, unplanned introduction to those people who matter in her life. And suddenly Gayle matters, too. Emma can't remember feeling such an emotive bond with another woman—well, not since her mom died.

So there's reason to feel good this morning, though she still feels far from good. Another cup of coffee, two Advil. She sits down at the kitchen table and stares out the window. It's a gray morning, starting to drizzle. She logs onto her phone, checks the weather. Heavy rain is in the forecast. Yet she sent Thomas to school without his raincoat. Shit. Her small motherly victory with the T-shirt suddenly feels different: a bad mom moment.

She wishes she could cancel her classes, remembers that she still has a pile of ungraded papers which students will surely start bugging her about, would be nice to take a mental health day and cut into that pile. But she's already cancelled too often. Gotta tough it out today.

She finishes her coffee and showers, lets the hot water soak her head. She feels a little better, maybe because the Advil's kicking in, too. She forces herself to sit down at the kitchen table again and grade a few papers. One B, one C, one D. And the D was probably generous. Same with the C, come to think of it.

On the way to college, she stops at Buchanan Elementary and drops off Thomas's raincoat at the office. Better to draw attention to her bad mom moment than to leave him at school without it; who cares if the secretary thinks she was negligent?

Eleven o'clock on the dot, and she strolls into the classroom at Penn State-Harrisburg, 108 Olmsted Building, her parka soaking wet, her hair back up in a clip to keep it dry, her travel mug full of more coffee. Her first class goes well enough, and at the end of class she announces her offer for extra credit for the resource guide. Two girls express interest. After class, only one student stops to ask if Emma has graded their last paper yet. "I'm still working on them," Emma says apologetically.

Onto her 12:30 class, upstairs in Olmsted 204. She finishes her coffee as she climbs the stairs, and her stomach rumbles. She should get some food in her stomach, something light, of course, but that will have to wait until after class.

She takes attendance, and the only absence is Aaron Campbell. He's missed the last three classes, still hasn't turned in the paper that Emma probably wouldn't have graded by now. Emma makes a note to submit an academic progress warning for him, and then ten minutes after class starts, he shuffles in, wearing a cheap plastic poncho, Crocs, and checkered pajama pants. His hair is matted down and he needs a shave.

"Nice to see you today, Aaron," Emma says, barely disguising her sarcasm.

"You, too," he says politely, and takes a seat at the back of the class.

At the end of class, Emma announces her offer for extra credit again. Three girls express interest, and one, a softball player, has a question: "Would a book on Jackie Robinson count?" Absolutely, Emma says.

As the class clears out, Aaron comes up to the instructor's desk, a sheepish look on his face, a paper in hand. He offers Emma the paper, apologizes for handing it in late.

"And I'm sorry I was late for class," he adds. "But I slept until 12:15."

"That's too much information, Aaron." She slides his late paper in her grading folder with the rest of the class's papers.

"What do you mean?" he asks.

"I appreciate the apology, but you didn't need to tell a professor how late you slept."

"Oh, right."

"And maybe you should do something about your sleeping habits."

He scratches his scruffy chin and nods, a heavy nod, as if this is an idea that deserves some serious thought. At least, Emma thinks, he's putting serious thought into something.

On her way to the food court, Emma wishes it were Tuesday, because if it were Tuesday she'd be teaching at Cumberland College, where she just might bump into Myles. Maybe tomorrow. Hopefully tomorrow.

***

Mid-afternoon, office hours, and Emma's slumped at the desk in the adjunct office, a vanilla-walled room on the third floor of Olmsted, someone's bottle of Zicam on the desk beside the computer, which left Emma nervous to touch the keyboard. So she hasn't. She has papers to grade anyway, and she's halfway through a paper that's no better than a C when her phone pings with a text. It's Myles.

"Our game was rained out, how about that dinner tonight?"

"Thomas has a game," she replies.

"It'll rain out too, believe me, bring him with us, we can do pizza."

She looks out the window—yeah, still raining. Not as heavy as before, but steady.

Another ping, a follow-up from Myles: "i've been thinking about you all day."

Her insides melt. She's falling hard for this guy, and he's apparently falling just as hard for her, and it feels so good, despite their differences in age and height, which really aren't that significant when you think about it, and yeah, she's been thinking about it, but not obsessing about it. Besides, it feels good just to feel good for a change. Yet she decides to mess with him, have a little fun in the moment.

"Yes, but on one condition," she replies. "You revise that last text and resend it with proper grammar."

"ha ha"

And then a minute later, she gets this: "I have been thinking about you all day."

That same melting feeling.

***

"You're a lot taller than my mom," Thomas says. He bites into a mozzarella stick.

"I'm taller than a lot of people," Myles says.

"And I'm shorter than a lot of people," Emma says.

"Yeah, I guess," Thomas says, mid-chew.

They're in a window booth at Two Brothers Pizza, the pizza joint on Main Street, clear plastic cups of soda in front of Thomas and Myles, water for Emma. It's a brightly lit place, and outside the rain has stopped, but a gray mist still hangs over the town. The seats are cracked red leather, and Emma's sitting on a piece of duct tape, but the pizza here is good, thick and cheesy. It's a popular spot with the college kids, and there are two tables of them nearby, but Emma doesn't recognize any of them, thank God.

The counter guy brings their pizza on a raised tray, a spatula jammed under the crust, and he cautions that it's hot. It's half pepperoni, half cheese; Emma's not a fan of pepperoni, especially on a weak stomach. She suggests they wait a minute before dishing it out.

"How old are you?" Thomas asks Myles.

Emma interjects: "That's not an appropriate question for an adult."

But she's dying to know the answer.

"It's okay," Myles says. "I'm forty-three. How old are you?"

So there it is; now she knows.

"I'm nine," Thomas says. "My mom is thirty-eight."

"So I'm out with a younger woman," Myles says dryly.

Thomas laughs. Emma slants her head, sends Myles a bemused look. "Okay, I think we can dig in now," she says.

Myles reaches for the spatula. "Let me get it," he says. "It still looks pretty hot."

As he carves three slices, Emma considers their age difference. Not as big as she'd feared, though Myles looks good for his age. And it's not that big of a deal, not in her late thirties. Ten or fifteen years ago—yeah, a bigger deal. She tells herself their ages are in the same ballpark, makes a mental note to say it that way to anyone who asks, because it's also kind of clever, and she's just glad they're here together, the three of them.

Myles dishes a cheese slice for Emma first, then pepperoni for Thomas and him.

"What's your favorite major league team?" Thomas asks Myles.

"I'd have to say the Phillies."

"Same," Thomas says.

"Who's your favorite player?" Thomas asks.

"Hmm," Myles says, biting into the tip of his slice. "Ever hear of Curt Schilling?"

"No." Thomas lifts his slice to his lips, decides it's too hot, drops it on his plate.

"I know," Emma says, blowing on the tip of her slice. "Still hot."

"Curt Schilling played when I was younger," Myles says. "He was a pitcher for the Phillies for a while, and later the Red Sox. He won a big playoff game with blood oozing out of his sock from an ankle injury. It's a legendary moment. You should know about it."

"That's cool," Thomas says. He takes a drink of soda, crunches an ice cube with it.

Their exchange brings a smile to Emma's face. She's never seen Thomas interact with a man like this; even when Abid was around, Thomas was too young to help carry this kind of conversation.

"I want to know more about the bloody sock guy," she says. What was his name—Shillington?"

"Schilling. Give it a google," Myles says, chomping into the middle of his slice.

"No," Emma says. "Why do we always have to google everything? Tell us the story."

Myles swallows his pizza. "Okay, okay," he agrees. "I think it was Game Six, yeah pretty sure, Game Six of the American League Championship Series, and the Red Sox have their back to the wall. They're down three games to two, so if they lose this game it's all over. And on top of that, they hadn't won a World Series in ages—a hundred years, something like that, so if they lose this one, it's another dagger in the heart of their fans. Schilling's their ace, so they need him to pitch, and his doctor puts sutures in his ankle so he can pitch. You can see the blood on his sock as the game goes on, but he pitches through it. A real profile in courage. The Sox win the game, and the next, so they go on to the World Series, and they sweep the Cardinals and win their first World Series in like a century."

"Wow, see?" Emma says. "That's a great story."

When they finish eating, there's one slice of cheese left on the metal pan and one mozzarella stick left in the red-plaid paper tray.

"Should we get a to-go box?" Emma asks "Or will one of you big guys finish those off?"

Thomas leans back and pats his belly. "I'm too full," he says.

Myles reaches for the mozzarella stick.

"This was the absolutely best way to spend a rainy evening," Emma tells Myles. "Why don't you come over to the house with us? I'll put on a pot of decaf."

Myles bites into the mozzarella stick and says, "Absolutely."

***

While Thomas goes upstairs to do homework, Emma and Myles sit at the little table in the kitchen and talk over mugs of decaf. Emma's eyes are bothering her again, and she rubs them with the heels of her hands.

"When you were twenty years old," she asks, "did you imagine your life would turn out the way it did?"

"Of course not," Myles says. "I thought I was going to be a big-time pitcher, but I was naïve."

"Is that what it is—naiveté?"

"I guess." He shrugs, sips his coffee.

"I don't know what it is, but I didn't imagine my life this way, either."

"What did you imagine?"

"I don't know—publications, awards, black-tie dinners. I was a valedictorian, then an Ivy League girl. Princeton. I felt like I had so much potential, and now, I don't know, it feels like all that potential is going unrealized, while I'm just trying to keep my head above water. I definitely didn't think life would be this hard."

"You didn't think you'd end up at this little kitchen table with an older guy who coaches Division Three baseball?"

"That's not what I meant. Seriously," she says. She reaches across the table and squeezes his hand.

"Just checking," he says.

"Spend the night, will you?" she asks, still grasping his hand. "I'd love it if you spent the night again."

"It won't be too weird for Thomas in the morning?"

"He really likes you. I can tell. And we've already been there, done that."

"You twisted my arm," he says.

"Good," she says with a little smile. "Just keep in mind, it's a school night, so we'll be up early."

"Fine by me."

She finishes her coffee, excuses herself, goes upstairs to check on Thomas, reminds him it's time to get ready for bed. When she comes back downstairs she's wearing only a baggy gray T-shirt, nothing else, which hangs over her hips but leaves her legs entirely exposed.

"That's a very sexy look," Myles says.

"I'm glad you think so."

The bedroom is warm, humidity in the air. She cracks open a window beside the bed. She sets the alarm, 6:30 a.m., rubs her eyes again. She pulls back the sheet, crawls into bed. Myles comes out of the bathroom, undresses and slides in beside her.

"Just hold me for a little while," she says.

"Of course."

Streetlight slides in through the crack in the window. Emma rolls onto her side, facing away from him. He snuggles up against her, wraps his arm around her belly. Soon he kisses the back of her neck, just a light kiss above the collar, then higher, just below her ear. She likes it.

She wiggles out of her T-shirt, and the foreplay is slow, tender, intense. The sex, too. When they finish, they lay on their backs, naked and quiet, an affectionate quietness, as the rain starts up again outside, and she falls asleep to the sound of the rain and the feeling of Myles's long, strong arm wrapped around her.

TEN

EMMA SLEEPS surprisingly well, wakes up only once, in the middle of the night when Myles gets up to pee. The temperature is dropping, so she gets up to close the window while Myles is in the bathroom, and when he comes back to bed she promptly falls back to sleep, curled up under the comforter, Myles breathing heavily beside her.

Myles doesn't stay for breakfast—he has an early visit from a recruit to prepare for, so he slips out while Thomas is getting dressed, leaving Emma at her bedroom door with a peck on the lips and a promise to call her soon. Emma gets Thomas off to school, after ensuring he's wearing a sweatshirt on a chilly morning, then decides to throw in a load of laundry before she gets ready for classes, because the laundry basket in her room and Thomas's room are both overflowing and she has only one pair of clean underwear left. She hauls a mixed load, mostly Thomas's clothes, plus a few pairs of her underwear, down to the basement and chucks it into the machine, relieved she's able to notch one domestic chore this morning.

But no.

The washing machine is broken. After it fills with water, the next cycle won't kick in. The little green wash-cycle light is flashing, as if it's trying to tell her something. She opens the lid, looks over the heap of clothes in the water, but what can she do? She bangs the lid shut.

She calls the landlord, who says he'll call a repairman, and then he calls back and says the earliest the repairman can come is Friday. Meanwhile, the clothes are just going to have to sit there. No time to deal with it now. Gotta get ready for class.

So she showers and dresses, into that last pair of clean underwear, puts her hair up in a clip, figures she'll drag the clothes to a laundromat after classes. Or after dinner. Or whenever, sometime soon. Maybe she should welcome this sort of sopping wet inconvenience, because a laundromat is just what she needs right now—she'll finally find time to grade that backed-up pile of papers while she waits on her clothes.

As Emma's leaving for class into the brisk but clear morning, pulling the front door closed, her brown leather teaching bag slung over her shoulder, her phone buzzes. She doesn't recognize the number, but it's local. Maybe it's the repairman, so she better answer.

It's a state trooper.

"Is this Emma Muller?" he asks.

"Emma Muller-Farooq, yes."

"I'm calling from Interstate 81. We're about a half mile east off Exit 61. I'm here with Mr. Joseph P. Muller. He says you're his daughter."

A clutch in her chest, she drops her bag on the porch. "Yes."

"We had a report of an elderly man wandering out here on the interstate. He says he has to be in Carlisle this morning to meet a truckload of beer."

"He's a retired beer truck driver," she explains.

"He also says he doesn't have a car and doesn't have a home, but he provided me with a Pennsylvania driver's license, which is still valid. It lists an address in Cumberland Borough."

She squeezes her eyes shut, tilts her head back, processing, processing. "Right," she says, then reopens her eyes and levels her head. "He's not doing well. He's living in the encampment under the bridge in Harrisburg."

"I see."

"Can I come get him?"

"Yes, I can release him into your custody, but I'll have to address the matter of his driver's license."

"What do you mean?"

"I'll have to file paperwork with the Department of Transportation to revoke it. He's clearly unable to function properly behind the wheel."

Emma rakes the fingers of her free hand through her hair. "Okay, fine," she says. "I guess he doesn't need it anymore."

He gives her instructions for meeting them at the state police barracks, and when they end the call, she sits down on the top step of the porch, drops her head into her hands, lets the tears flow.

***

She cancels both of her classes, citing a family emergency, but she doesn't fret about it because this is a legit family emergency, and she hasn't cancelled that many at Cumberland yet this semester—only once back in February when Thomas was sick. So she doesn't feel too bad about that, at least.

There are times when Emma wishes she weren't an only child, wishes she had a sibling in her life, someone she could count on for invitations to holiday dinners and late-night phone conversations after a bad day. Usually she wishes for a sister, but sometimes an older brother, a guy who would readily help with home and car maintenance and come to Thomas's baseball games with her. And the state police barracks.

She knows why she's an only child. She remembers it vaguely as the day she was whisked off to Grandma's house, because Mom suddenly became sick and Dad rushed her to the hospital. It was a sultry summer afternoon, and Grandma made chocolate chip cookies, but she seemed worried and distracted, not her usual buoyant self, and though the cookies were yummy, Emma felt the same sense of apprehension. Finally the phone rang, her dad calling with an update, and Grandma took the news and wiped a tear from her eye, then hung up and told Emma that her mom would be okay. "So that's the good news," Grandma said.

"What's the bad news?" Emma asked.

"Don't worry about it," Grandma said. "It's adult stuff."

Later, when Emma was a teenager, her mom confessed: At three months pregnant, she'd miscarried. Her second in three years. Her doctors advised her not to try again, and they didn't.

Sometimes when she closes her eyes, Emma can see her mom reappear. The woman who carried Emma into the world also bequeathed certain physical attributes: golden hair and big chest, a bad back made worse from pounding the hard tile floors during years of hospital shifts. Mom had a taut face and a small nose, and while she always wore her gold hair up in a bun at the hospital, on summer days she let it down and it was beautiful. As Emma grew up, people often said they looked like sisters.

So when Emma closes her eyes, she can see her mom's reflection in the mirror as they sit together at Emma's bedroom bureau, Mom showing her how to apply makeup for the first time. Or see her spinning Elvis Presley records on the old turntable in their dining room, shaking her hips and urging Emma to dance along. Or see her perched in the front row at CASH stadium during Emma's graduation, beaming over the valedictorian in the family. Or see the distraught and exhausted look on her face as she came home from the hospital without a sibling for Emma.

Colleen Muller, nee Llywelyn, Welsh-Irish, the granddaughter of a Welshman who arrived in Central Pennsylvania to work on the railroads and an Irishman who found work at a lumber company. Colleen remained a blue-collar girl—her dad an auto mechanic and mom a grade school secretary, and Colleen was the first member of her family to go to college, Bloomsburg University, the closest state school with a nursing program. Joe Muller was her high school sweetheart, a fullback on the football team with broad shoulders, a hard chin, and while she went to college, he stayed home and then drove a truck, but they stuck together. She had modest expectations for life, never hoped for much beyond good health, a steady job, and a roof over her head, but Emma always knew Colleen had high hopes for her daughter. Emma misses her terribly. Misses having someone to lean on when she needs it, and boy, does she need it.

***

When Emma pulls into the parking lot of the state police barracks, she shuts off the engine and texts Myles: "Thanks for another nice night last night. My morning is off to a terrible, horrible, no good, very bad start, BTW."

Before getting out of the car, she pauses to collect herself. Angles the rearview mirror down, looks herself over. Deep breath, then she opens the car door.

Her phone pings with a reply from Myles: "oh no what's wrong?"

"I'll have to explain it all later, but it's my dad." She sends it, one leg in the car, one leg out, then remembers that's not the entire story, so a quick follow-up: "Oh, and our washing machine is broken, with a full load of wet clothes inside."

"i'm sorry, anything i can do to help?"

"Can you fix a washing machine?"

"i doubt it but i'd be happy to look at it"

"It's okay, but please work on your grammar."

"Yes, professor."

Another deep breath, and she climbs out of the car.

Inside, the barracks smell like a locker room doused with cleaning chemicals. The trooper and her dad come out from behind a heavy brown security door. The trooper's a middle-aged black guy, and tall, almost as tall as Myles—why so many tall guys in her life all of a sudden? Her dad is wearing his camouflage sweatshirt, with the hood down, and his gray hair is ruffled. He seems agitated, tapping his foot on the floor as Emma introduces herself. The trooper speaks calmly, tells Emma he's in the process of filing the paperwork to revoke her dad's drivers license, suggests she contact county senior services to see if there's anything they can help with.

"They have a number of different services," the trooper says. "Everything from transportation to hot meals, but they might not visit the homeless camp."

"Yes, thank you," she says. "Anything else?"

"That's it on our end," the trooper says, turning to her dad. "And you be safe, Mr. Muller."

Emma's in a hurry to get out of there, so she's the first one out the door, holds it open for her dad, who's two steps behind, walking with his usual hitch. The morning chill is still in the air.

"Please let me make a doctor appointment for you," Emma says, leading the way across the parking lot.

"For what?"

A stiff breeze crosses the lot, the wind in their faces.

"For you, for whatever it is you're dealing with."

"I'm fine," he grumbles.

She stops, throws her hands out. "Dad, we're at a state police barracks. They picked you up for wandering out on the interstate. I'm making a doctor's appointment."

"I'm not going."

"I'm making one anyway," she says, starting toward the car again. "How's that?"

"You do what you want, but I'm not going."

She points to her little blue Honda. "This is my car. Get in."

When he gets to the car he stops, looking down at the tire, the front one on the passenger side.

"Your tire's low," he says.

She huffs, walks around the front of the car, and yes, sure enough, there's a bulge of half-deflated black rubber where the tire meets the ground.

"Shit," she says. "Does this mean I need a new tire?"

"Don't know," he says. "Stop at a gas station, and I'll put air in it for you."

"I appreciate it," she says, and she realizes it's the first time in a long time she's been grateful to him—for anything. "Now, please get in the car."

He complies. Sitting beside him in the car, she catches a putrid whiff of his body odor, and she makes a mental note to add deodorant to her next weekly care package.

They come to a gas station a half-mile down the road, and she pulls up at the air pump beside the building. He doesn't budge. She looks at him, raised eyebrows. "Well?" she says.

"Well, what?"

"You said you'd put air in my tire. I don't know how to do it."

"Oh, okay."

He opens the door. "Which tire is it?"

"Front passenger side."

"Okay."

It takes him a minute to fill it.

"Keep an eye on that tire," he says as he climbs back in the car, "in case it has a slow leak."

"Thank you very much." It feels so strange to say it. When's the last time she said that to her dad?

"Where are we going now?"

"I'll drive you back to your neighborhood," she says as she backs away from the pump. She doesn't know what else to call it. Doesn't seem right calling it his home, because she still thinks of their old red-brick that went to sheriff's sale as his home, and she hates to say homeless camp, or even tent. So, his neighborhood.

Crossing the I-83 bridge, Emma notices a billboard for the Marines. Underneath a photo of several Marines, a mix of fresh-faced men and women lined up in their dress blues, it reads, "A Sense Of Belonging In The Marines."

Yeah, Emma thinks, I'd like a sense of belonging.

But the Marines? No, not for me.

I'll keep looking.

***

Emma calls senior services when she gets home. She's already decided to back off of her threat to make a doctor appointment, because she knows he won't go and she doesn't need that drama. Yet senior services is worth a try. But no, they're no help, won't visit the encampment, just as the trooper suspected. The woman on the phone is polite, sounds older, and Emma suspects she's a volunteer. The woman says they can open a file on her father.

"What good will that do him?" Emma asks.

"Then we'll have a file on him," the woman says.

"Right, I get that, but what is the benefit of the file?"

"It will be on file."

"Okay, why not," Emma says with a roll of her eyes. "Let's do the file." And Emma gives her the info needed to open the file.

Before Thomas gets home from school, she finds time to grade a few papers, then it's off to baseball practice, then home for Taco

Tuesday. With dinner wrapped up, dishes in the dishwasher, and their wet laundry in the trunk, Emma heads to the laundromat, Thomas in the passenger seat, still wearing his baseball stuff with soiled practice pants, which he'll just have to wear again tomorrow. He brought his backpack so he can do homework at the laundromat while she grades more papers. But first, a pit stop.

She wants to see the old house.

She also wants Thomas to see it, wants him to understand and appreciate where he came from, on both continents. It's why his name is Thomas: To accompany his Pakistani surname, she wanted a first name that evokes memories of men like Jefferson, Edison, and Paine, and sounded perfectly American. His father agreed, and now that she looks back, it's one of the few favors he did them.

She's avoided the house since moving back—an emotional burden she didn't need to add to all of the rest. But today, after the episode with her dad, she feels the need to see it, to reconnect with her own history, what's left of it.

It's red brick, three stories, big front porch, circa 1930. Address 216 Beale Street, a tidy residential street on the south side of town. She parks on Beale, across the street from the house, winds down her window. Can't park in front of the house because of an industrial-size trash bin out front; someone is renovating it. It's dusk.

"That's where I grew up," she says to Thomas, who leans over for a better look.

"Who lives there now?" he asks.

"Nobody. That's why that big trash bin is there. Someone is doing work on it for whoever lives there next."

There's a lot of work to do. The front steps are crumbling apart, the screen door has no screen, a bedroom window is broken and patched with duct tape, the paint on the eaves is chipping, the roof has thick charcoal-colored streaks. And that's just the outside. She hasn't been inside since her mother died three years ago.

"It was a good place to grow up," she says.

"Were there a lot of kids on your block?" Thomas asks.

"Yeah, there were." She points to the house two doors down.

"Tracey grew up in that yellow house with the driveway. And beside her was a boy named Eddie Douglas. And on the corner was a big Catholic family, the Schmittingers, who had eight kids."

Emma looks back at her old house, the big front porch, empty except for a broom angled against the wall by the door. There used to be a wooden porch swing, and her mom loved that swing. So did Emma. She closes her eyes and glimpses a moment from her childhood, sitting on the swing beside her mother, with her gold hair down, their feet and legs bare in the summer heat, comparing their suntans after a week at the Jersey Shore, a time when she felt secure and loved.

A red pickup thunders down the block, whips into the driveway at Tracey's old house. A fat bearded guy in work boots and an untucked shirt gets out, staggers into the house. Emma wonders if he's drunk, but she stops herself before saying it to Thomas.

"Isn't that Tracey's house?" Thomas asks.

"It was, but not anymore. Her parents moved to a townhouse community out in the township."

"Who lives there now?"

"I don't know," Emma says faintly. As she puts the car in gear, she realizes there's so much she doesn't know about this place any more.

ELEVEN

EMMA DREAMS about her mom that night. It's a new version of a dream she's had before—she's a little girl, and they visit the corner store for milk and a popsicle for her. This dream ends bizarrely, with the old-timer behind the counter warning them that the store is starting to melt, then the three of them hurry outside and stand on the sidewalk and watch the whole building melt into a blob.

Bad dreams. Seems like those are the only dreams she has.

That dream, minus the melting, is a scene from a real-life memory, one of her very first, albeit a nice memory. Late afternoon on a Saturday in early summer, an orange sun descending west of town, the security of her mom's hand gripping Emma's on the way to the store. At the counter, the old-timer asked how old she was. Five, she bragged.

"You're a special little girl," the old-timer said.

"She's very special," her mom concurred.

Emma rubs her eyes with her fingertips, shakes off the weirdness of the melting store as she wakes up, but her mom's memory still lingers. Would life be any different if she were still alive? At the very least, there would be someone to take care of her dad, someone who was very good at taking care of people. And Emma would still have someone in her life she could talk to, confide in, someone to tell her she's special.

She didn't sleep well; it was a restless sleep, maybe because of the strangeness of her dream, or maybe because of everything else that's on her mind—her dad, the house, the washing machine, the daily challenge of creating a happy and healthy childhood for Thomas, and the parental anxiety that comes with meeting that challenge. And let's not forget the number of papers she still has to grade. She sits up, and her back is stiff. She stretches, arms back, then up in the air, then back again. Doesn't help much.

She wishes she could sleep for a few extra hours. Or days, or weeks.

But no, it's Wednesday, which means a school day for Thomas, gotta get him up and on his way, then two classes at Penn State Harrisburg—which means she can't even hope to bump into Myles today. Then another baseball practice, dinner and the dishes, then get ready to do it all again tomorrow, just hope nothing shitty happens along the way.

So she pushes through her morning routine—calls Thomas, reminds him to brush his teeth, brews her coffee, pours his juice, plates his Pop-Tart, asks if he really did brush his teeth, checks the weather, instructs him to wear a sweatshirt over his new green Hornets jersey, which is now clean. Then a kiss on his cheek, have a great day, and he's off to the bus stop. She tries stretching her back again, but it still doesn't help much.

Coffee mug in hand, still feeling groggy from a bad night's sleep, Emma sits down at the computer, which is upstairs in the rental's third bedroom, on a cheap IKEA desk beside a ten-year-old StairMaster which Emma never has time to use any more. She logs onto her email account, which she'd completely neglected yesterday because of everything else that was going on, and she double-blinks at the screen as she takes in the sight of her mailbox, full of new messages from people she doesn't know, with subject lines that read things like *Resource Guide, Book Ideas,* and *Books Our Children Should Read!*

So many: ten, twelve, fifteen, twenty? How did they know to get in touch so soon? Gayle Brungard, that's how. Gayle got on it, messaged everyone on her district contact list about their plans for the resource guide, and people responded.

Emma clicks on one. It's from a woman named Lisa Dunn, suggesting *The Colors of Us* by Karen Katz and *Under My Hijab* by Hena Kahn. Emma types a quick response: Thank you so much! Then she opens a notebook, starts a list. Another emailer recommends *Who Was Jackie Robinson?* by Gail Herman—of course, Emma should have thought of that one, because Thomas is reading it now. She records it in her notebook, types the same response. Then another, and another.

She doesn't have time to respond to all of them this morning, so she'll have to finish later. Still, she's heartened. She leans back in her chair, stares at the screen, all of those emails, half opened, half unopened, all full of kindness and purpose. She cracks a smile and lets out a satisfied sigh, as she realizes she's doing something special.

***

Leslie Rozman, associate dean of students, is on the phone. Myles recognizes the number on the little screen of his desk phone, and with it comes a sense of dread. Always does. But usually she calls on Monday mornings, after campus security has busted some of his ballplayers at a weekend party. A Wednesday call is unusual; this must be something out of the ordinary.

"Do you have a few minutes?" Leslie asks. "I need to talk to you about something."

"Always for you, Leslie."

"Very funny, but this is serious. I'll be down in a few."

As soon as she enters his office, folder in hand, she closes the door. She sits down in one of the green plastic chairs that recruits and their parents normally sit in. She's wearing cat-eye glasses and a knee-length beige dress, and she sits with her knees together, opens the folder in her lap.

"We had an incident over the weekend. You may have heard about it," she says.

"I don't think I did."

"Someone put a toilet on the roof of the union building."

Myles lets out a little laugh, then stops himself. "I'm sorry," he says. "Seriously?"

"Yes, seriously." She stares right through him.

He leans back in his desk chair, looks up at the ceiling, as the realization hits him: "And I'm guessing it was ballplayers."

"Yes, it was."

"How do we know?"

"They were spotted on a stairwell security camera, and we tracked their identification card swipes at the doors."

He drops his head back to eye level, leans forward, elbows on his desk. "I didn't know we had security cameras in the stairwells."

"In case of sexual assault."

"Where did they take it from?"

"A second-floor bathroom."

"Who did it?"

She lowers her glasses on her nose, looks over the papers in her folder. "Three of them: Thad Roboski, Jacob Starkey, and Shawn McCord."

"Oh, no, not Starkey. He's our best pitcher. And McCord's our shortstop."

"Regardless."

Myles closes his eyes and nods. "Yes, regardless."

"I'm glad you understand."

"What's the penalty?" he asks as he opens his eyes.

"They're barred from participation in extra-curriculars for the rest of the semester."

Myles winces.

"We have to set an example," Leslie says. "We don't want this sort of prank proliferating."

"Of course," Myles says, trying his best to sound agreeable.

"We also need you to talk to the rest of the baseball team. Make it clear to them that we won't tolerate this sort of thing."

"I'll talk to them," he says. "But listen, just listen. Is there any chance we can talk about a lighter punishment?"

"No, the dean was adamant. He wants their punishment to serve as a deterrent."

"Okay, fine."

She pushes her glasses back up on her nose. "Thank you for your cooperation."

He releases a long groan when she leaves, grips his head in his hands. Then he rotates in his desk chair, looks at the season schedule he keeps posted on his wall. No Starkey, no McCord. And Starkey was scheduled to pitch in today's rain makeup against Gettysburg College. How the hell can he make this work?

He can't. He'll be lucky to finish this season .500. This is why he never shoots higher any more: You just never know. You never know when guys are going to blow their arm out, botch a routine grounder, or haul a toilet on top of the union building.

He texts Emma: "Guess who's having a terrible, horrible day today?"

She replies in a minute: "Oh, no. I'm sorry. I hope it gets better." And then she sends a quick follow-up: "At least your grammar is perfect today!"

***

Emma's back is still sore, and those damn bleachers never help, so she decides to go for a walk along the outfield fence. At least out there she'll be closer to Thomas's position—the outfield. That doesn't bother her, though, and it doesn't bother her that he's always inserted in the last spot in the batting lineup. He still doesn't have a hit. More importantly, however, he hasn't been harassed by Justin or anyone else lately. Emma can't imagine Justin has had a change of heart toward Thomas; he must be heeding his dad's advice to be politically correct. But whatever, as long as he's not bothering Thomas. It nags at her, though, that Thomas is hitless, because she knows going hitless is weighing on him, and one hit, just one damned hit, would be like an explosion of sunshine in his world.

It's another sunny but brisk day, a breeze kicking up and whipping across the field. Out beyond the fence, though, trees are budding, and the wind isn't so bad. Emma leans on the fence in leftfield. She likes it out here, likes the smell of the outfield grass and the relative quiet away from the bleachers, and she loves the little wave Thomas gives her when he jogs out to his position.

He comes up to bat in the third, Astros leading the Pirates 6-1. There's a runner on third, two outs. The Pirates pitcher is accurate but doesn't throw very hard. As Thomas adjusts his feet in the batter's box, Emma taps her jeans pocket. Oh shit, she forgot her magic dust.

How could she?

But what's it matter, really? That stuff doesn't work anyway.

Emma raises her hands above her head and claps. "Let's go, Thomas!"

The first pitch is low, at the ankles. Thomas steps into it, eager to swing, but he checks himself. Ball one. The next pitch comes right down the middle, and Thomas hacks at it. It's a late swing, but he makes solid contact, and the ball scoots past the pitcher, between the first and second basemen, and rolls into the outfield. The runner on third sprints home. Safe at first, Thomas thrusts both fists above his head like a world conqueror.

Emma claps hard and high above her head again. "Wooooo, hooooo!"

***

The magic dust is sitting on the desk beside their computer. That's where she left that little bottle this morning when she checked emails; she picked it up after sending Thomas off to school and carried it around until she sat down at the computer. So maybe she shouldn't write off the power of the magic dust so soon—though she didn't have it in her possession for Thomas's big first hit, she did possess it that morning. And here it is at her desk, the very spot she had that wonderful epiphany after seeing all of those warm-hearted emails about all those fantastic books for kids.

Thomas is tucked into bed, dinner and homework wrapped up, and Emma's back at the computer to finish logging all of the suggestions and responding to everyone who sent them. Several more have come in since the morning. There are some redundancies—a few recommended *The Undefeated* by Kwame Alexander, for example, as well as *They Called Us Enemy* by George Takei—but that's to be expected. She'll also have to vet some of the titles, because she's not familiar with all of them—but no problem. She still gives everyone the same grateful reply: Thank you very much!

It's been a good day, a really good day. For a change.

TWELVE

THE FIRST TIME Gayle saw men in hoods in her hometown, she was riding her bike home from cheerleading practice on a Saturday morning. She had to cross Main Street to get back to her neighborhood, and that's where they were, milling about on a corner by the hardware store. Gayle was so unnerved that she swerved, narrowly missed a streetlamp, then hit the brakes and dragged her feet to stop. Then she just gaped at them—five of them, wearing work boots and jeans underneath their sheet-like outfit and holding homemade signs such as "Jews Will Not Replace Us" and "Blood and Soil." She'd heard rumors they were organizing, but it hadn't felt real to her, hadn't really infiltrated her safe sixteen-year-old life, so she hadn't thought much about it. But seeing them in person, she felt it in her gut, the indignation.

The Ku Klux Klan had been rallying one Saturday every month on a street corner in the quaint downtown in Boyertown. It was 1995, the middle of the Clinton years, and white-supremacists and militias in rural swaths of Pennsylvania were mobilizing. Her county, Berks County, was a hotbed.

Gayle came from a good Republican family. Dad was president of both the local bank and the school board. Grandma had been a GOP committeewoman dating back to the Eisenhower campaigns. They were Catholics who believed in stopping abortion, standing up to the Communists, and keeping your fiscal house in order. So did young Gayle, a sophomore in high school with excellent grades who had her sights set on advanced placement courses and then college. She also knew right from wrong, and what she saw that morning was wrong.

Her best friend, Cindy Steinberg, was Jewish, so those signs touched Gayle personally, too. Replace us? How ignorant. Cindy was also a cheerleader, but she lived in the other direction, out in the township, so she didn't have to come this way after practice. Thank God. As Gayle waited for the light to turn green, she thought about riding over and saying something to those ingrates, something like *Go crawl back into your holes*, but no, no. Keep your head and don't provoke them. Don't pay them any more attention than they're getting, because that's what they really want. She could hear Dad saying that as soon as she got home. So when the light turned, she pedaled through the intersection, picking up speed along the way, giving them only a quick glance out of the corner of her eye, and spitting on the curbside as she sped past.

***

Thursday night, and Gayle has a headache. Probably going to develop into a full-blown migraine, because they usually do, but right now it's just the light throb. She takes three Advil and brews a cup of ginger tea, her go-to home remedy. She sits at the island in the kitchen, the smell of her spicy pork and broccoli lingering, tries to breathe evenly. The house is quiet, finally. Her son is finished drumming, so he's now upstairs on his computer, and her husband took over the rec room, watching a basketball game, smoking one of those damned cigars. It's not the drumming that caused the headache, though. It's Clarissa.

Clarissa isn't home yet. That means theater practice ran late, or they decided to go somewhere afterwards, the pizza place or the burrito place, probably to complain about their parents or teachers and how backwards they are. Gayle's trying her best to be supportive, though, not backwards. An ally, that's the term. Gayle wants to be an ally.

Halfway through her tea, and there are headlights in the driveway. Clarissa's home. Gayle wraps both hands around her teacup.

Clarissa's not happy. Gayle can tell the instant she sees her step into the kitchen. She can read her looks. This one is tight-lipped with hot eyes. She's a pretty girl with pale skin, despite her recent decision to dye her hair coal black, a look meant to carry significance.

Clarissa throws a ticket on the island. "Look at what I got."

Gayle picks it up, lowers her glasses on her nose so she can read it. "What's it for?"

"Running a red light. These local cops are bozos."

This is a problem, not so much the ticket itself, but the timing. This makes two things they have to inform Clarissa's dad about, and he won't be happy about either one.

"What happened?" Gayle asks.

"He said I kicked it in the ass to get through a yellow light, then gave me a lecture about kicking it in the ass. I didn't tell him the only reason he stopped me was because he had nothing else to do, but I wanted to. Really wanted to."

"I'm glad you didn't," Gayle says. She's also surprised Clarissa didn't. She's usually the kind of girl who speaks her mind.

Standing on the other side of the island, Clarissa throws her hands on her hips, facing her mom directly, then her face softens and her shoulders slack. "Oh, no," she says. She's looking right at Gayle's cup of tea.

"What?" Gayle asks, looking up from the ticket, peering above the rim of her glasses.

"Migraine?" Clarissa asks. She can read her mom, too.

"Not yet, but I think one is coming on."

"Does that mean you talked to Dad, or does that mean you didn't talk to Dad?"

Gayle drops the ticket on the counter. "This will mean points off your license," she says.

"I know that, Mom."

"I'm sure you do. I was just saying." She sips her tea.

"And you're avoiding my question. Did you talk to Dad?"

Gayle takes off her glasses, rubs her temples. "No, not yet."

Clarissa drops her left hand from her hip, throws her left hip out. "It's a month away, Mom. A month."

Junior prom. Clarissa's going with her girlfriend Amelia, but her dad still doesn't know his daughter is out. It's a family secret Clarissa has shared with Gayle for the past six months, because her dad surely won't take it well.

"I know," Gayle says.

"It's time," Clarissa says.

"Maybe I need a little more time," Gayle says.

"Whatever." She turns, opens a cabinet for a water glass. Slams the cabinet door.

Gayle puts her glasses back on. "That's not fair. I've tried to be supportive."

Clarissa goes to the fridge, then stops, turns back toward her mom. "Fair?" she smirks. "You realize life will never be fair to me, right? Not now, not ever."

"I'll pay your ticket," Gayle says.

Clarissa turns back to the fridge, starts filling her glass from the water dispenser. "Like that fixes everything," she says with a sarcastic shrug of her shoulders.

"It fixes something for you."

"What are you trying to say?" She stops pouring, her glass only half full, turns back toward her mother. "My life needs all this fixing?"

Gayle pinches her eyes shut, reopens them. "I'm just trying to help with what I can."

"But you can't help with Dad."

"I'm trying to help with Dad. Tonight's not the right time."

"Maybe I'll tell him. I'll just blurt it out—'Hey Dad I'm gay.' Then it will be over with. He's going to freak out either way."

"Maybe," Gayle acknowledges, with a sad nod.

***

Downstairs in the rec room, the smell of Doug's cigar is heavy. Always is, and Gayle hates it, but she puts up with it. His Padrons, a coffee-colored Nicaraguan cigar he orders by mail, cost eighty-five bucks for a pack of five, and Gayle knows to allow him certain indulgences. Doug is reclined on the La-Z-Boy, in his stocking feet, his blue Brooks Brothers shirt untucked, collar open, a bottle of Heineken beside his ashtray on the little table to his right. Gayle catches the score on the bottom of the big screen—Milwaukee 86, Philadelphia 65—but she asks anyway.

"What's the score?" she says as she eases into the chair to Doug's left.

"It's a rout," he complains, stubbing out his cigar. "No point in watching much longer. I should go to bed soon."

"What's your day like tomorrow?"

"Not bad. Just morning meetings. I want to squeeze in nine holes in the afternoon." He takes a swig of beer.

He's still a handsome man, thick salt-and-pepper hair, only a little fleshiness in his face. It's funny, how much his daughter resembles him. Same deep brown eyes, same high cheekbones and broad jawline, same skin tone that sunburns too easily. But that's where the similarities end. Emotionally, spiritually, politically, they couldn't be more different.

"Let's go out to dinner tomorrow," Gayle says. "I need to get out."

"Why? Something happen?"

"Clarissa got a ticket," she says. "She ran a red light."

"Oh, Christ. Already? She just got her license."

"I know, and this will be points on her license. I'm not sure how many."

"How much is it gonna cost us?" He picks up his beer bottle, twirls it, watches the last couple of ounces swirl around.

"Two-hundred and twenty dollars, with the fees."

He moans boorishly.

She reaches over and pats the back of his hand. She's the kind of woman who knows how to handle men like him. Well, usually. Times are changing, the human variables getting more complicated.

"I want a good mojito tomorrow," Gayle says, fully cognizant of the change in topics. "I feel a migraine coming on, and I want something to look forward to. Let's go somewhere with good mojitos tomorrow."

"That Cuban place in Harrisburg?"

"Perfect. I'll make a reservation tomorrow. Do you remember the name?"

"Los Tres something or other."

"I'll google it," Gayle says. "In the meantime, don't say anything to Clarissa about the ticket. I handled it. She's dealing with a lot."

"Like what?" He finishes his beer, plunks the bottle on the side table.

"You know. Stuff."

***

Los Tres Cubanos sits on a corner in a riverside neighborhood on the south side of Harrisburg. It's surrounded by redbrick rowhomes that are old but quaint and well-kept. It's a small, narrow place with Latin tunes drifting through the stereo system and a bust of Hemingway on a windowsill.

Doug had a few beers at golf, got some color in his face and seems to be enjoying himself. But he's struggling with the menu—hates it when he can't pronounce things.

"Forget it," he says finally, the waitress waiting patiently at their table. "I'll just have the red snapper. With salsa verde, right? That I can pronounce."

"Good choice," the waitress says, turning to Gayle.

"I'll have the same," Gayle says. "It does look very good."

"And I'll have another beer, too," Doug says, waving his green bottle of Presidente at the waitress.

She's not going to bring it up today. She decided that much already. Not the day after a migraine, not after the ticket. But Doug does seem to be in a good mood, after a little golf and before a nice spring weekend, with more golf likely. This just might be the kind of circumstances that would be the best possible way to do it—not that there's a good way to do it, not that he'll take it well. It's just that in a public place like this, after a good day of golf, with a happy little beer buzz and good food on the way, and just the two of them, which means she's the only person who has to absorb his animus, it might be the best way to do it. But Clarissa bears some responsibility here, too: No more tickets, nothing like that to complicate things ahead of time. They'll have to have that talk.

And who knows, maybe Doug will surprise her. Every once in a while, that actually happens. She just needs to take him somewhere he can pronounce the menu.

THIRTEEN

MADELINE GARVANITIS has dug up twelve books on diversity, sent them to Emma in one email which ends with this: "I hope this meets the criteria for extra credit!!!" Emma told her classes they only needed one book for extra credit, and Madeline has submitted more than all of her other students combined. Madeline apparently likes to cover her bases, especially after she's endured the pain of her first ever B-plus. All twelve are already on Emma's list, so they're among the more common titles. Madeline probably googled them. Still, a promise is a promise, and maybe Madeline learned something about some of the books during her search, so Emma notes the credit in her grade book.

"Yes, they qualify," Emma types back. "Thank you very much!"

Friday morning, and Emma is back at her upstairs desk, in her plaid pajama pants and baggy gray T-shirt, with plans to curate her list. No classes today, and though she still has papers to grade, this will be a good day to research every book that was suggested, read some reviews, make sure each one is appropriate for the school district's Diversity Committee. Some of the suggestions aren't even books—some are videos, documentaries, and Web sites, which seem like good ideas, but she wants to be absolutely comfortable with everything she puts on the list, so she'll watch segments of every video and examine every Web site. She also has to wait for the washer repairman, who's due before noon, and she should also pay bills today, at least one of which is overdue.

Before she logs off her Cumberland College email, however, another one arrives, this one from the English chair, Suzanne Dodd, marked high importance with a red exclamation point, with the subject heading "Announcing a Resignation." It's the department secretary, Frances Eddinger, a pleasant and super-efficient woman in her mid-forties who, according to Suzanne's email, is moving west to Colorado because her husband has landed a new job out there. The department will hold a goodbye party in two weeks, so everyone is encouraged to mark their calendars, and the job opening is being posted, so they hope to have a replacement on board soon, perhaps even before the end of the semester.

Emma likes Frances a good deal, even though she's been teaching there less than a year and doesn't know her all that well. Emma also suspects Frances puts up with too much, especially from some of the tenured professors, but she always seems to handle their petty requests, micro-aggressions, and blatant condescension with professionalism. Emma will miss her; she suspects the whole department will, whether some of them realize it or not.

Back to work. One book at a time. Or Web site or documentary, whichever the case may be. She won't have time to get to them all today—it's going to be a long list, an impressive list, and just the thought of the final product warms her heart—but that's okay. Put a dent in it, at least, hopefully a big dent.

The repairman arrives, a short chummy guy with a pencil-thin mustache, spends an hour in the basement tinkering. He calls upstairs just before noon, and Emma, still in her pajama pants, meets him on the stairway, where he gives her bad news: The unit can't be repaired, needs replacing. He explains why in terms Emma doesn't understand, and she explains that she's just a renter, asks him to call the landlord.

Okay, okay, she tells herself as she heads back to her desk. This is an inconvenience, but it's not the end of the world. You'll deal. And hopefully the landlord will get a new one in here soon.

Better put the list aside for now, move on to life's necessary tasks. Bills. They're waiting for her in a stack on the side of the desk, alongside her checkbook. She's put them off long enough. So she saves her Word document with the resource guide—she has made significant progress on it this morning, will revisit it later this weekend—and slides the bills and checkbook in front of her, picks up a blue pen, blows out a sigh mixed with doubt and encouragement. She needs the encouragement, doubts there will be much left in her checking account when she's done.

She wonders how much Frances makes. Not a lot, but more than an adjunct, in all likelihood. It's a full-time job, after all, comes with full benefits. And it's one job at one location—no need to travel to other campuses every other day. Something appealing about all of that. Something appealing about filling your gas tank or buying a pack of chicken without shuddering at the price.

No, no, she tells herself. You're not a secretary, so stop thinking about it. Stop right there. You're a valedictorian, a Princeton girl, a woman of letters. Just pay the damn bills, and don't overreact. It would also break your mother's heart if she knew this thought had even crossed your mind. You may be an adjunct now, underpaid, underappreciated, overstressed, but things will work out—eventually?

So she starts writing the checks. The old-fashioned way, because she never bothered to set up her accounts to pay them electronically. First rent, the big one. Sign, lick, seal, stamp. Then cable, which is a few days late, but still within the grace period, so she should be fine, as long as she mails it out this weekend. Sign, lick, seal, stamp. Then their Obamacare premium, thank God for Obamacare, and her student loans. Sign, lick, seal, stamp. Then the credit cards, which aren't much, because they haven't spent much, except Old Schooners, the national retail chain which brilliantly markets its kidswear. Shit, she forgot about that visit to Old Schooners over the winter. When Thomas needed larger pairs of jeans. And it's overdue. Has a thirty-dollar late charge tacked on. Shit, shit, shit. It's the second time that's happened to her. Last time, she called and begged forgiveness, threw herself on the mercy of Old Schooners, and they dropped it, called it a one-time courtesy. Hmm. She drops the pen, rocks her head back, thinking—how to get a two-time courtesy?

Her hold time isn't long, only about five minutes, and the call is being recorded for quality assurance. When a human being comes on the line, it's a woman, and her voice sounds young. Emma's strategy: Tell it like it is. Emma asks the young woman for her name.

"Laura."

"Listen, Laura," Emma says plaintively. "Money's really tight, so we don't shop much, and this late fee is almost the same amount as the jeans we bought."

"I see," Laura says, non-committal.

"Last time this happened, you guys waived the fee. Any chance you can do that again?"

"We can do that as a one-time courtesy, but only one time."

"Right, I figured that," Emma says. "But let me explain our entire situation to you. Do you have a family, Laura?"

"Um, I'd rather not say."

"I get it. You don't know if I'm some sort of wacko, right?"

"I'm sure you're not," Laura says.

"Let me tell you about myself," Emma says, and she gets up from her chair, pacing in front of the desk. "I'm a single mom, thirty-eight years old. My son is nine years old and he's Pakistani, and we live in central Pennsylvania, which is one of those red spots you see on the television map every election night, so it isn't very welcoming to people of color. We moved here because my husband, or my ex-husband, is a shit, a real shit. He told me he wanted a divorce in a text message—that's right, a fucking text message, because he was having an affair and he couldn't deal with the fact that our little boy was sick. I guess he couldn't deal with much. He pays child support, but I told him I didn't want any alimony from him, because I wanted to make it on my own, without his charity. You know what I mean, right? But that means we don't get a whole lot from him. I grew up here in central Pennsylvania, so I figured moving here would be a good thing, lower cost of living and more of a support network. But I have no support network. My mother died at the beginning of the pandemic, and my dad lost his mind, then lost the house, and now he lives in a tent under a bridge. I'm an adjunct—do you know what an adjunct is? Cheap college labor. We teach part-time for just a few thousand dollars per class, so I have to teach at two different colleges. No benefits, no job security, and those poverty-level wages. This winter my son needed new jeans, so I took him out to Old Schooners, and then the bills piled up, and maybe one or two slipped my mind, and now you guys are slapping a thirty-dollar late fee on me, and it's the last thing I need right now."

"I'm sorry," Laura says.

"That's it? Sorry isn't helping me very much."

"I wish there was more I could do, but waiving the fee is a one-time courtesy."

Emma falls back in the desk chair, blows a defeated sigh. "That's it? That's all you've got for me, Laura?"

"I'm afraid so."

"I guess I'm going to write this check," Emma says. "And then I'm going to cancel this card. How's that?"

"Let me talk to a supervisor," Laura says.

Emma sags into her chair. It's an empty threat, an idea that popped into Emma's head at the last moment. Thomas loves Old Schooners, and their prices are good, so she won't cancel the card. So much for telling it like it is, but hey, sometimes you gotta do what you gotta do.

When Laura comes back on the line, she says they can waive the fee one last time.

"I have to stress that this is the last time we can offer any fee waivers on this account," Laura says.

"Of course," Emma says. "You're a doll, Laura. Thank you very much."

Sign, lick, seal, stamp.

***

It's a quiet Friday night. Myles is out of town with the baseball team for a weekend series in Scranton—and thankfully, Sounders never followed up about that guitar player he wanted Emma to see at the coffee shop—so she and Thomas order a pizza and watch a movie together. After the movie, Thomas heads to his room and Emma takes a bath, sits and soaks, with her phone propped against the tile behind the sink, streaming a pop music mix.

She's tired. After she did the bills, finally pulled off her pajama pants and grabbed a quick shower and late lunch, she went back to working on the resource guide, plowed through it with a purpose, put off grading all of those papers, again. She put more than a dent in it. When she meets Gayle again on Sunday, she'll suggest they move forward with it, submit it to the entire committee. And it really is a remarkable list. She envisions it as a model for other school districts. Just wait until word about it gets out. Thirty-three books, sixteen articles, nine videos, eight Web sites, six documentaries. Harriet Tubman, Rosa Parks, James Baldwin, Thurgood Marshall, Harvey Milk, the Anti-Defamation League, Black Lives Matter, the National Child Traumatic Stress Network. Articles from Stanford University, Georgetown University, Education Week, the National Museum of African American History and Culture. With a simple click of their mouse, any kid or teacher in the school district, her school district, the one she grew up in, and now her son's school district, can find the kinds of books and stories that help us get through the tough times, connect to the people and organizations that have made a difference in this world.

Yet her back hurts, of course, and her eyes are sore. All that screen time, all that time hunched at her desk today. Maybe eye drops would help—she should stop at the drug store tomorrow. And hopefully the bath will help. If not, two Advil before bed. She slides down in the tub, the water lapping her shoulders, closes her eyes, tries to relax, let the music from her phone manage her mood—Adele is belting out something emotive and soulful, *When We Were Young.*

The secretary job. Wait, where did that thought come from? Her eyes pop open. What happened to Adele, and the mood, and when we were young? Why is a job like that piercing her thoughts? Bills, that's why. The damned bills. Yeah, it would be nice if it were easier paying the bills. If she didn't have to stress over every thirty-dollar late fee, if she didn't always feel as if she were hanging on by a thread. If she could find a nicer place for her and Thomas, someplace that really felt like home. And where all the appliances worked.

But no, no. Get a grip. Would administration even consider you for a job like that? Probably not. They'd consider you overqualified. Because you are.

An old FM rock song is streaming now, a voice she can't place, singing about needing a little help. She closes her eyes again, lolls her head back, the water lapping up behind her ears, as she takes in the song, which strikes an emotional chord: a little help. But why does she even pay attention to the lyrics? It's some sort of curse, this overqualified mind of hers that examines and self-reflects and frets and sweats. Can't just hum along. Even after the accomplishments of the past few days—the list, Thomas's hit, and hey, bills are paid, without any late fees—she frets and sweats. But of course, she still has a lot to fret and sweat about. Where are the manuals or roadmaps for dealing with this shit? Where is the Adulting 101 class?

If only she could just hum along.

***

After her bath, belt tightened on her pink terrycloth robe, she checks on Thomas, pokes her head in his bedroom, says "Hey."

He says, "Hey."

She steps into the doorway, leans against the doorframe. Outside, a storm has kicked up. Hard, wind-driven rain, a steady patter against the bedroom windows. A crack of thunder, followed immediately by another. Yet here in his bedroom, it feels cozy and safe.

Thomas is reading. He's sitting up in bed, on top of his red-white-and-blue baseball sheets, a book on Roberto Clemente propped in his lap, with a warm light from the lamp beside his bed.

"I thought you were reading a Jackie Robinson book?" Emma asks.

"I'm done with it," he says.

"Oh, good."

"Did you know," he asks, "that when Clemente was a little boy, he was so poor he had to make his own bat from a tree branch?"

"No, I didn't."

"He was from Puerto Rico."

"I didn't know that either. What team did he play for?" She forks her fingers through her damp hair.

"The Pirates."

"That's Pittsburgh, right?"

He glowers at her from the corner of his eyes, says, "Yes, Mom."

"See, I know some things about baseball."

He shakes his head dismissively. "Everybody knows that."

"Oh, really?"

He drops the book in his lap. "Can I get a Pirates shirt?" he asks. "Do they sell them at Old Schooners?"

FOURTEEN

FRANCES SEEMS FLUSTERED. Tuesday morning, fifteen minutes before class, the smell of manure wafting across campus, and Emma has ducked into the English office in Irving Hall to check her mailbox. Frances is standing at her desk, eyes bouncing around, from doorway to phone to computer screen, as if looking for answers somewhere, anywhere.

"Thaddeus is freaking out," Frances says. "He can't poop."

Thaddeus Webber, the British poetry professor, the only professor on campus with a degree from Harvard, fully tenured for the past twenty years. Emma has never talked to him, seen him only once, waddling across campus in a flannel shirt and faded jeans, with a shock of mussy white hair, carrying a small volume of poetry in one hand, but she's heard he can be goofy. A minute earlier, as she approached Frances's office, Emma saw his office door bang shut down the hall, so he's apparently retreated to his office.

"Why can't he poop?" Emma asks, eyes raised, stupefied. "And why is this any of your business?"

This is most definitely a job she doesn't want.

"The toilet is missing," Frances explains, as she rakes both hands through her hair. "From the basement men's room, which is where Thaddeus likes to take his morning poop."

Emma does a double take. "You're kidding me, right? I feel like I've just stepped into the Twilight Zone or someplace like that."

"Not kidding," Frances says. "It's missing, and he's very upset, so I've just called maintenance."

"How does a toilet go missing?"

Frances shrugs.

"And why can't he poop somewhere else?"

"I don't know," Frances says. "He has his routines, I guess."

A campus cop appears in the doorway. He's a pudgy guy with a military haircut, says he received a report of a missing toilet.

"I called maintenance about it," Frances says, and she seems even more confused.

"They called us," the cop says.

Emma takes a step backward, further away from the doorway. It's a small office, and she wants to watch this whole exchange without being in anyone's way. The cop steps in front of Frances's desk, places both hands on hips. He's taking this very seriously.

"It's the second missing toilet incident we've had," the cop explains. "The last one was in the union building. Which bathroom is it this time?"

"The basement men's room," Frances says.

"Any indication where the toilet went?" the cop asks.

"I don't know," Frances says, shoulders drooping. "I don't track the toilets."

"I'll check it out," he says with a nod of confidence, and he's gone.

"There you have it," Emma says. "Campus security is on the case. Will that mollify Thaddeus?"

"Who knows," Frances says, falling into her chair.

At last, Emma checks her mailbox. Nothing in it of any significance.

On her way out the door, Emma says, "You don't make enough money to deal with shit like this. No pun intended."

"Colorado," Frances says, "here we come."

***

The next couple of days, as the central Pennsylvania weather turns warmer, the dogwood and redbud tress in full bloom, the scent of lilac bushes and grape wildflowers in the air, red robins and blackbirds reappearing in the sky, Thomas starts racking up strikeouts again, and Myles turns mopey over his team's losing streak, which ensued after the first toilet incident on campus, the first time Emma's seen that side of him. And Emma finds herself stressing over something new:

the list. The Diversity Committee is about to review it at a Thursday night meeting. That was Gayle's suggestion when Emma met her for coffee again on Sunday. Gayle had looked it over Sunday morning and said it was a very fine draft, looked "good to go."

For some reason, though, Gayle didn't leave Emma feeling very confident about it. It wasn't anything Gayle said; she just didn't seem the same, didn't radiate that sense of control and confidence that Emma detected when they first met. Instead, Gayle seemed distracted, weary. Her eyes looked tired, and she kept checking her phone while she and Emma chatted and sipped their coffee. Emma didn't want to pry, though, so she didn't ask if something was wrong. The list was good to go, so Emma accepted that at face value.

Still, Emma drives to the committee meeting Thursday night fighting back doubts and trying to calm her nerves. What kinds of questions should she expect? What if someone grills her over the quality of some of the sources—can she adequately defend them? Did she really put enough time into this project? Or did she rush it, too overwhelmed by the rest of her life to do it right?

She's dressed nicely, the same belted blue dress she wore to class earlier in the day. And she's brought her leather teaching bag, partly because it has the pens and notebook she'll need to take notes, but mostly because it conveys professionalism.

She's on time, thank God. Squeezed in a dinner of Hamburger Helper, the Philly Cheesesteak flavor, Thomas's favorite, and dropped him off at Tracey's. After she parks at the high school, she reaches into her purse for her eye drops, pinches a drop into each eye. She even has two minutes to spare as she approaches the school doors, slings her teaching bag over her shoulder and mutes her phone.

The Diversity Committee meets in the school cafeteria, which is often converted to event space in the evenings. It's been renovated since Emma's high school years—opened up and brightened up to resemble a food court, with glossy tile walls and bigger windows—so Emma feels little sense of nostalgia. For tonight, the tables have been rearranged with a head table fronting the main serving area and a single guest table across from it. Evening sun slants in through the windows in the back. The smell of Brussels sprouts lingers.

Gayle is sitting at the head table, leaning into a conversation with Sounders, who's seated beside her. When Gayle spots Emma, she springs out of her seat and winds around the head table, meets Emma at the space between the tables and gives her a little hug.

"I'm nervous," Emma says.

"Don't be," Gayle says. "What's that old line from *The Brady Bunch*? Just imagine everyone in their underwear."

"Ha," Emma chuckles. "That just might help."

"It really is an excellent list, especially for a draft," Gayle says, then turns toward the head table. "Let me introduce you to some committee members."

So Emma meets Emily Satchell, a gray-haired history teacher who's taught at the high school since Emma was a kid, though Emma never had her class; and Dennis Graham, a young music teacher who's wearing a tie-dyed rainbow T-shirt; and Anna Heffner, the middle school guidance counselor; and Grace Miller, a parent whose daughter is a tenth grader. Each one shakes Emma's hand and offer brief compliments about Emma's work on the list. Only one is a person of color—Grace is black—and Emma's reminded that diversity is a relatively new thing here, because when Emma attended CASH, this small central Pennsylvania town was overwhelmingly straight and white, a parochial fold of flag-waving Bush voters and devoted Rush Limbaugh listeners who, unless they were paying for gas or soda at a convenience store, never even met a Muslim, and even when they were paying for their gas or soda, still considered them conniving terrorists who were likely plotting next to blow up Three Mile Island, which sits just south of Harrisburg on the Susquehanna River. Emma knew one black girl in high school, who sat beside her in English class junior year, and no one who had come out as lesbian or gay or bi or trans or queer. The black girl's name was Kylee Voss, a shy girl who ran cross country and track and spent most of her time hanging out with her teammates, then went off to Shippensburg University and disappeared from Emma's life. All the more reason to do what they're doing here tonight.

Sounders hovers at the head table, watching as Emma meets the other committee members. As if he needs some sort of reintroduction.

Which feels strange, because she saw him again on Sunday at the coffee shop with Gayle, at which time he pretty much agreed with Gayle on everything, but then Emma successfully avoided walking through the parking lot with him, afraid he might ask her back for guitar night or something. So maybe he feels snubbed? He steps forward after the introductions are finished, offers his usual limp handshake.

"Nice to see you again," he says with an air of formality.

"Yes, you too," Emma says, same formal tone.

Emma takes a seat at the guest table, the only person there, and as the others settle into their seats at the head table, she peers around the cafeteria, trying to picture the scene during the lunch hour. Where do the jocks sit? The band kids, the gamers, and the LGBTQ+ kids? How many black and brown kids are there, and do they integrate at all? Where will Thomas sit? Will he have friends to sit with? But of course he will—right? Oh, God, she hopes she's right.

Gayle starts the meeting. She seems herself again, welcomes everyone and officially introduces Emma with the same focus and confidence that Emma detected when they were first acquainted, so whatever was bothering or distracting Gayle on Sunday must be resolved, or at least has settled down. Emma hopes it's resolved.

"Can I say a few words?" Emma asks.

"Of course," Gayle says.

Emma clears her throat, squares her shoulders. She didn't plan on this, but suddenly she recognizes that she has an audience, and this is too important to let any opportunity pass.

"I want to tell you a little about myself," she begins. "I grew up here and graduated from CASH, as valedictorian. I moved away to New York and then moved back last year with my son, whose father is Pakistani, and I can see how much my hometown is changing, for better and worse. I know that my son isn't alone. He's not the only student of color in this district. And I know how difficult it is for those kids sometimes. Just being different is hard enough, but sometimes things happen. Real things that really affect these kids. What we're doing here, I'm absolutely certain, has the potential to make a difference in their lives. I teach college English—I have classes at

Cumberland and Penn State-Harrisburg—and I felt comfortable and qualified doing this work. In fact, I was really happy to do it. So thank you so much for taking on this project and for asking me to be involved and for being there for our kids."

There's quiet. Nods and smiles at the head table. Gayle says, "We understand."

"Yes, very good," Sounders says. "Now, let's get to work."

First, questions. Who offered recommendations for all of the sources? Did Emma research each source for reliability? Appropriateness? Emma's answers seem to satisfy everyone—a lot of affirmative nodding at the head table. The discussion turns to how best to organize the sources, how to present the list to the board. What should the finished product look like? Should it be professionally formatted, into a .pdf with graphics? Yes, yes, more affirmative nods. Dennis Graham says he's pretty good at graphic design, so he'd be happy to do that.

They decide to meet again next week, same place and time, review the formatted version of the list, consider any last-minute questions or concerns that might arise, before sending it to the school board. The school board meets the following Thursday.

"Wouldn't it be great," Gayle says, "if this was in place in time for the beginning of next school year?"

Everyone nods.

FIFTEEN

"I'm just going to tell him," Clarissa says. "Blurt it out, just like that—hey Dad, I'm a lesbian, so deal with it, okay?"

Friday morning, and she and Amelia have skipped school, driven over to Harrisburg, stopped for breakfast burritos on Second Street, then walked over to the river and spread blankets in the grass under a sun-soaked sky. They're wearing halter tops and shorts with Banana Boat rubbed into their skin. Behind them, joggers and bicyclists and dog-walkers trickle by on the riverside path. On a bench to their right, about ten yards away, an old guy is nursing a tall beer in a paper bag.

"Maybe he'll send you to conversion camp," Amelia says, deadpan.

"Not funny."

"I don't know which is worse," Amelia says, "not having a dad or having an asshole for a dad."

"I don't know either," Clarissa says, and that's how she wants to leave it. She knows better to compare their situations, both of which are shitty. Amelia's dad left when she was twelve.

Amelia lifts herself onto her elbows, and a serious look crosses her face. She's light-skinned too, much like Clarissa, but with soft freckles and short reddish hair. "At least your mom's been cool," she says.

"Well, sort of." She stays flat on her back.

Clarissa hasn't brought up the topic with her mom since the night she got a ticket, and though home life has settled into a truce-like atmosphere, the clock is ticking toward junior prom, driving up Clarissa's anxiety. And next week, the three of them are scheduled to visit Bryn Mawr College, Clarissa's top choice, and the thought of spending four hours in the car together isn't helping. Just the thought of college isn't helping: Amelia's looking at state schools, Shippensburg and Bloomsburg, so Clarissa knows the time will come when they'll be several hours apart, and then who knows. Their relationship is so damn easy, that's how Clarissa thinks about it, and she recognizes the irony, because the outside world has such a hard time with it, but every interaction between them, from their most casual chats to their most tender moments, comes so easily. So easy that when Clarissa began to realize her sexuality, last fall, she initially wondered if her feelings were inspired by who Amelia is as a friend, or who she is as a young woman. Now she knows it was both. It's why she agreed to skip school today—Amelia's idea—despite the risk. A big risk, considering her mom's recent lecture about avoiding any more tickets or trouble of any sort while she tries to prep her dad for the news. But still, she wanted to take advantage of the awesome weather and the time with Amelia.

Life is coming at her hard and fast, and there's nothing she can do to stop it.

Clarissa raises herself on her elbows, gazes out at the river, muddy and fast-moving, full of recent rains and melted snow from upstate, and on the other side, the West Shore, with the narrow riverfront borough of Wormleysburg running along the river and the million-dollar homes of the town of Lemoyne on the cliff above them. West of them, the upscale suburb of Camp Hill, and then their hometown, Cumberland.

"I feel like I'm a million miles from home right now," she says.

"Is that a good thing or a bad thing?" Amelia asks.

"Definitely a good thing." She nods for emphasis.

"Have you ever heard the West Shore described as the White Shore?" Amelia asks.

"Why—because that's where all the white people live?"

"Yup." She waves away a fly.

"Hmm," Clarissa says. "Makes sense."

"I can't believe we live on the White Shore."

"I know, really."

Clarissa rolls onto her stomach, looking eastward into the city, away from the West Shore.

***

"i got caught"

Late Friday afternoon, and Clarissa is sitting on her bed rubbing aloe into her skin, hoping her mom doesn't ask how she got so much color today, when she gets the text from Amelia.

"shit, how?"

"someone from the school called our house, i guess one of those random calls they do, then my mom called the principal, afraid i was abducted or something"

"nobody called here, i blew by my mom when i got home and she didn't say anything"

"don't worry i didn't rat you out, told the principal i skipped with a friend from camp hill"

"u r a great partner in crime"

"lol"

"how much trouble r u in?"

"too much"

"seriously"

"2 days of in school suspension, not allowed to drive the car for a month"

"ouch, i have my car tho"

"u r my new chauffer"

"lol"

A knock on her door.

"Yes?"

"It's me," her mom says. "Can I come in?"

Clarissa drops her phone, chucks the aloe into a drawer in her bedside table, rolls over, buries her face in her pillows. "Okay."

Her mom opens the door partway, sticks her head inside. "Everything okay?"

"I don't feel very well."

"Did something happen today?" Her tone is sincere. She doesn't know.

"No, I just don't feel very well." She covers her head with her forearm.

"Headache? Stomach ache? What?"

"Headache."

"Ah, it's Friday night."

"I know, but I can't help it."

"We're thinking about ordering Chinese."

"That's fine. Just get me some wonton."

"That's all?"

"And an egg roll."

"Got it. Wonton and an egg roll. Want some Advil?"

"No, that's okay."

"Let me bring you some Advil."

"It makes me nauseous sometimes."

"Okay, but let me know if you change your mind."

"I won't."

Her mom closes the door gently without saying anything more. At least she realizes that her daughter rarely changes her mind.

SIXTEEN

"They loved it," Emma brags.

She's sitting on one of the plastic chairs on her back porch, wearing shorts and flip-flops, glass of wine in hand. It's a lovely Friday evening, the sun setting with an orange glow, the lilac bushes full and fragrant on the side of the yard, and she's hosting her first little picnic, even though the grass is long and weedy because the landlord hasn't mowed it lately. Tracey is sharing a glass of chardonnay with her on the porch, the kids are scootering in the alley behind the yard, and Myles is tinkering with the old grill, trying to get it started.

"Absolutely loved it," Emma continues. "And it's probably going to the full school board the Thursday after next."

"Is there any propane in here?" Myles asks. He's on his knees at the grill, one arm swaying the tank from side to side.

"I don't know," Emma says. "I thought you could take care of it. You said you could."

"But I assumed there would be propane in it," Myles says. He lets go of the tank, stands up and dusts off his knees. "Let me try to explain this. It's like a car, which needs gas. Even if you get all the parts working properly, the car won't run without gas."

"Okay, smart guy," Emma says. "I get it. So the grill won't work."

He picks up his green bottle of Yuengling, takes a slug. "It might. But only if it has propane. So I don't know."

"So what are we going to do with the burgers and dogs?"

"Go get propane, and then give it a try," Myles says. "Or cook them on the stove."

"Or just order pizzas?" Tracey suggests.

"Pizzas are on me," Myles says, yanking his phone from his pocket. "What does everyone want?"

***

The pizza boxes are still open, lying on the floor boards of the porch, two pepperoni slices hardening in the late-night air. Emma's wearing her Princeton sweatshirt, still in shorts and flip-flops, another glass of wine in hand. Myles has just cracked another beer, his fifth—or is it his sixth? Ah hell, what's it matter? He didn't start until after six o'clock, so he obeyed his own rule. He and Emma are slouched in the porch chairs, a bright, three-quarter moon in the sky, and Thomas is in bed. Myles feels content, surprisingly content, especially considering all the losing he's endured lately. Hasn't won a game since the toilet suspensions were handed down.

"Will you come to one of Thomas's baseball games?" Emma asks. "He would love that, and I would love that."

"I'd like to, but it's hard—you know, our schedule, practices and everything. It's my job."

"I know, I know," she says, tilting her wine glass. "But if I could just spend one inning in the stands with this tall and handsome college baseball coach, so all the other Cumberland parents could see us there rooting for Thomas, it would be so damn cool."

He wishes he could, genuinely does. Wants to be there for her. Since his marriage dissolved, there have been plenty of women, but none he's felt this way about. Pretty much a series of flings that ended after a date or two, or just a hook-up at the casino. A divorced kindergarten teacher from Camp Hill, a long-legged athletic trainer from York College, a young lobbyist from Harrisburg, a thirty-something bartender with tattoos up and down both arms. His longest post-divorce relationship was three weeks with a redheaded dental assistant named Julie. They met at his dental appointment. She was a little younger than him, just like Emma. They went out to eat a few times, and he slept over at her apartment twice, but then a bad dream broke them up. Julie told him that she'd dreamt Myles cheated on her with her best friend, and she couldn't get over it. But, Myles pleaded, it was just a dream. She pressed him: Why did your marriage break up? He admitted that he cheated, but it wasn't with his wife's best friend. Even so, she said, my dream says something about you.

"Send me his schedule," Myles says. "Maybe I can work something out."

"I'll do that til morrow—I mean tomorrow," Emma says, then cracks a cute, embarrassed smile. "Too much wine."

"It's okay," Myles says. "It's been a great night."

Emma holds up her wine glass, studies it against the moonlight. "I've been drunk twice in the past ten years," she says, her tone only half-serious. "And both times have been with you. What's that about?"

"I have that effect on people," Myles deadpans.

"Hah. You're a good guy, though. I really believe that."

"Thank you," he says. "And you're a great gal. A really great gal."

"Thank you," she says proudly and drunkenly. She pushes herself out of the chair, stands at the edge of the porch, looks up at the sky. It really is a beautiful night, starry and clear, just a little chill in the air, the nicest night of the spring so far, the promise of summer looming. She sits down on the edge of the porch.

"Come sit with me," she says, patting the spot beside her.

"Sure," he says. Their shoulders and knees rub against each other, and they take in the spring sky together.

Waving a finger up at the sky, she points out the North Star, then the Big Dipper. She explains that they're easy to spot on clear nights, how the Big Dipper is like a kitchen ladle in the north sky, how the two stars at the end of the cup point to the North Star.

"How do you remember that stuff?" he asks.

"I'm a college professor. Don't you forget it." She blows up at a stray lock of hair.

"But you're an English professor."

"And a Princeton graduate before that, and a valedictorian before that, so we know stuff. Don't forget that, either."

"Got it, professor," he says obediently, then takes a sip of beer.

She gives a satisfied nod, takes a drink of wine. Places her hand on his knee, squeezes it affectionately.

"Have you ever had sex outside?" she asks.

"Huh?"

"You heard me."

"Can I plead the Fifth?"

"Hmm," she says. "Okay, but I'll take that as a yes. It's okay. We're adults now."

He puts a hand on his lower back, gives it an exaggerated stretch. "Oh, yeah. We're adults. I can even feel it."

"You're good at changing the topic. It's called diversion."

He shrugs.

"But I'm not going to let you change the topic," she says, squeezing his knee again, tilting her head provocatively, flashing bedroom eyes at him. "I want to have sex outside."

"Seriously?"

"Yeah, seriously. Under the stars. Isn't it romantic?"

She leans in for a kiss, a wet, boozy kiss. After a minute, he pulls back, looks from side to side at the other houses. "What about the neighbors?" he asks.

"The twin beside us is vacant," she says, stretching her neck to look beyond it. "And the house beside that looks all dark, so they must be in bed." She turns her head the other way, where a large lilac bush abuts the neighbor's fence. "And over here the bushes block the view."

"Then what are we waiting for?" Myles says.

She hops up, bolts into the house, finds an old blanket stuffed in a closet, carries it outside, takes Myles by the hand, leads him down the porch steps, spreads the blanket beside the lilacs on the long, unmowed grass. Down on their knees together, they kiss again, then wiggle off their shorts. Still wearing her sweatshirt and bra, Emma climbs on top.

"Wait a minute," she says, stopping mid-grind. "I can't see the stars. You get on top."

"Whatever you're into."

They switch positions.

"Is that better?" he asks, after he re-enters her.

"Much better. Thank you."

She wraps her arms around his back. He moves slowly, gently. She looks past his shoulder at the night sky. The moon hangs low and lush. Stars glisten. She hears the music of the night—songbirds trilling softly in the trees, an engine revving somewhere down Cedar Street, the purr of the HVAC alongside the house, and she's humming along.

SEVENTEEN

THEY TAKE THE AUDI to Bryn Mawr. Her dad's car, black with gray leather seats. He never lets her mom drive, let alone Clarissa, so the Audi was a given. Clarissa, who still hasn't been behind the wheel of the Audi, is stretched out in the back seat, earbuds in while she searches her playlist, her mom thumbing her phone in the passenger seat.

"I'm having lunch with Ted Vance tomorrow," her dad says, one hand on the wheel, eyes straight ahead, after merging into the eastbound lanes on the turnpike. "I heard he wants to retire next year."

Her mom stops thumbing. "Really? That's interesting."

Ted Vance is the West Shore's longtime state senator, held down the seat since the Reagan years, hasn't had a primary opponent since the Clinton years, and given the district's heavy Republican registration edge, that means he's been a re-election lock for a couple of decades. It's Ted's seat.

Clarissa stops searching her playlist, pulls out one of her earbuds. This discussion is worth eavesdropping on.

"Who told you he wants to retire?" Mom asks. She slides her phone into the console between the seats.

"Don Haggerty, his chief of staff," Dad says. "I talked to Don this morning, but he told me the retirement buzz should stay hush-hush for now."

"Don's pretty reliable." Mom says.

"Oh, he's very reliable."

"Why do you think he told you that?" Mom asks.

Dad turns his face slightly, left eye on the highway, right eye in Mom's direction.

"My guess?" he says. "He wanted me to be prepared for it, so I can play my cards the right way."

"How do you want to play your cards?" Mom asks.

He shifts his face back to the left, both eyes on the highway. He's thinking.

"Well?" Mom asks.

"I know Ted pretty well," he says, and his voice his measured, his professional voice, a lawyer's voice. "We've golfed together several times, and I think he has a lot of confidence in me. An endorsement from him would be huge."

Mom shifts in her seat, her whole body angled toward Dad.

"So you're interested in Ted's seat?"

"Yes."

She reaches over and pats his thigh, his tan chinos. "I'm glad," she says.

They cruise past a turnpike plaza, a Sunoco and a Roy Rogers, from which two cars want to merge back onto the highway, so Dad checks his mirrors, flicks on his turn signal, allows the cars to merge.

Clarissa doesn't want to hear any more. She replaces her second earbud, revisits her playlist, settles on Lizzo: *Exactly how I feel*. She sees what's coming. The next several weeks, months—years?—will be consumed by Dad's political ambitions. What's best for Dad will be best for the family; everything else will just have to take a back seat. Yeah, that's how it's gonna be, even if Clarissa's ready to come out, and come out fully, to everyone, not just the people who can deal with it, rather than remain stuck where she is now, in this shitty, half-out limbo.

***

Bryn Mawr College is tucked inside the old and moneyed Main Line just outside of Philadelphia, a sanctum of Gothic architecture and liberalism along New Gulph Road. An all-girls school, founded by Quakers, one of the most liberal in the country. Does Dad realize that? He probably just looks at the rankings, and it ranks high. If she likes this tour as much as she likes everything she's heard and read about the school, Clarissa plans to apply under early decision, so if she gets accepted, and she sees no reason why she shouldn't, with her killer grades and a 1480 on the SATs, that's where she'll enroll.

Their tour guide is a perky Asian girl named Chloe, wearing an unbuttoned gray sweater over jean shorts and a gold T-shirt that reads "MAWRTYR." One other prospective student is on the tour, a tall black girl named Morgan who's touring with her mother. When Chloe asks the girls where they're from, Morgan says Washington, D.C.

"I'm from some little town you never heard of in the middle of Pennsylvania," Clarissa says.

"It's a suburb of Harrisburg—Cumberland," Mom says, as if she needs to clarify something.

"Cool," Chloe says, as their group descends the concrete steps outside the admissions building. "What do you both want to major in?"

"Physics," Morgan says.

"Political science," Clarissa says.

Mom and Dad arch their eyebrows. Shoot each other a look that says, *What's happening here?*

"Really?" Mom says.

"Cool," Chloe says. She's two steps ahead of the group, leading them on the trail that winds into the heart of campus.

"What happened to environmental studies?" Mom asks.

"I don't know," Clarissa says, her head on a swivel, soaking up her surroundings, the budding trees and gray-stone Gothic buildings and late-morning sun. "I've been thinking about political science lately."

Well, yeah, sort of. She's been thinking about it since she put Lizzo in her ear on the car ride, so technically, yeah, she's been thinking about it.

"I see," Mom says.

"Maybe someday I'll run for Ted's seat," Clarissa says.

"Who's Ted?" Chloe asks.

"He's our state senator," Clarissa says.

"Cool," Chloe says.

Clarissa is enjoying every step she takes. This place already feels like home. She's also enjoying her control over the discussion. She's enjoying the vexed looks on Mom and Dad's faces. But there's still this big pot of crap in her life—time to stir it.

"Maybe I'll run against Dad someday," she says. "Of course, I'll have to run as a Democrat."

Mom sidles up against her, whispers in her ear, "Not funny."

"I'm not trying to be funny," Clarissa says in her own sharp whisper.

Dad, who looks sufficiently uptight in his chinos and red golf shirt, as out of place as February Christmas lights, is holding onto his silence, holding on tight, lips locked, face strained.

Morgan and her mom keep their silence, too. They slow their steps for an extra yard or two of distance. They recognize a messed-up white family when they see one.

"We'll definitely stop by the Political Science Department," Chloe says. "Physics, too."

"Let's be sure to stop by Environmental Studies as well," Mom says.

"For sure," Chloe says.

***

Lunch is a quiet and awkward affair at a Vietnamese place on Lancaster Avenue, but the shrimp rice vermicelli is fantastic, better than Harrisburg's one and only Vietnamese restaurant, a dumpy little joint on Third Street. Dad eats his Vietnamese hoagie without complaining—it also looks very tasty, so he has no reason to complain—yet Clarissa wonders if he ordered it only because he can pronounce it and it reminds him of something American. Mom nips at her chicken noodle soup. Clarissa picked the restaurant, and Mom and Dad complied, Clarissa sensing they were preparing to do battle over her college choice, and of course they're smart enough to choose their battles wisely, so they didn't want to argue over a lunch spot.

Back on the turnpike, westward toward Harrisburg, the backseat is stuffy, the afternoon sun beating into the car while they ate. Clarissa thinks about Morgan, feels a swell of regret that they hardly spoke to each other on the tour. Should have made an effort to connect with another girl her age who's also trying to chart a future in this broken world and is crossing paths with her. But then again, it's hard with parents around, sending each other looks, whispering in your ear, so maybe Morgan understood, felt the same way. Still, Clarissa should have tried. She would have loved to have simply said, *Believe me, I'm not like these people.*

Finally, Mom broaches the subject they avoided at lunch: "So what did you think?"

"It's definitely my first choice," Clarissa says. "I'm going to apply for early decision."

"It's the only college you've visited," Dad says. "How do you know it's your first choice if you haven't seen any other colleges?"

"I've read about them, talked to people. I know what I'm looking for," Clarissa says.

"Before you apply, why don't we visit one more?" Dad asks. "What about Penn State?"

"Can you turn up the air conditioning, please?" Clarissa asks.

Mom adjusts the knob. "You'd get in the Honors Program at Penn State, no doubt," she says.

"No, there's no point," Clarissa says.

"Why not?" Dad asks.

"There's no way I'm going to some big, testosterone-charged football school," Clarissa says. "No way."

"Just think about it," Mom says.

Clarissa feels her mom's eyes coming at her from the rearview mirror.

"Okay, I'll think about it," Clarissa says, then cocks her head, lets a pause hang in the air, scratches her chin mockingly with thumb and forefinger. "I just thought about it, and no way."

***

Wednesday morning, kids off to school, empty cereal bowls stacked in the sink, morning sun glowing in the windows, and Gayle gets a peck on the cheek at the kitchen island. She smiles at him, a good-luck smile, wraps her fingers around his upper arm, holds tight for a moment. "Text me after lunch," she says. "Let me know how it goes."

But he won't. Not in the middle of a workday. She'll have to text him, and then he may or may not reply, depending on his mood and how his day is going. But that's okay—he's a lawyer and a local politician, and she understands the lay of the land. And she knows how to get what she wants regardless. So if she wants to know how it went before he gets home this evening, she'll have to go see him. No problem. She calls a friend, Maryanne McLain, whose husband served as Doug's campaign treasurer in his county commissioner race, and suggests they meet for lunch—how about that cute new bistro on Main Street, the one that's just down the block from the law office?

Another warm day, so Gayle dresses light, a yellow midi dress with leather sandals. Lunch is pleasant—she orders the Caesar salad with chicken, while Maryanne orders shrimp salad—and Gayle deliberately avoids talk about anything heavy, especially politics. Plenty of time for that later, if it comes to that, and Doug's lunch is what's on her mind.

After lunch with Maryanne, she stops by Doug's office. He's not back yet. A good sign? She makes chit-chat with his secretary while she waits. When he finally returns, his chin is up and he takes long, purposeful strides into the office. Another good sign?

"Everything okay?" he asks Gayle when he sees her sitting in the waiting area.

"You tell me. How was your lunch?"

"Come on in," he says, checking his watch. "I have five minutes. I'll bring you up to speed."

In those five minutes, Doug tells her that they ate at Tavern on the Hill, a popular spot for the Harrisburg power set which overlooks the river, where Ted told him he's announcing his retirement next week, but he'll finish out his term. That will give interested candidates a year to prepare for the primary. Ted said he hopes Doug is interested; he didn't mention the word "endorse," but it was implied. They're golfing together Saturday.

So, another campaign. This one for higher office: the state legislature. And who knows after that—the governor's mansion?

Congress? Okay, maybe she's getting ahead of herself there, but then again, maybe not. Doug is not that old, the future is bright.

Gayle feels up to it. So exciting. They can do this. When she leaves the office, stepping onto the warm sidewalk of Main Street, she starts a mental to-do list: volunteers, and by now, they have a network already in place; nominating petitions; financial statements and other paperwork; fundraising; signs and media; appearances at chicken barbeques. Yeah, they can do this. Done it before. The only problem— her daughter has something very important to tell her father, the candidate.

EIGHTEEN

FOURTH-GRADE LUNCH, Thursday, chicken nuggets on the menu. Thomas sits at the end of a table with Michael Baxter and Ashley Clay, two of his frequent lunch partners, wearing his green Hornets jersey. They've just returned from morning recess, their throats dry and their skin clammy from running around and sweating. Ashley is complaining about tag; she hasn't gotten the chance to pick in forever, and Danielle Fossberger gets too much say. She asks, "Who made Danielle boss, anyway?"

Thomas gulps his apple juice, gives Ashley a shrug.

Something splashes on the side of his neck. It feels slimy, gross. He reaches up and wipes at it with his fingertips. It's brown. Chocolate pudding.

"Go back where you came from."

The words come at him from his right, a boy's voice, spoken as if they were spit at him. A salvo of haughty giggles comes next. Thomas looks up to his right, sees a group of boys passing him with trays in hand, Justin Bass smack in the middle.

Startled, hurt, embarrassed, Thomas turns his eyes away, drops his gaze to his tray. Justin and company move on, find seats two tables away. Thomas picks up his napkin, wipes off his neck and fingers.

"Aren't you going to tell on them?" Ashley asks.

"I don't know," Thomas says. He balls up the pudding-stained napkin, sets it on the corner of his tray.

"You should," Ashley says.

"They're jerks," Michael Baxter says.

"If you don't tell, I will," Ashley says. "I saw it."

"Who did it?" Michael asks.

"I don't know, but one of them," Ashley says.

Thomas scans the cafeteria, above the din of chattering chicken-nugget munchers, looking for the cafeteria aides. He spots them both, a heavyset older woman and a stringy-haired younger woman, leaning against the wall by the entrance, talking to each other. He screws his eyes closed, unsure of what to do, wishing he weren't here in this loud and crowded and tortuous place. When he opens his eyes, he looks back down at his tray, picks up a chicken nugget.

"Aren't you gonna tell?" Ashley asks.

"I don't know," Thomas says quietly. He takes a small bite of nugget.

"Then I will," Ashley says.

"No, don't," Thomas says in mid-chew.

"Why not?"

Thomas looks back at the aides, finishes chewing. "I will. I'll tell."

"Good," Ashley says. "I hope so."

Thomas looks over at Justin and company, two tables away, babbling and beaming and feeding their faces. He looks back at his tray—three nuggets left, in addition to the half-nugget left in his hand. He pops the half-nugget into his mouth.

Ashley eyeballs him. He finishes his nugget, picks up another.

"I thought you were gonna tell," Ashley says.

"Yeah, you should tell," Michael says. "I would."

"I am," Thomas says. "After I eat my chicken nuggets."

He bites into his next nugget, and the next, and the next. Five minutes left in lunch, and he finishes his last nugget, takes a final drink of his apple juice, gets up and walks over to the cafeteria aides, head down every step of way, and he tells them what happened.

***

Eric Sounders is calling. Emma recognizes the number by now. Hopefully it's a call about the Diversity Committee's work or the upcoming school board meeting, which is just a week away, not a Friday night date. So she wants to answer this call even though she's working with a Cumberland College student, who's sitting with her at the desk in the drab adjunct office in Irving Hall.

"I have to take this," Emma tells the student, a sad-eyed girl named Sophie. "Look over your third page in the meantime. Look closer for grammar errors."

Sophie makes a face, her sad eyes looking even sadder, but complies nonetheless.

"Ms. Muller-Farooq?" It's Sounders' voice, but why so formal? She blinks in confusion.

"Yes."

"This is Eric Sounders at Buchanan Elementary School."

"Yes, I know you. Remember?"

"Yes, right," he says, then clears his throat. "I'm calling about Thomas. There was an incident today at lunch."

"What kind of incident?"

"Someone flicked pudding at him, and someone said something inappropriate to him."

"What did they say?"

He clears his throat again. "To go back to where he came from."

Emma recoils in her desk chair. The phone comes away from her ear. A thump in her gut.

She replaces the phone beside her cheek. "Who," she says, "who said it?"

"That's the thing," Sounders says. "We don't know, exactly. It was a group of boys."

"You don't know?" Emma says, incredulous.

"That's right."

"I'm coming in there," Emma says.

"That's not necessary."

"Yes, it is."

"If you insist."

"I'll be there in fifteen minutes," she says. "Maybe less."

"That's fine."

She thumbs off her phone, drops it on the desk, spits out a wretched sigh. "I have to go," she tells Sophie. "Family emergency."

"Okay?" Sophie says. Her tone suggests more than uncertainty— it suggests something akin to abandonment.

"Can you take your paper to the Writing Center?"

A wounded look crosses Sophie's face.

"It's a family emergency," Emma says, tucking her phone in her purse, logging off her computer, then standing up to leave. "Believe me."

Emma blows out of Irving Hall, teaching bag hanging off her shoulder, into a steamy afternoon. A late-spring heat wave has hit Central Pennsylvania, and the manure smell is particularly strong today. She hustles to her car, whips out of the parking lot, and speeds across town, through the very last millisecond of two yellow lights on the way; one might have actually turned to red, but no cops on her tail. At Thomas's school, the front driveway is parked up with school buses waiting for the three-o'clock bell, so Emma has to wind her way over to the parking lot, finds a spot in the back.

Sounders is waiting for her. He's standing in his office doorway, making small talk with his secretary. He's wearing a baggy brown sweater over a loosely knotted green tie. Emma recalls that he was dressed in a similar outfit the first day she met him, so maybe it's his look, or maybe he just doesn't know how to tie a tie and pick out a sweater. He waves Emma inside. "Thank you for coming in," he says.

"Really?" Emma says. "You must say that to all the parents, because you told me we could handle it over the phone."

He hesitates, eyes floating as he searches for a reply. "We welcome all of our parents," he says.

"Gotcha."

He closes the door with an unusual gentleness, as if he doesn't want to wake someone, follows Emma inside. In front of his desk, she stops suddenly. There's only one chair this time. The other one has been moved to the corner. She does a double-take.

"You moved it, didn't you?" she says.

"The chair? Yes." He settles into his desk chair.

"Why? Don't two parents come in here most of the time?"

"Sometimes, yes, but I remember how uncomfortable it made you."

She sits in the lone chair, her purse in her lap. "That's nice of you, I think," she says. She glares at the chair in the corner—she still doesn't like it, because it still reminds her that she's a single mom.

"But anyway," she says, and turns her gaze to Sounders.

"Yes, anyway."

"What happened?"

He readjusts himself in his seat.

"It happened at lunch. A group of boys was walking to their table, and as they passed Thomas, someone flicked pudding onto the back of his neck, and someone told him to, um, to go back to where he came from."

Emma leans forward, eyes drilling into him. "And who did it?"

Sounders lets out a sorry little huff. "We don't know," he says. "It was a group of four boys. I talked to everyone involved. Nobody who was sitting with Thomas saw who did it, and the four boys in the group all deny saying it themselves, and they all say they don't know who did it. This happens sometimes. Kids protect their friends like that."

"And who's protecting Thomas?"

He readjusts again. "I understand how you feel. I talked to him. He seems to be doing pretty well, under the circumstances."

"Right," she snorts. "Kids are resilient. Isn't that what you told me the last time?"

"Yes, I believe so."

"Was Justin Bass in that group of four boys?" she asks.

"He was."

"So it was probably him."

"I wouldn't say that for certain. It could have just as easily been one of his friends."

"I'm not so sure about that."

"And I'm not either. We're not sure about much here, but we're doing everything we can. And if we're not sure about something, there's not much we can do, unfortunately."

Emma grinds her jaw, breathing hot through her nose. "So what's going to happen to them?" she asks.

"I called the parents of all four boys. I was able to reach all but one, and I'll keep trying his after school. With the others, I asked them to talk to their son at home about the situation, and to see if they can help us get to the bottom of it."

"Did you talk to Justin's parents?"

"Yes."

"And that's all you'll say."

"Correct. That's all I can say."

She leans back in her chair, and her chest and shoulders sink. Is this stuff ever going to stop? How do you make it stop? To her boy, her only son, the person who matters more than anything in the world to her. What can she do? It'll take more than a book list, so much more, but at least she's doing her part, right? She is, isn't she? She rubs her forehead. The weight of this is too much. Her head feels like a brick is strapped on top of it.

Sounders leans forward. "I'm upset about this, too," he says. "If it helps in any way."

"Not really." She closes her eyes, holds them tight. She doesn't want to cry in here.

When she opens her eyes, he's nodding sympathetically.

Times like this—and why are there so many times like this?—Emma sometimes wishes she could just float away from this world, but then she realizes she could never float away without Thomas. Which causes her to immediately regret and then forget the whole idea of floating away. So never mind. She's here, she's staying. She pinches her eyes with finger and thumb. They're moist.

"Are you going to the committee meeting tonight?" he asks. Somehow it sounds as if he's asking for a date, or maybe that's just how she perceives it.

"I don't know," she says. "I was planning on it, but now ... this. I might just prefer a big glass of wine."

She shouldn't have said that. Doesn't want to lead him on.

"Understandable," he says. "I'll be there, but I don't think you need to be. It will be mostly discussion about the presentation—how does it look now that it's been formatted? And then it's off to the full board."

"Is it going to make a difference?" she asks.

He pauses, takes in the question.

"It's not going to change everything," he says. "But it's a step in the right direction, and yes, it will make a difference, for some kids in particular, and that will make it worthwhile."

***

Baseball practice, a soupy-hot Thursday afternoon, and Emma drops off Thomas at the field and hangs around for a few minutes to watch him blend in with the team. She wants to stay for the entire practice, but when she suggested that to him after school he shot it right down. He'd be embarrassed—none of the parents stay for practice, he said. So she'll stick to her word, because she doesn't want to make things worse, though she's racked with worry. She'll be back before long, though. She's wearing gym shorts and her Nike sneakers, planning a walk around the neighborhood while he practices. "It's a nice day," she told Thomas. "And I want to get some exercise."

She walks out past the outfield, turns around at a shaded spot under a patch of trees, scouts the boys from a distance, and Thomas seems fine. The boys are warming up along the third-base line, where he and a teammate are throwing nicely, no sign of tension. The other boy is short and spindly, appears to be Evan, also a sub who strikes out a lot, a really nice kid, so she's glad to see Thomas paired with him. She lingers a minute as they lob a ball back and forth, suspects Thomas doesn't see her, but he will eventually, so she stretches her back then turns and heads into town, carrying her worries with her.

She crosses Main Street and heads for the college, the baseball field, where the Hornets are playing a game against some team in gray and blue. Again, she finds a spot under a tree beyond the outfield fence, watches the other guy in her life as he does his job. Myles is standing along the third-base line, flashing signals to batters, ear taps, chin taps, nose taps, shoulder taps. He looks so sharp, so athletic, in his home white uniform with the green and gold lettering, yet she can sense his frustration even from three hundred yards away. He paces back and forth after each series of signals. His Hornets are losing, again. The score is 3-0. They haven't won a game since his best players were suspended, and she knows it's shaping up as the worst season in his career. He told her recently that his teams have always hovered around .500, and he was okay with that, and she respected that about him, and thought it showed the right winning-isn't-everything perspective. Yet this long losing streak is clearly weighing on him.

The batter strikes out. Inning over. The blue-and-gray team hustles off the field. Myles slogs back to his dugout, head low, wipes his brow. Then he lifts his head and claps, and his voice carries across the field as the Hornets jog out to their positions: "Let's go! Let's see some defense!"

Emma wishes there were something she could do for him. She'll call him later, for certain. Offer to make him dinner this weekend, maybe suggest they take a blanket outside under the stars after Thomas is in bed. That should cheer him up.

Back to her walk—she really does want to get some exercise. Too many tacos and pizzas and glasses of wine lately, and she feels like she's put on a couple of pounds. She stretches her back again and leaves campus behind, strides purposefully back into the residential neighborhoods of Cumberland. Locust Street, Oak Street, then Hanover Street. A light sweat on her forehead. As she crosses Hanover, an old guy is mowing his lawn, and the smell of cut grass wafts down the sidewalk. On just about every block, she passes the home of a childhood friend or an old boyfriend, and she wonders which of their families still live there, which have moved out to the township or down to Florida or the Carolinas. It's a guessing game; she's been out of touch with them for so long. Some of the homes are tidy and well-kept, others run-down with weedy lawns and junked-up front porches.

Across Main Street, her side of town—not where she lives now, but where she grew up. She still thinks of it as her side of town. Chestnut Street, Race Street, Mill Street. Now her arms and chest are moist with sweat, too, and she pinches her damp shirt away from her chest—gotta pick up one of those sports bras.

At the end of Mill Street, the home of an old boyfriend is adorned with Trump flags and "Biden Sucks" flags. It's not the only Trump house in town—there's another on the way out of town, on the west side of town just off Main Street, but this is the first one she's seen on her side of town. It's a battered ranch house with soiled white siding and yellow shutters, an overgrown lawn and rusted-out boat in the gravel driveway, and the whole property looks so ugly. When she was in tenth grade, she dated a soccer player named Dylan who lived there. Could his parents still live there? Could Dylan live there now, after his parents moved on to some other place, be it heaven or Earth? Emma also wonders: Is this still her side of town? She should recognize where she is, conservative Central Pennsylvania, because she knew she'd see stuff like this when she decided to move back home. But not here, not this close to home. So much hate, so much ignorance. She wishes she could wield some sort of shield to protect herself from it—and Thomas, yes, especially Thomas—but it often sneaks up on her. So whoever lives there now, whether it's Dylan or his parents or someone else, she doesn't want to know. It doesn't matter. They are who they are. The flags flap as a gentle spring wind blows past, and she shakes her head glumly, keeps moving.

Yeah, it's gonna take a lot more than a book list to change things around here, but at least the school district is doing something, something real, something which, as Sounders says, is a step in the right direction, and she's part of the effort, so there's that. Maybe that will be her shield.

Soon she finds herself at the old Dickinson Elementary School, her school, now Benders Dance Studio. She knew it was no longer a school, because Thomas attends its replacement, but this is the first time she's been here since moving back home. She stops, gazes at the square red-brick building, remembers herself bounding up the steps, pink book bag in tow, her whole life in front of her. Beside the building, the tall chain-link fence is gone. It used to surround the playground, where she skipped rope and kicked kickballs, but now the playground is a parking lot, an empty one with graying asphalt and fading white lines. Is this an off-night for the dancers, or has this place gone belly up? It looks lonely, and it's sad, being here, looking at this empty place which was once full of children, their laughs, their games, their squabbles, their innocence and ambitions. Emma's shoulders sag, and her heart with it. This is too much, and now she feels completely empty—Thomas's awful day and the ugly Trump house and now her shuttered school. Why hasn't she been here sooner? Is it because she knew how it would hit her? A little piece of her life, and a piece of her, a bright-eyed, rope-skipping girl who saw so much potential in this world, gone for good.

NINETEEN

"Let's go to the beach," Myles says.

"Now?" Emma asks. Late Friday night, the heat has taken a little break, the subtle sounds of the backyard stir in the air, and she and Myles are on the blanket in the grass, wearing only T-shirts, lying on their back, staring up at a crescent moon, catching their breath after sex.

"No, not now," Myles says. "As soon as school lets out. You and me and Thomas. We'll book a place. I really need to get away for a while, and I think you do, too. When's the last time you were at the beach?"

Good question: When is the last time? Several years. Thomas was about five, and they went to Asbury Park, where she and Abid were able to reminisce about the night they met. At the time, Asbury Park was enjoying a renaissance, overcoming much of the blight and neglect that had seeped into the aging beach city in the late twentieth century, with new shops on the boardwalk, new condos in the beachfront neighborhoods, and a vibrant bar and restaurant strip. Maybe, on some level, they thought the same would happen to their relationship, but no.

"I don't know," Emma says. "Money's really tight right now."

"Don't worry about that," Myles says. "I'll cover it. And if we go right after school lets out, it won't be peak season, so the rates won't be bad, and if we get a place with a kitchen, we don't have to eat out. We could go to Ocean City or Wildwood, someplace with a big boardwalk. Thomas would love it."

"He would," she agrees.

The word *float* comes to her again, but unlike yesterday, when she wished she could float away, the connotation is pleasant. She imagines herself in the ocean, floating on her back, gazing up at a cloudless sky, not a worry in the world. Such a tempting thought. But it's a big step in their relationship. Is it moving too fast? Or is this the norm for thirty- and forty-something flames? It feels right, though, everything about it. Maybe she should count her lucky stars: She's found a good guy, tall and handsome, who relates wonderfully to her son and seems to genuinely care about her.

She rolls onto her side, straps her arm across his chest. "It's a nice thought," she says.

"Is that a yes?"

"I don't know. Maybe. Let me think about it."

"I'll look up rentals this weekend. I won't book one, but I'll look. I'll bet I can find a nice one in a good location."

"What if we just did a weekend?"

"Weekends are so short," he says.

"I know, but it just feels more practical."

"I'll check dates and prices for both. Early June, right?"

She kisses his cheek. "That's fine. Early June."

He rolls onto his side, drapes an arm across her half-naked hip, peers into her eyes.

"Maybe it will help convince you if I confessed something," he says.

"What's that?"

On a nearby street, a speeding car with a loud muffler gashes the nighttime quiet.

"I think I'm falling in love," he says.

"Well," she says, breaking into a smile. "That's quite a confession."

"I mean it," he says.

She brushes his cheek.

"I'm glad," she says. "Because I think I am, too."

***

Her dad is not answering his phone. Saturday morning, and she's called three times, and each time it goes to voicemail. She's parked beside the encampment, hasn't left the driver's seat, and doesn't want to, not until her dad appears. The engine is still running, air conditioning cranked, another steamy day in the making, and there's a hairy, shirtless guy sitting on the curb who already looks drunk. He's drinking something out of a paper bag. Could Dad's battery be dead? Who the hell knows? But she knows this: She doesn't want to go anywhere near his tent to check on him, and she doesn't want to be here very long. She dropped Thomas off at the baseball field before coming over, because they woke up late, Myles rushing off without coffee or a shower to prepare for a doubleheader, and she figured she could make her weekly drop-off during Thomas's pre-game warmups, even though she's still stung by the lunchroom incident and wasn't completely comfortable leaving him alone with his teammates.

One more time, and still no answer. Good thing the bags in her trunk are full of non-perishables, SpaghettiOs and applesauce, plus deodorant, because she's heading back to the baseball field. She'll stop back here this afternoon.

Bottom of the first, and she finds a spot in the bleachers, on the side closest to the dugout, because that's where she wants to be—as close to the boys as possible, just in case someone says something cruel. She's not close enough to hear them talk to each other, or to do much about it, but that's where she wants to be.

Top of the first, Thomas is in the dugout as a sub again, and her phone buzzes. It's her dad.

"Did you call?" he asks.

"Yes, is everything alright?"

"I guess so," he says.

An Astro hits a home run, and cheers go up all around her.

"I stopped over about an hour ago," Emma says. "Where were you?"

"I must have been sleeping."

At home plate, the Astro who homered—is it Justin Bass, that little shit?—is welcomed by a gaggle of jubilant teammates. Yeah, it's Justin Bass.

"I have some things for you," she tells her dad. "I'll come back over in about an hour. Don't go anywhere, and keep your phone on."

This is no way to live. For either of them. But nothing she can do about that on this phone call, so she says goodbye and ends the call, watches another Astro strut to the plate.

The beach—the suggestion drifts back into her consciousness, because hell yeah, she could use a week at the beach, and particularly the Maryland or South Jersey beaches, which shouldn't remind her too much of Abid. But, but, but. Could she really relax if she were that far away from her dad for a week? Could she be jumping into something too quickly with Myles? Did they really discuss being in love last night?

She rewinds that discussion in her head. She qualified it, at least, didn't declare it outright—*I think I am.*

Maybe she had too much wine. That seems to be happening to her these days. Or maybe she was simply caught up in a nice moment. After all, it was a nice moment, and she doesn't get many of those.

TWENTY

"We do not have kitty litter in the high school bathrooms," says the silver-haired man in the blue suit. "I can assure you."

It's the school board meeting, which started ten minutes ago at the Educational Service Center, and Emma has just arrived. The board room isn't crowded, maybe because it's raining outside or because the school year is winding to a close. The board is seated in a U-shaped set of tables at the front, each with their own microphone and bottle of water and stack of paper, and in the middle of the U is a single microphone, for the public comment period.

As Emma shakes the rain out of her umbrella in the back of the board room, she also tries to shake the worry about her tire, which is low again, but she drove here on it anyway, hoping it would hold up a little longer, determined to attend this meeting. She recognizes the man in the blue suit, despite signs of age—Richard Weaver, the high school principal, who's been principal since she was a high schooler twenty years earlier. He's sitting in the front row with Eric Sounders and a few other administrator types, and his silver hair is perfect, as it always was, before it turned silver, yet he looks displeased.

"Then why," says the woman at the microphone, "did I read about it on Facebook?" She's a thin woman wearing wire-rim glasses. She has flat half-gray hair that hangs below her shoulders. She's holding a yellow legal pad.

"Whoever posted that didn't have their facts straight," Weaver says. "I believe it was taken down because it wasn't factual."

"But it's true that some kids identify as cats now," the woman says with absolute certainty. "And they want kitty litter in the bathrooms. I heard one of them is the daughter of a teacher. I won't mention her name, but a lot of people are talking about it."

"The only thing I can tell you," Weaver says, sounding exasperated now, "is that we do not have kitty litter in the bathrooms."

The woman makes a notation on her legal pad.

Emma tiptoes up to the second row of seats, where other members of the Diversity Committee are sitting, and squeezes past their knees into a middle seat. She's wearing the same outfit she taught in that day—blue notch-neck blouse over dress chinos, with her bottle of magic dust tucked in her pocket. She sits right beside Grace Miller, the parent, who rolls her eyebrows at the woman at the microphone. Beside Grace is Dennis Graham, the music teacher, who's wearing his tie-dyed rainbow T-shirt again and is shaking his head at the woman at the mic.

"Thank you for your comments," says the board chairman, seated in the middle of the U. "I believe Principal Weaver has answered your question."

Why, Emma wonders, are bathrooms such complicated places around here these days?

She's bemused, though. She's been looking forward to this night, the final approval of the Diversity Committee's work, and this local crackpot is not going to ruin it for her. She *needs* this—needs the reinforcement and recognition from an official body that every single kid matters, her only son included, no matter which faraway country their grandparents were born in, or whatever else makes them seem different. She *needs* to feel better about her son's place in this world, at least their little corner of the world. Especially after last week's lunchroom incident, because those conversations that the parents were supposed to have with their boys resulted in no leads; whoever had done it had gotten away with it. So yeah, she's been dealing with a lot lately, a whole helluva lot, and she really, really needs this.

The chairman declares an end to the public comment period, and the woman with the notepad slinks back to a seat, her face pained and stiff. The board moves on with its agenda, starting with approval of the minutes of the last meeting, and Emma takes a closer look at her surroundings. It's a windowless room, and hanging on each side wall is a framed copy of the district mission statement: "The mission of the Cumberland School District is to provide educational opportunities through which ALL STUDENTS strive to achieve their full potential." Long tubes of bright lights hum overhead. She counts the men and women at the board table: eleven total, and nine are men, so Gayle is one of only two women, and are all white. Gayle doesn't look happy, maybe because of the bathroom nonsense they just had to endure. The men at the ends, each wearing dark suit and tie, are the superintendent and solicitor, according to the nameplates in front of them. The other nine, the board members, aren't as well-dressed—the men in open-collared shirts, the women in bright spring blouses.

Emma takes a closer look at the chairman, the man in the middle. Didn't Myles say his brother was on the board? She squints to read his nameplate—Ron Halprin, Chair. Yes, that's him. He doesn't look like Myles, though. His face is fleshier, his hair thinner, and even sitting down, he looks shorter. Small world, Emma thinks, and an even smaller town. He plows through the agenda—the board quickly and unanimously approves new hires, a variety of reports, a bid for new computers, another bid for HVAC work at the middle school. Last on the agenda: Diversity Committee.

"I have a motion," Ron Halprin says as they reach the last item.

Emma finds herself breathing easily, thinking of what's about to happen. A motion to approve, then a second, and possibly some questions or a short debate, and maybe one or two board members will object to something on the list, because unreasonable people are everywhere, especially these days, but any objections will most certainly be voted down by the reasonable majority, and the list will be in place, a beam of light into a life where almost every day feels like a rainy day. She pats her pocket with the magic dust in it, a reminder she has good luck on her side.

"In response to concerns raised by several parents and board members," Ron Halprin begins, reading from a single sheet of paper, "the books and other resources on the proposed list titled Resource Guide from the Diversity Committee, unless reviewed and approved by the board for use by all students, may not be taught in any classroom or made available in any library in the Cumberland Area School District."

Wait, what did he say? May *not*?

Her breath stops. A murmur starts up.

"Huh?" Grace Miller says.

"What the hell?" Dennis Graham says.

"Yeah," Emma says. "What the hell?"

Emma and Grace and Dennis exchange quick glances, their jaws hanging open.

"Is there a second?" Ron Halprin asks.

"Wait a minute," Gayle Brungard says, leaning forward in her seat, as if ready to jump out of it.

"Are you seconding?" Ron asks her.

"Of course not."

"We need a second before we can have any debate," Ron says.

Gayle's face tightens.

"I'll second," says another board member, a man. Emma doesn't catch his name. She feels something pulling at her gut—it's this, this incomprehensible moment, the may *not*.

Blood rushes to her face. Her hands start shaking.

"What's going on here?" Emma barks at the school board.

Ron Halprin pats a hand in her direction. "Please, ma'am," he says. "No public comments. The public comment period is over."

"May *not*?" Emma says, throwing both of her shaky hands in the air, fingers spread wide in bewilderment. "Did you say, 'May *not*'?"

"I did," Ron says coolly, "and the public comment period is over, so please, no more comments from the public."

"But we had no idea you were going to say *not*," Emma says.

"I don't want to have to escort you from the building," Ron says.

"Oh, really?" Emma says. She breathes heavily through her nose, nostrils flaring.

Grace Miller puts her hand on Emma's knee. "Just sit tight."

"Can we move on with the motion?" Ron asks, looking around at the board members.

Several nod yes. Not Gayle. Her jaw is set tight.

"The motion is open for debate," Ron says.

"I have questions," Gayle says. "A lot of questions, starting with this: Why the abrupt turnaround? I thought the board was supportive of a Diversity Committee."

"We were," Ron says. "But not this proposal."

"Did you say *we*?" Gayle asks.

"Yes," Ron says, waving his hand at other board members. "Several of us discussed it this week, and we shared it with some members of the community, and we have a number of concerns."

Gayle: "Concerns with books?"

Ron: "Yes, books like this."

Gayle: "What's wrong with books like this?"

Ron: "They're divisive."

Gayle: "Seriously?"

Ron lets out a little huff.

Emma looks at Grace Miller and says, "I can't believe what I'm hearing. It's like bizarro world." She says it loud enough to be heard halfway across the room, but no one pays her any attention.

Gayle crosses her hands on the table in front of her, fingers locked, knuckles turning white, and eyes the other board members. "This motion is a very serious statement about this board's moral priorities," she says. "I hope everyone realizes that."

She's met with blank looks.

She turns her attention back to Ron. "And what's this language about reviews? It's completely vague. What's the process? What's the timeframe?"

"We'll do the review," Ron says. "The board."

Someone sneezes loudly. It's the kook who's worried about kitty litter in the bathrooms. She takes a crumpled tissue from her pocket, wipes her nose.

"So," Gayle says, "the same group of people who've already decided they don't like these books and resources get to decide whether they like these books and resources. Right? That's not a review—this is a ban. Under this motion, these books and resources are gone for good."

"Look," Ron says, "we don't want this sort of thing being forced down our kids' throats. We don't want them coming home from school feeling guilty about being white."

Gayle: "This isn't about how the white kids feel."

Ron: "But it is. We have to keep the interests of all kids in mind."

Gayle: "Huh?"

Ron: "There's also a Web link here to a Black Lives Matter site. You realize they're Marxists, don't you?"

Gayle: "I don't know what you're talking about, and I'm not sure you do, either."

Ron: "And why is this list so one-sided? Why aren't there books with other perspectives, like police and firefighters?"

Grace Miller leans into Emma's ear and whispers, "Yeah, bizarro world."

Gayle furrows her brow, eyeballing Ron. "I don't understand what you mean."

"Police and firefighters," Ron says. "Why don't we have books and Web sites on this list that tell our kids what their perspective is?"

"Why are you under the impression police and firefighters oppose diversity?" Gayle asks.

"They might have a different perspective," Ron says. "And that's what I'm saying. We want different perspectives."

Gayle: "That makes no sense to me."

Ron: "Well, obviously."

Gayle: "None of this makes any sense to me."

Emma: "Me either!"

Ron: "Ma'am, this is the last time I'm going to say it. Public comment is over."

"Call the question," says another board member, the same one who seconded the motion. Emma gets a look at him this time—he's older, probably the oldest on the board, white hair and pink face, white Polo shirt.

Ron waves his hand dismissively, looks down at the papers in front of him. "Yeah, I'm calling the question," he says.

Gayle glances around at the rest of the board again. "I'm guessing no one else feels the same way I do," she says. "It saddens me so much."

"We have a motion on the floor," Ron says.

The vote is 8-1. Motion passes.

TWENTY-ONE

EMMA ISN'T LEAVING. Not yet. She refuses to. She and Grace and Dennis form a little huddle beside their row of seats. They shake their heads, exchange baffled looks.

"Apparently we expected too much from a district in Central Pennsylvania," Dennis says.

"What did we expect?" Emma says. "That they wouldn't be a bunch of racist pigs?"

"Yep," Dennis says.

A young woman with a notebook and small tape recorder approaches their huddle. She was sitting on the end of the third row during the meeting. She has straight brown hair, tortoiseshell glasses, and she's wearing a yellow parka, unzipped. She identifies herself as a reporter from the *Harrisburg Telegraph*.

She looks at Emma. "You seemed very upset about the vote on the books."

"I guess it was obvious, huh?" Emma says.

The reporter shakes her head yes. She presses a button on her tape recorder, slides it underneath her notebook, holds them together in the same hand, pen in the other. "Can I ask you," she says, "why you feel so strongly about it?"

Emma pauses, realizes she's about to be quoted, tries to collect her thoughts. But they don't seem to collect, they just start pouring out: "I'm livid, and confused, very confused. We were under the impression this board cared about diversity and wanted to do something constructive for our kids. My son is Pakistani, because his father is Pakistani, yet I grew up here. It's my home school district, and I was a valedictorian here, by the way, and I can tell you it's not easy for a little boy with Pakistani roots to be growing up here. So I agreed to work on this resource guide, because it's a great thing for a school district like this, and I'm livid, absolutely livid, about what just happened here."

The reporter scrambles to get it all down.

Gayle steps up to the group, beside Emma, wearing a forlorn expression, holding her hands behind her back. "I'm sorry," she says. "So sorry."

"What the hell happened?" Dennis asks.

"I think we just got a lesson in politics," Gayle says. "If you want to bury something, create a committee to study it. That's why they agreed to create our committee. They never thought we would actually *do* anything."

"Can I quote you on that?" the reporter asks.

"Absolutely," Gayle says.

The reporter turns her shoulders so she's directly facing Gayle. "Can I ask you about the review?" she asks. "You seemed skeptical, said it's really a ban. Why?"

"It's a ban," Gayle says flatly. "Let's not kid ourselves. If you were paying attention tonight, you saw this board has no interest in taking a legitimate look at any of the resources on that list. That language about a review is nothing more than a public relations cover. It allows them to say they're really just reviewing them, when in fact they're banning these books."

"Where can I get a copy of this list?" the reporter asks.

"Give me your email," Gayle says, pulling her phone from her front pocket. "I'll email it to you."

The reporter spells out her email.

"Look closely at the books and other resources on that list," Grace Miller tells the reporter. "These are diverse books and resources, and that's all they are. Books by people of color, or LGBTQ authors. Clearly, there is no legitimate reason to ban them—or review them, or whatever you want to call it."

The reporter jots down Grace's comment, asks for her name, then turns to Emma, asks for her name, and the spelling. The room is clearing out, and she says, "Thank you for your time. I want to go catch the superintendent."

"Thank you for covering this," Grace says.

"You should have the list on your email account," Gayle says. "Please call me if you need clarification on anything, even if it's late. I don't mind."

"Will do," the reporter says. She does a beeline to the superintendent, who's talking with Weaver and Sounders at the end of the board table.

The rest of the board is gone. All eight of them.

Emma rubs her forehead.

"Did I call them racist pigs?" Emma asks.

"I believe so, yes," Dennis says.

"To the reporter?"

"No, just to us, before the reporter came over," Dennis says.

Emma blinks, feels a tinge of relief. "Good. That wouldn't have been helpful," she says.

"What would be helpful?" Grace asks.

"I don't know," Gayle says with a sigh. "An eight-to-one vote is tough, really tough."

Dennis keeps his eyes on Gayle. "Did you know this was coming?" he asks.

"I had about two minutes of advance notice," Gayle says. "The superintendent pulled me aside right before the meeting and told me about it. I wish I'd had time to give everyone else some advance notice."

A sloop-shouldered maintenance worker pushes his cart into the room. He empties a trash can by the doorway. The reporter concludes her interview with the superintendent, heads towards the door. The superintendent, along with Weaver and Sounders, walks slowly toward Emma and her allies.

"I know this is a big disappointment," the superintendent says. He's a tall man, taller than Weaver, about the same height as Sounders, and mostly bald. He's standing next to Emma, close enough that she catches a whiff of his coffee breath.

"That's an understatement," Dennis says. "It's crushing."

The superintendent nods.

"Anything we can do now?" Grace asks.

"It looks like it's going to get some press coverage," the superintendent says. "So there might be some public pressure that results."

"Not enough to overcome an eight-to-one vote," Gayle says.

"I'd say keep fighting the good fight," the superintendent says. "Sometimes meaningful change takes time."

He says goodnight and leaves; Weaver leaves, too. Sounders lingers. The maintenance worker pushes his cart to the front of the room, empties a trash can behind the board table.

Emma looks at the empty seats at the board table. "I know Ron Halprin," she says. "Well, not personally, but I know of him. I'm dating his brother. Can you believe that?"

"Dating the brother of a racist pig?" Dennis asks.

Gayle reaches over and rubs Emma's back.

"Yeah," Emma says. "I guess so."

TWENTY-TWO

"Who the hell is Ron Halprin?"

Emma's in the car, rain pelting the windshield, wipers slapping back and forth, hair and blouse wet because she didn't bother with her umbrella when she left the building. It's dark now, and she's pulling out of the parking lot, hoping her low tire will hold up until she gets home, but she couldn't wait another minute until she called Myles.

"My brother. Why?"

"I know he's your brother." Her voice is clipped. "But do you know who he really is?"

"I'm not sure what you mean."

"He's a pig, okay. I'm sorry to be like this—wait, no, I'm not sorry, because it's the truth. He's a racist fucking pig."

"Did something happen?"

She huffs through her nostrils.

"Yeah, something happened, and he made it happen. Your brother, Ron Halprin, chairman of the Cumberland School Board."

She comes to a stop sign, swipes a wet lock of hair away from her eyes. Another car crosses in front of her.

"What did he do?"

"He torpedoed our resource guide. Do you remember I told you about it? It was for kids of color, and I was the one who compiled it?"

"Okay, so you met my brother. Yeah, he can be like that."

She starts through the intersection.

"No, we didn't meet, not like people normally meet. I went to the school board meeting, and I sat there stunned as he pushed through a motion to ban the books on our list. He escaped right after the meeting, along with everyone else who voted for that racist fucking motion, so that he didn't have to meet me."

"Oh, boy," Myles says wearily.

"He also threatened to have me removed from the meeting. Yeah, your brother did that."

"Why?"

"Because I spoke up. I had the temerity to speak up when it wasn't the public comment period."

"Wow."

"That's it? Wow—that's the best you can do?"

"I don't know what else to say right now."

Another stop sign. She glances right to left quickly, starts through the intersection.

"It's going to get media coverage," she says. "There was a reporter there asking about it afterward, so he's going to look like a racist pig in the paper tomorrow. As he should."

"I wouldn't say he's a racist," Myles says.

"Are you kidding me?"

"Why don't you come over? We can talk about it."

"I have to pick up Thomas. He's at Tracey's."

At Main Street, she comes to a red light. She squeezes her eyes closed, stretches her neck straight back, still holding the phone against her ear.

"Why don't you call me when you get home?" Myles says. "Take some time to cool off."

She opens her eyes, snaps her head forward. "Oh, you think I need to cool off." Her tone is jagged.

"You sound really upset."

"As I should be."

"Okay, okay."

The light turns green, and she turns onto Main Street.

"Why aren't you upset?" she asks.

"I am."

"You don't sound like it. And if you are, you're only upset because I'm upset."

The rain picks up, beating hard against the windshield. Visibility is affected, so she taps the brakes. Rainwater backs up at a storm drain, her car rolling through the puddle.

"Look, I get it," he says. "I just wish you weren't so upset."

"Is he your older brother or younger brother?"

"Older, by two years."

"Married? Kids?"

"Yes, still married. Two kids, both girls."

"What's he do for a living?"

"He sells fire equipment."

"That's interesting," she says. "He's used to throwing water on things."

Myles pauses. "Um, I guess."

She turns onto the street that leads to Tracey's house.

"You know," she says, "I find it interesting that during this whole phone conversation, you never once offered to call your brother."

"I try not to talk politics with him."

"Oh, really?"

"Yeah."

She shakes her head disbelievingly. "But this isn't about politics. It's about basic human decency."

"Okay," he says grudgingly. "If you want me to call him, I'll call him, but I don't think it will help anything. I know how he is."

"So do I."

"What do you want me to tell him?"

"Did you catch what I just said—the part about basic human decency?"

"Yes, got it."

She pulls up in front of Tracey's house. Rain is still coming down hard.

"I have to go," she says. "But I have one other question—do you know how to fix a tire?"

"What do you mean?"

"One of my tires is low. My dad said it might be a slow leak."

"I can put air in it for you, if that's what you mean, but you might need a new tire."

She groans.

"I'll come over tomorrow morning and look at it, if you want," Myles says.

"Okay, fine, but I have to go now. I'm here, at Tracey's, and I have to get Thomas."

"Listen," he says. "Call me later. I'll be up."

"Maybe," she says. "That's the best I can do right now."

She ends the call, cuts the ignition, hits the headlights, and a sob comes tumbling out of her. Then another. Uncontrollable, guttural sobs. Tears roll down her cheeks, saliva oozes from her lower lip, drips off her chin as she sits there alone in the dark car in the rain.

A minute passes, and then another, and the rain slows to a drizzle, and her sobs become a whimper. She wipes the spit off her chin with her forearm. She's panting now.

"Oh God," she says to the empty vehicle. "Oh God, oh God, oh God."

How could she be so naïve? Is that the right word, naïve? Or was she delusional? Just plain stupid? To believe that she'd be able to pioneer something progressive and meaningful in a backward town, to believe she'd actually be able to make a difference in an ugly world. To believe that she had some sort of control over how the rest of this place saw her only son, and the other kids like him. Was she kidding herself all along? Or just riding a little wave of hope as long as she could, delaying the inevitable, that heartbreaking moment that she's experiencing right now, when she's splashed in the face with the hard, cold truth.

She closes her eyes, rubs her eyelids with her knuckles.

Oh God, oh God, oh God.

***

Clarissa's sitting at the island in the kitchen, eating peanut butter out of the jar with a spoon. Beads of rain cover the window above the sink. Her mom comes home, shakes out her umbrella in the foyer.

"Yuck," her mom says as she walks into the kitchen. "Why are you eating out of the jar like that?"

Clarissa doesn't respond right away. She dips her spoon back in the jar, scoops another dollop of peanut butter, lays it on her tongue. "I like it," she says.

"But you know how much I hate it," Gayle says. There's an unusual edge to her voice.

"Are you in a bad mood?"

"I had a bad board meeting. Very bad."

"So is this a bad time to ask if we're ready to tell dad about me and Amelia? The prom is coming up soon, you know."

Gayle massages her temples with her fingertips.

"What happened at the board meeting?" Clarissa asks.

Gayle opens a cupboard, finds a wine glass.

"Let's just say this town can be very closed-minded sometimes."

"I know that," Clarissa says. "But why?"

Gayle uncorks a bottle of red. "Maybe I need something stronger tonight," she says.

"Wow, that must have been one really bad board meeting," Clarissa says.

"Yeah, believe me." She pours a glass.

"You have to tell me," Clarissa says. She scoops another lob of peanut butter.

Gayle takes a drink of wine, then pulls out a stool, sits at the island across from Clarissa. She lets out a sad sigh.

"Tell me," Clarissa says.

Gayle gives an agreeable little nod. "I chair our Diversity Committee, and we put together a resource list for kids, books and Web sites, things like that, and the rest of the board went behind my back, decided to ban them all."

"You're fucking kidding me." She holds her spoon in the air.

"Watch your language. That won't help anything."

"I hate this town," Clarissa says.

"Stop it."

"No, I do."

Gayle wraps both hands around her wine glass, lowers her head.

"So is there anything you can do?" Clarissa asks.

"The vote was eight to one, so I don't think so. It's going to get media coverage, though. A reporter from the *Telegraph* was there, and she was asking questions about it afterward."

"It should." She sticks her spoon in the jar, pushes it aside.

"Where's your dad?"

"Downstairs, doing dad things—watching sports, smoking a cigar, drinking his man drinks. You're not expecting him to offer moral support for this, are you?"

Gayle shakes off the question. "Where's your brother?"

"Upstairs. With his bedroom door closed, I think. I don't wanna know what he's doing in there."

Gayle drinks her wine.

Clarissa wraps both hands around her head. "I just can't believe they did that," she says. "Did you ask them why they did it?"

"Of course," Gayle says. "Ron Halprin, the chairman, spearheaded it, and he just spewed a bunch of nonsense. I was fighting a losing battle."

Clarissa unwraps her head. "But it's a battle worth fighting," she says.

***

Myles cracks a beer. He didn't want to drink tonight, but it's late enough, well past six o'clock, so no need to feel guilty. And he could really use a beer after that phone call with Emma. And before he calls Ron.

He takes a chug, wipes his lip. Sits at the square table in his kitchen. Checks his phone battery—35 percent. That's enough for a call like this, because it certainly won't last long. Ron isn't easy to talk to when it comes to things like this.

And what to say? Besides the line Emma fed him? He rehearses it in his mind: this is about basic human decency. But what does it matter? Why even worry about what else to say? Ron doesn't listen.

Another chug of beer. Another wipe of his lip. He stares at his phone screen, all those colorful little icons. Hell, just get it over with.

So he logs onto his contacts, enters the R, and Ron's contact comes up first. He thumbs the call button.

Voicemail. Relief. He leaves a brief message: "Hey, it's Myles, give me a ring when you get a chance."

***

At this hour, the newsroom is mostly empty. Regular cutbacks over the years have thinned out the staff, so some of the desks are permanently empty, and except for the sports staff and a single police reporter, few reporters work late. But thankfully the education reporter has been deemed a priority, so Wanda Nicholls, though only twenty-six years old and younger than some of those who got pink slips, still has a job, as long as she's willing to get out at night and cover those school board meetings, which used to be pretty bland, budgets and test scores and the occasional labor matter, but lately have become more heated, cultural stuff, mask mandates and bathroom policies and race. And thank God she still has a job here, because she's not the type for public relations—which is where most of her ex-colleagues ended up after their layoffs—even though it pays better. No, Wanda's not a spinster; she likes to be in the thick of things, and has to tell it like it is. As she crosses the newsroom, she flips back the wet hood of her yellow parka, detects the smell of takeout pizza, hears a breathless male voice on the police scanner, an accident with injuries somewhere.

The scanner report grips the night city editor's attention, so Wanda waits beside her desk until it's over. The editor is Jennie Barr, a portly middle-aged woman with a tinny voice. Jennie stretches her neck, calls halfway across the room to the police reporter: "Jim, did you get that?"

"Got it," Jim says.

Jennie picks up a half-eaten slice of pizza, takes a hurried bite. "Jesus," she says to Wanda, mouth half full. "So many accidents tonight. Must be really bad out there."

"It is," Wanda says.

"So what's up?" Jennie asks. That tinny voice always bugs Wanda.

"I think I have something good here," Wanda says.

Jennie raises her eyebrows.

"They banned a list of books tonight in Cumberland," Wanda says. "Books on diversity."

"You're kidding me." She wipes her mouth with a stained napkin.

"Nope."

"Anyone there who was upset about it?"

"Oh, yeah," Wanda says. "Just a small group, a couple parents, one teacher, one of the board members. But I have great quotes from them."

"Can you get me three-hundred words in thirty minutes?" Another quick bite of pizza.

"Yup."

"Good," Jennie says, as she chomps her pizza. "We should get it up on the Web site tonight. And I wouldn't be surprised if the wires pick it up."

TWENTY-THREE

BULLSHIT—it's so bullshit. But it's so Cumberland, so White Shore—banning books. This is the shit she has to deal with, the reality of her life, and yet another reason why she's absolutely dying to get away from here, and why she's so glad she applied early decision to Bryn Mawr. Even though it will put distance between her and Amelia.

Clarissa's sitting on top of her bed, legs crossed, multiple pillows stacked behind her back. Her door is closed. She texts Amelia: "my mom just told me the school board banned a bunch of books on diversity, do u fucking believe that????"

"do i believe it, yeah, this is fucking cumberland pennsylvania, or should i say pennsyltucky"

"yeah really, or pennsylbama"

"hah, or pennsylssippi"

"lol"

"this place will never change"

"my mom told me there was a reporter there from the telegraph, so i wanna see the story and i hope they make those people look like the idiots they are"

A delay, and a minute later Amelia texts back: "i just checked their web site, and no story yet"

Clarissa logs onto Twitter, searches for the *Harrisburg Telegraph*, but nothing there either. Their last tweet was three hours ago, a warning about heavy evening thunderstorms with the possibility of flash flooding.

***

Myles pops open another beer. Then he's back on his cushy brown couch, the Phillies post-game show on his big screen, but he pays no attention to the two ex-jocks debating the talent level in the bullpen. He's wondering what the odds are: His own brother and his new girlfriend, each with their own forceful personality, at the same school board meeting, opposite sides of a hot-button issue, his brother threating to kick out his girlfriend, and his girlfriend's head, that beautiful little blonde head, ready to explode.

"Million to one," he says to the ex-jocks on the screen.

Ron has always been headstrong and opinionated. Should have, could have gone to a good college, because he had the grades for it, but instead he went to community college, because he was certain that's where the value was in higher education. Earned his Associates Degree in business, then decided he was ready to start making money. Started in sales for a pretzel company, and shortly thereafter joined the local fire company as a volunteer. Wasn't into politics, not until Sept. 11. As he drove around central Pennsylvania each day to his clients at grocery stores, he started listening to talk radio, Rush Limbaugh and a couple of local yakkers, soon decided Fox News was the only network he could trust, and all of a sudden he was spouting "support the troops" and theories about Saddam Hussein's terrorist ties to Myles when they saw each other on holidays.

After five years of selling pretzels, Ron started his own fire equipment business, which has flourished. Five years after that, with both of his daughters in school, he decided to run for school board, determined to hold down his taxes and reign in the teacher's union, and after his second term, he was voted board president. Still listens to talk radio during the workday, then watches Fox News at night, still spouts off to Myles once in a while, still believes Muslim terrorists are an existential threat. And now he believes murderers and rapists are pouring across the Mexican border, climate change is a hoax, and the 2020 election was stolen from Donald Trump. He even refuses to watch NFL football anymore, disgusted by players kneeling during the national anthem and the Washington Redskins, who used to hold training camp here in central Pennsylvania back when he was a kid, bowing to pressure from the progressives and changing their name.

But he's Myles's only brother, only sibling, in fact. So Myles doesn't argue with him, always tries to steer the conversation somewhere more palatable. Myles doesn't listen to talk radio, rarely watches cable news, doesn't vote. What's the point—one vote out of all those zillions? Besides, politics is such a turn-off, only divides people nowadays, so it's better to just avoid it. Even with his ballplayers, when he instructs them on their social media use, he tells them to avoid party pics and political posts. And now, evidence that it is indeed best not to talk politics—look at what it's doing to his new relationship already.

His cell buzzes. Ron is calling back.

Myles takes a big swig of beer, picks up his phone, stares at the screen. Green button, red button. Accept or decline.

He does nothing. Just watches the screen as the call disappears to voicemail.

***

Just before 11 p.m., the story is posted: "Cumberland School Board Votes To Ban Books On Diversity."

Clarissa's still holed up in her bedroom, lying across her bed on her belly, the rest of the house quiet, when she sees the story. She clicks on it immediately, reads it carefully.

Her mom is quoted extensively, and Clarissa's proud of her—doesn't give her mom enough credit sometimes, but tonight she has to hand it to her. She put up a fight with that asshole, Ron Halprin. Clarissa knows his daughter, Maddie. They're in the same grade, took the same algebra class together last year, but they hardly interact. It's a big school, and Maddie's dating a football player, hangs out in a separate crowd. Still, Clarissa could track her down easily enough on Snapchat or Instagram, would love to message her—*Hey, your dad is a total racist and homophobic asshole, just so you know.*

But no, no. Bad idea. That'll come back to haunt her, for sure.

Think, think. What can she do? Gotta be something she can do.

***

Emma dreams that their house burns down. The house she grew up in. It's vivid, her and her mom and her dad standing on the sidewalk watching orange flames shoot out of the roof. Her mom is young and pretty, her dad lean and strong, and Emma's a little girl. She feels small, tiny really, and she's gripping her mom's skirt. Her mom's arm is wrapped around her shoulders. Nobody is there to help. No firefighters, no neighbors. Just the three of them, and there's nothing they can do but watch the flames tear through their house.

Emma wakes with a start. Oh, thank God, she thinks, just a dream. But still, another bad dream, and she's unnerved. And those flames, clearly orange, bright and hot. Which doesn't make sense, because she'd read somewhere that people only dream in black and white. Then again, nothing makes sense any more.

At least she fell asleep. A few hours earlier, she was afraid she wouldn't. So upset about what had happened at the board meeting, she tossed and turned and punched her pillow hopelessly for at least an hour, until finally the emotional exhaustion pulled her into sleep. But now, the red digits on her alarm clock showing 4:39, she's so unnerved that she knows more sleep is going to be hard to come by.

And it is.

Less than. She feels less than. Less than everyone else around her. Less than the other moms with happy suburban families, less than the other professors with good secure jobs, less than those eight votes on the school board. And it's not just because of the vote—it was that exchange with Ron Halprin, the way he shushed her and suggested kicking her out, as if her presence was completely unnecessary, as if she doesn't even matter. Why is the world, her own world, too, right here in her backyard, so unkind sometimes? She feels hollow inside, as if something is sucking the life out of her, as if she has a slow leak.

And Myles. Why was he such a dolt last night? So indifferent? And how much does he have in common with this brother of his, this Ron Halprin character? She rolls her head across her pillow, disgusted. He's so good with Thomas, so good about the little things, from shoulder massages to next-day texts. So good looking, especially for his age, so good in bed. That relationship seemed so promising, until now, all of a sudden. So much potential, or so she thought. Kind of like his baseball career—a major league prospect who didn't quite have what it takes. Didn't have that extra something, that inner substance that it takes to stick. Sure, things seemed good, but she really didn't know him all that well. Maybe now she's getting to know the real Myles.

She sits up, hugs herself.

The magic dust. It's sitting on the bedside table, the shape of the bottle barely visible in the shadowy darkness. Last night, without thinking about it, she took it out of her pocket and set it there when she undressed. She picks it up, throws it at the trash can, in the corner of the room, where it bounces off the wall and hits the floor. That shit doesn't work.

She sighs. Three hours of sleep. That's about how much she got, and that's gonna have to do today, because more sleep is out of the question. At least she doesn't have to teach today. Maybe a nap later. Oh, the joy of a nap—when was the last time she experienced that?

Oh, the joy of anything.

She pines for a persuasive reason to get out of bed, because she doesn't want to just lay here and let her mind scour her life, but at the same time, facing the world today is too much of a challenge. But there are no good reasons—she can't go back to sleep, that's it. So she crawls out of bed, pulls on her slippers and a baggy old sweatshirt. There's a middle-of-the-night chill in the house. Over in the corner of the room, she bends down and picks up the magic dust, finally deposits it in the trash can. What the hell was she thinking with that stuff? There's no magic in her world.

Downstairs, she starts a pot of coffee, pulls her folder of ungraded papers from her teaching bag. Plops them on the kitchen table; maybe grading some of these will help take her mind off of things.

And it does. But not for the better, because the first paper is bad— yet another guy writing about legalizing marijuana, and he seems to have completely forgotten what a comma is, as well as an apostrophe, as well as a paragraph. Was he high when he wrote it? She should put a new rule in place—no more papers on legalizing marijuana in her class. Or lowering the drinking age, for that matter. Sure enough, the next paper is about lowering the drinking age. And it's bad, too. It seems this guy never met an extraneous word or phrase he didn't like. The paper is cluttered with them. Redundancies, too. He must have mentioned five different ways how unfair it is that he can fight for his country but not legally drink a beer.

Next up: Madeline Garvanitis's paper. Climate change. Good topic, at least. At least the girl wants a better world, somehow. Emma takes a sip of coffee, then holds the first page up in front of her—perfect formatting, but no surprise there. Still, she doesn't feel like reading it, doesn't feel like dealing with anything from Madeline Garvanitis right now, even though it's most likely a good paper. But what if it's not quite good enough? What if—God forbid!—it's a B? She tucks the paper back into the middle of the pile; she'll get to it later.

She grades two more papers from students who are unlikely to complain about their grades—both of which are Bs—then stands up to stretch her back. Rubs her eyes and checks the clock, and it's 6:02 a.m. Doesn't have to wake Thomas for another half-hour.

She's in no hurry to wake Thomas anyway, no hurry to tell him it's time to get up and face another day in this world of theirs. Especially today. He doesn't completely understand his world yet, doesn't completely understand why people tell him to go back to where he came from, but someday he will, and oh how she wishes she could make it better somehow.

She refills her coffee, peeks out the window. The rain has stopped, but there's still no sign of the sun. Looks like a gray day out there. But of course. Already feels like a gray day to her. Is this really home now, this place where she grew up as a valedictorian with so much promise? Or is this place, this time, just too different now? Moving back here with Thomas might have been a monumental mistake, but where else? Not everyone has a place to go. And not her, apparently.

She decides to take a break from grading, from thinking about her life. She wanders into the living room, slumps into the couch. Clicks on the television, surfs some channels, not really paying attention as she passes up one channel after another. Until a local morning news show grabs her attention.

The news crew is at Cumberland Area High School. The curvy concrete canopy outside the main entrance is unmistakable. The reporter is a blonde twenty-something, wearing a tight purple dress and bright pink lipstick. The chyron at the bottom of the screen reads: CUMBERLAND SCHOOL BOARD BANS BOOKS ON DIVERSITY.

Emma sits up straight, turns the volume up a notch.

"We reached out to the school board president this morning," the reporter is saying. "His name is Ron Halprin, and he explained to us that the ban isn't really a ban. He said critics of the move are making too much of it, and there's a process in place that allows a board review of any book on the list. But I'm here with a CASH student who isn't buying that explanation."

The reporter turns slightly to her left, and the camera pans along with her, to a girl with pale skin and coal-black hair.

"I'm here with Clarissa Brungard, a junior at CASH. Clarissa, tell us your opinion of the book ban."

Brungard, was it? Did Emma hear that right? Is she thinking clearly enough to process it? Could that be Gayle's daughter?

The reporter flicks her wrist, tilting her microphone to Clarissa. The chyron changes to CLARISSA BRUNGARD, CASH STUDENT.

Yes, it must be Gayle's daughter.

"I'm livid," Clarissa says. "I heard about this last night after the vote, and I was up all night. I was that upset, because our district is sending us the message that if you're different, if you have a different skin color or different identity, then you don't matter. Well, we're going to show how much we matter. A bunch of us students have organized a walkout, fifth period, after lunch. And we're going to keep it up every day until the school board reverses this ban."

Clarissa stops with a huff. The reporter tilts the microphone back.

"Do you think a walkout will have any effect on the school board?" the reporter asks.

Emma leans forward, feels a little stirring inside.

"If it doesn't," Clarissa says, the microphone tilted back her way, "then they don't understand their own students. I know this is central Pennsylvania, a conservative place and everything, but we're not all white and straight, and some of us can use all the support we can get. Me, for instance." Clarissa steadies her gaze, looks straight into the camera. "I'm a lesbian."

TWENTY-FOUR

EMMA SAYS TO HERSELF: I like this girl.

She's up on the edge of the couch, spine arched, watching Clarissa finish pleading her case. This girl is spunky. And fearless. Yeah, good for her.

When the blonde reporter with the bright pink lipstick sends it back to the studio, Emma springs off the couch, looking for her phone. Where the hell is it? Oh, right—still upstairs on the bedside table, where her charger's plugged in. She rushes up the stairs, grabs it and texts Gayle: "Is that your daughter on television? She's great. So great."

Might be the caffeine, or the spirit she felt coming through the screen from Clarissa Brungard, but Emma feels suddenly emboldened. She's not in this alone. She also envies that girl, her fortitude, fighting the good fight on live television. Maybe it comes easier when you're younger. Maybe Emma was like that at one time, too, and maybe there's a little bit of that left inside somewhere. Maybe some part of her is still the girl she used to be.

***

"What did she say?" Doug asks sharply.

He and Gayle are standing on opposite sides of the kitchen island, a fresh pot of coffee on the counter. Doug's dressed in his Friday casual slacks and red Polo shirt, has an empty mug in hand, hasn't poured his coffee yet. The little television mounted under the cabinet is tuned to the local morning news.

"I think you heard her," Gayle says.

"Is she making that up?" Doug asks. "I know she tends toward the dramatic."

"No," Gayle says somberly. "She's not making it up."

"How do you know?"

Full mug in hand, Gayle leans back against the counter and takes a cautious sip of her coffee. Her phone pings with a text, but she ignores it.

"She's been confiding in me," Gayle says.

His eyes dash back and forth, between her and the little television. "She told you she's a lesbian?"

Gayle nods.

"So she's not making this up?"

"She's not."

"Oh, wonderful," he says. "Just wonderful."

Her phone pings with another next, but she ignores this one, too. "We didn't know how to tell you," she says.

He looks down at his empty mug, angrily.

"But we wanted to tell you," Gayle says.

He looks up at her. "Oh, really."

"Yes, we did."

"It didn't seem that hard for her to tell a whole television audience," he says, as he starts pacing alongside the kitchen island. "She just blurted it out on live television pretty easily."

Gayle shrugs.

"Is this why she dyed her hair black?" he asks, as he turns to pace the other way. "Is that some sort of a lesbian thing?"

"I don't know."

Another ping from her phone.

"Who keeps texting you?" he asks. "Is it her?"

Gayle reaches out and picks up her phone, scans the list of texts.

"No," she says, and puts the phone back on the counter. "Various people. This ban is big news in the school district. I'll probably hear from a lot of people today."

"Plus they just heard your daughter announce on live television that she's a lesbian. That's pretty big news, too, wouldn't you say?" He's still pacing, with one hand on his hip, empty mug in the other.

"I don't think it's anyone else's business."

"But it's *our* business." He stops pacing, sets down his empty mug, faces Gayle.

"It's *her* business," Gayle says. "It's Clarissa's business. Don't make this about you."

"But I'm the one laying the groundwork for a Senate campaign."

"Please believe me," she says. "This isn't easy for her."

He pushes the empty coffee mug toward the middle of the island.

"I'm leaving," he says. "I'll stop for coffee on the way to the office."

"What are you going to say to your daughter when you come home?"

He doesn't answer, leaves the question hanging there. He stomps into the hallway, reaches into the closet for his briefcase. After he shoves the closet door shut, Gayle keeps her eyes trained on him, through the kitchen-hall entryway, waiting for an answer. "I'm not sure," he grumbles, turning toward the front door.

"Try telling her you love her."

***

Myles wakes up early, ten minutes before his alarm goes off. Could be the guilt weighing on his mind from not talking to his brother last night, or a sense of responsibility, knowing he should check Emma's tire as soon as possible. Either way, his mind is muddled.

He takes a quick shower, which does little to clear his head, yanks on sweatpants and a Hornets Baseball pullover. Pours his coffee in a travel mug.

He pulls up behind Emma's Honda, which is parked right in front of her house, the street and sidewalk still wet from the heavy nighttime rains. He looks over her tires, and sure enough, one is low. Still looks drivable, though, at least for a little while, so he'll offer to take it to the shop on Main Street. He takes a big swig of coffee, plods toward the house.

His toe catches a lip in the sidewalk, and he stumbles. He manages to catch his balance, but coffee spills onto his pullover. He wipes at it with his hand, but it leaves a stain. Don't stress about this, dude—you have more to worry about than coffee spills right now.

As he wipes his sneakers on Emma's welcome mat, he's reminded of the first time he rang this doorbell, that feeling that he was out of his league with this adorable English professor when she invited him over for their first dinner. He has to muster the courage to press the doorbell.

Emma answers in less than a minute, coffee mug in hand, holds the door open as an invitation for him to enter.

"Thank you for coming over," she says, an awkward formality in her voice.

"You're welcome," he says, and he steps inside. She takes a step back, doesn't seem to notice his coffee stain.

She wipes a loose strand of hair away from her eyes.

Um, now what to say? Should he broach the topic of that conversation with his brother that didn't happen, or just get right to the tire?

The tire.

"So I just looked at your tire," he says.

"And?" she says, nipping at her coffee.

"And it's definitely low, but I think it's drivable, at least locally. If you like, I can take it over to the shop on Main Street."

"Do you think I need a new tire?"

"I don't know. Maybe. Or maybe they can repair it."

"They can repair leaky tires?"

"Sometimes."

"Huh. Who knew."

He takes his last remaining drink of coffee. "A small favor," he says. "Can I get a wet paper towel?"

"For the tire?"

"No," he says, pointing at his stained pullover. "I tripped outside."

"Oh, yeah, sure." She disappears into the kitchen, comes out promptly with a wet, wadded paper towel.

"Here you go," she says.

"Thank you." He notices that same awkward formality in his own voice.

He dabs at the stain.

"What time do you think they open?" she asks.

"Eight o'clock, probably. I'll take it over now if you want."

"I'll get you my keys." She turns toward a coat rack in the corner, where her purse is hanging, and she digs out her keys.

As she hands them over, she asks, "Did you talk to your brother last night?"

"Um, no. We played phone tag," he lies. But is it a lie? What exactly is phone tag, anyway? Even if you deliberately avoid the call-back, can you consider it phone tag? Even if you can, it still feels like a lie.

***

Wanda dreads Fridays. She's lived in Harrisburg four years, and though there's more of a night life than that crummy railroad town she grew up in, she usually has nothing to do. At least on Saturday there's a Harrisburg Young Professionals mixer, but this Friday night, like most, will probably serve as yet another reminder that she's five years out of college and still can't find a guy. A reminder she doesn't need—last Friday she watched a cheesy Netflix movie and sat on her lumpy couch and cried. Most of her friends from Penn State and her hometown, Altoona, which is stuck in nowhere-land between Pittsburgh and State College, are getting engaged and married. Not Wanda. She's still waiting for somebody. Her last relationship was a three-week blunder with a young lobbyist who, she soon learned, was juggling multiple women, and the last guy she heard from on a dating site had a profile that led with this: "I pee sitting down." She can't even get a dog, because her landlord won't allow it.

So she hits her snooze button three times, in no hurry to face this day. Her editors never complain if she straggles into the office a little late after a night shift.

When she finally drags herself out of bed and shuffles into the bathroom, she's reminded about last night's story—damn interesting, wasn't it? The wires should have picked it up, she thinks as she sits down to pee. (It's strange how conscious she is now of her womanly peeing needs since she heard from that weirdo.) But that story gives her something to look forward to: She'd love to see it circulated on the wires, appearing on news sites everywhere, because even if the wires wouldn't attach her byline, it would still be her work, and she could text friends and family and have a little something to brag about.

A career woman. Maybe that's what she's destined to be. Okay, so be it. Or is it okay? Aren't those women lonely and miserable?

At least she has a cool apartment, even though she should replace some of the furniture, old stuff she brought from her parents' basement in Altoona. It's a third-floor apartment in a 1920s building in midtown Harrisburg, along Front Street, windows overlooking the Susquehanna River. Still wearing her cotton pajama pants and blue Penn State T-shirt, she makes a cup of tea and sits at her little desk by the window, logs onto her laptop. As it starts up, she peeks out the window. It's a soggy morning, and the only person she sees is a bag lady in a brown ski cap lumbering down the riverside trail.

She checks the wires first, and yep, they picked up her story: "Pennsylvania School Board Bans Books On Diversity." The dateline is Harrisburg, Pa., but no byline, just as she suspected. Still, it's hers, and she knows it.

She checks her work email next, and she has one that was sent about an hour ago from the editor-in-chief, Norm Baker:

Hi Wanda,

Nice job on your story last night. Let's be sure to follow up on it today, and stick with it to see where it goes. That story has legs.

Thanks,

Norm

This, she concludes, must be the life of a career woman.

TWENTY-FIVE

TEN A.M. and Emma feels strung out already. It's the lack of sleep, the surge of caffeine, the whirlpool of emotions. But there's also something intoxicating about what's happening at the high school today. Her high school.

She'll go, no doubt. Assuming she has a car. She wants to be around as many people as possible who feel the same way she does, to feel their youthful energy, their hope of making positive change. She needs this, needs something to hold onto.

She's showered and dressed—just jeans and her Princeton sweatshirt, but that's perfect for a student protest, and she looks out the front window, down the street. No sign of Myles and her car. She thinks about calling him to ask about it, but she just doesn't feel like talking to him right now, not while he's dodging his connection to this book ban that hit her like a fastball to the head. Phone tag—really? How hard is it to talk to your own brother? Then again, maybe she should call to check on the tire, not just to find out its status, but because if he's sitting in the waiting area of the auto shop, he should have plenty of time to end that game of phone tag, and she can suggest just that.

Though it was nice of him to do this. She has to admit that.

She wonders if he'd have offered to take care of her tire if this book ban hadn't happened, if he stepped up only because he's feeling some semblance of guilt over how poorly his very own brother treated her and how he himself tried to avoid the whole situation. Maybe, maybe not. Remember, he's good at the little things. In the larger scheme of life, tires are little things.

Still, it was nice of him to do this.

Meantime, might as well take advantage of that caffeine-fueled energy, take care of some domestic duties while she waits for Myles and her car. She throws a load of laundry into that brand new washing machine, one thing in her life she can count on right now. She pours her last cup of detergent in the bin, tells herself to add laundry detergent to her shopping list, which she keeps in a drawer in the kitchen, then realizes she'll probably forget about that little responsibility by the time she gets back upstairs, because in terms of her life's responsibilities, this one's way down on the list. So she brings the empty jug upstairs with her. It will serve as her reminder.

As she's climbing the basement stairs, jug in hand, the doorbell rings. Must be Myles. Good, finally.

When she opens the door, the look on his face suggests accomplishment. He's holding a to-go cup of coffee in one hand, and a little clear plastic baggie in the other. He shows her the baggie as he steps inside. There's a small screw in the pouch.

"What is that?" she asks.

"That's what was causing your slow leak."

"So it's repaired?" she asks. She takes the baggie from him, sets the empty jug on the coffee table, looks over the screw.

"Yes, good to go," Myles says. He pulls her keys out of his sweatpants pocket, sets them on the coffee table beside the jug.

"And they give you the screw back?"

"Yeah. To show you what they found, I guess."

"That's weird. Do I need it for any reason?"

"No, I'd just throw it away." He blows on the black plastic lid of his coffee cup.

"What do I owe you?" she asks. The question feels loaded—she's referring to money, but she wonders if he'll take it to mean something else. Forgiveness, too?

"Don't worry about it," he says casually. "It's on me."

"No, I want to pay. How much was it?" She heads toward the coat rack in the corner, where her purse hangs. She pulls out her wallet.

"It was just twenty bucks," he says. "Please, don't worry about it."

She's pretty sure she has a twenty-dollar bill. She clicks open her wallet, and yes, she has one.

She holds it out for him, but he won't take it. He waves a hand at her, shaking off her money, takes a step sideways.

She lays the bill on the coffee table. "I'm putting it here," she says. "I really wish you'd take it."

"It's not a big deal," he says.

Maybe not, but she doesn't want to feel like she owes him too much right now.

They stand there for a moment, the silence weighing heavy. She scratches behind her ear. He blows on his coffee again.

"Thank you," she says, "for taking care of my tire."

"You're welcome."

More silence, heavier.

"So," she says.

"So."

She looks down at the twenty. It's there, she offered it, and she gave him a proper thank you on top of it. No reason to avoid the more important issue any longer.

"So did you talk to your brother yet?"

He tilts his head downward, rubs the back of his neck. "No, we haven't connected," he says.

She feels the muscles tighten in her face. "I see."

"I'm sure he's not eager to talk to me," he says. "That's how it is with us when it comes to politics."

"Or are you the one who's not eager to talk to him?"

He takes a cautious sip of his coffee. "I guess it's complicated," he says. "Talking politics, that is."

She feels something splinter inside—why does he keep saying that? How hard can it be, when it's clearly so important to her? She shoots him a wide-eyed look. "Are you fucking kidding me?"

"Don't get upset. I'm just saying."

"What are you saying?"

Another delicate sip of coffee. "You don't know my brother. That's all."

"I'm fully aware that I don't know your brother. It's why I asked if you could talk to him. I'm starting to wonder if I don't know you very well, either."

His eyebrows twitch. His chest sags. She picks up the twenty, thrusts it toward him. "Please take this," she says.

***

News vans are parked outside the high school. Three of them, all from Harrisburg stations. Plus a smaller red van from one of the radio stations. The reporters mill about, chatting with their camera operators, or checking their hair and makeup in handheld mirrors, or just waiting. It's noon.

A pearly sky. A warm spring afternoon. The air smells clean and fresh, the ridges of the Pennsylvania mountaintops turning green in the distance.

Emma has arrived early, too. She figured she'd be early, because she didn't know exactly when fifth period began, but she also figured she'd rather be early than late. She stands off to the side, hands stuffed in her jeans pockets.

Richard Weaver appears, a school security guard at his side, his silver hair typically perfect. They stop outside the school's main doors and scout the row of news vans. The security guard crosses his arms; Weaver stands upright, clasps his hands behind his back.

At 12:15, a trickle of students emerges from the main doors: two, then two more. Then the doors remained closed for a moment. Emma scans the rest of the school, the doors at the ends of the building, which remain shuttered. Oh, God, she thinks, please let there be more than four students. Then two more emerge, and the doors close for another moment.

Emma spots the reporter from the *Telegraph*, the same one she talked to last night, notebook in hand, accompanied by a photographer, a portly middle-aged man. They just arrived; they must know when fifth period began.

And then a pack of students blows through the doors, one after another holding the doors open for the kids behind them.

Boys, girls, tall and small, slim and round, white, yellow, brown, black. Hair long and flowing, or held up in a clip, or cut at the shoulders, or short and buzzed—blonde, brown, black, red, blue, green, pink. Baby faces, zitty faces, and guys with unshaven teenage scruff. They're wearing sweatpants, gym shorts, chino shorts, long skirts, short skirts, khakis, tight jeans, loose jeans, jeans with gaping holes in the knees. White leather sneakers, colored canvas sneakers, flats, dressy boots, motorcycle boots. Sweatshirts, denim jackets, long-sleeve T-shirts, short-sleeve T-shirts, untucked collared shirts; some of the girls show a sliver of belly, some of them have their sweatshirt wrapped around their waist. Some hold hands. They talk breezily among themselves, a low murmur coming from the pack.

Emma's heart swells. This is something she can hold onto.

The pack moves slowly underneath the curvy concrete canopy outside the main entrance, down the long driveway in front of the school, past the row of news vans. Behind them, three more white boys emerge from the school, tall and athletic-looking, each wearing gym shorts and sneakers, two of them wearing a CASH Lacrosse sweatshirt. Weaver stops them, interrogates them. They shake their heads sheepishly in response, then they turn around, heads bowed, and head back inside the school. Back to class for those guys.

Certain protestors peel away from the pack, stand for interviews with reporters. Emma looks for the black-haired Brungard girl, sees her talking to the newspaper reporter by the news vans. Emma moseys over to them, hands still in her pockets, stands off to the side, just out of earshot.

"Excuse me," Emma says when they finish talking, as the reporter turns away to interview another student. "Are you Gayle Brungard's daughter?"

Clarissa seems unfazed by the question. She's getting used to questions from adults. "Yes," she says matter-of-factly.

"Can I give you a hug?" Emma asks.

"Um—"

"I'm Emma Muller-Farooq. I compiled the list that was banned last night. I worked with your mom on it."

"Oh, my God," Clarissa says, and her shoulders wilt, her face melts. "Yes."

As Emma wraps her arms around her, she wonders who needed the hug the most.

TWENTY-SIX

FOR FRIDAY EVENING, Gayle orders pizzas, because she doesn't feel like cooking and doesn't feel like going out in public—too much turmoil in her own world to interact with the rest of the world right now. She spent the entire afternoon on the couch with a migraine, took three Advil and a nap, then brewed a cup of ginger tea when she woke up, ignoring her phone most of time, and now her headache is subsiding, thankfully.

Because it's not going to be a pleasant night.

Nobody's home yet. Her son is at a buddy's house and her husband is playing golf, hopefully without drinking too much. He should be home soon. She doesn't know where Clarissa is. She texted her but hasn't received a response.

She decides to keep busy for the time being, so she empties the dishwasher and wipes down the counters. It's half-dark outside, dusky light creeping in through the windows above the kitchen sink.

The pizzas come, one cheese and one meat lovers, their usual family order; she and Clarissa prefer cheese while her husband and son like meat lovers. Gayle sticks them in the oven to keep them warm. She flicks on the recessed lights in the ceiling, brews another cup of ginger tea. She pulls up a stool, sits down at the kitchen island with her tea.

The Audi pulls into the driveway first.

Gayle massages her temples.

She can tell by his gait and the look in his eyes that he's been drinking.

"Hello," she says stiffly.

"Good afternoon," he says, and heads straight to the refrigerator, pulls out a green bottle of imported beer.

"Evening," she says. "I'd say it's evening now."

He uncaps the beer bottle. "Is that a problem?"

She sips her tea. "No," she says. "Not if we're one big, happy family."

"What's that supposed to mean?"

"I'll tell you what it means: At some point this evening, your daughter is going to come home. Have you thought about what you're going to say to her?"

"About what?" He takes a gulp of beer.

"You know exactly what I'm talking about."

"You mean that performance she gave on television?" He makes a mocking face.

"It wasn't a performance. It was real."

"Oh, come on," he says. "You know her as well as I do. You know how theatrical she is."

"I probably know her better than you do, and yes, she can be theatrical, but this is real."

"Bullshit."

"How much have you been drinking?" Her eyes bore through him.

"Does it matter?"

"Yes, it matters. I've been dreading this evening all day, and if you've had too much to drink, it's not going to help matters."

He takes another drink, defiantly.

She looks away from him, irritably.

"What's the plan for dinner?" he asks. "I'm hungry."

"I ordered pizza," she says, still looking away. "The boxes are in the oven."

"Meat lovers?"

"Yes, there's a meat lovers."

He pokes his head in the oven, pulls out one of the brown pizza boxes, drops it on the counter. He sets down his beer, takes a slice and bites into it. A piece of sausage rolls off his slice, onto the floor.

"We have plates, you know," Gayle says.

He shrugs her off, munching.

"Are you going to pick that up?" Gayle asks.

"Sure," he says, bending down to pick it up. He tosses it into the back of the pizza box.

Gayle gets up and goes to the cupboard, takes out a plate and hands it to him. "Here you go," she says.

He shrugs again but accepts it.

They hear the low rumble of a car pulling into the driveway, the ignition cutting off, the metallic thud of a car door closing. Clarissa.

Gayle looks at her husband uneasily. "I hope you handle this the right way," she says.

He takes another bite of pizza. She sits back down on the stool.

They hear the turn of the doorknob, the squeak in the door hinges, the one that Doug keeps promising to silence with a squirt of WD-40, and then the *cla-bump* of the door closing.

When Clarissa steps into the kitchen, keys dangling in her hand, she looks exhausted. Her eyes are baggy, oily strands of her hair tucked behind her ears.

Two long seconds of silence. Gayle knows neither her husband or daughter will say anything first, but she gives them those two seconds nonetheless, just in case. And then she breaks it: "How are you doing?" she asks Clarissa.

"How do you think I'm doing?" She's standing in front of the kitchen entranceway, not ready to step all the way in.

"I don't know," Gayle says. "But I know it's been quite a day."

"Yeah," Clarissa snickers. "Quite a day."

"I'm glad you didn't stay out too late," Gayle says.

Clarissa looks down at the floor, sucks in her cheeks. It's something she does during stressful moments, but she doesn't know why. She holds the insides of her cheeks in her teeth, careful not to bite down. Then she lifts her gaze and takes in the sight of her dad. He's leaning against the counter on the opposite side of the kitchen, finishing off a slice of pizza. He tosses the crust into a pizza box.

"I ordered pizza," her mom says. "Cheese is in the oven."

"I'm not hungry."

Her dad turns to grab a bottle of beer which has been sitting beside him on the counter, but he doesn't take a drink. He holds it against his chest, and as his head turns back, eyes sweeping the big airy kitchen, his gaze catches Clarissa's. They stare at each other, silently. The light from the ceiling feels too bright. She still doesn't want to bite down on her cheeks.

Her mom looks at her dad, then at Clarissa, then pinches her eyes with the tips of her fingers. She never hides her frustration.

"I'm going downstairs to watch some basketball," her dad says, and he walks out of the kitchen, through the back entranceway, toward the basement stairwell.

Clarissa doesn't watch her dad leave. She looks at her mom instead, as if she might be able to offer an explanation. But her mom just gives a sad little shake of her head.

Clarissa releases her cheeks. "So that's how it's going to be?" she asks.

"That's how it's going to be," her mom says.

***

"I really, really, really want someone to hang out with tonight," Emma texts Tracey on Saturday morning. "I want to drink wine and forget about the world. Can we do an adult sleepover?"

Ten minutes later, Tracey texts back: "Ha, i can't do a sleepover but I can come over for wine, can i bring the girls?"

"Of course. I meant to invite the girls, too, but no wine for them."

After dropping off her dad's care packages, which, thankfully, goes without any additional complications, Emma stops at the liquor store and grabs one bottle of white and one bottle of red. Ah, screw it, she thinks, and picks up an extra bottle of each.

Tracey and her girls arrive at 6:45, and the girls blow into the living room, little balls of energy. Thomas is sitting on the floor in front of the television, playing a video game, and the three of them immediately agree to watch a movie.

"My God, they're so agreeable," Emma says.

"I know, really," Tracey says.

"I wonder," Emma says, "at what age do kids stop being so agreeable, because adults sure aren't."

"Believe me," Tracey says, "my girls can argue."

"Okay," Emma says, "so maybe we're all cursed by it."

Emma asks the kids if they want popcorn, and they do, so she microwaves a bag for them, dumps it into a large bowl, hauls it into the living room and sets it on the floor in front of the kids.

"How about you?" she asks Tracey. "Glass of wine? Please, please say yes."

Tracey chuckles and asks for white, so Emma opens the bottle, pours them each a glass, and they head out to the back porch. It's a pleasant evening, an apricot sun disappearing in the west. The grass needs mowed, but Emma doesn't care about it enough to pester the landlord. They sit in the plastic porch chairs and Emma holds up her glass in a toast: "To Saturday night," she says. "You have no idea how badly I need this. I'm starting to understand why people are driven to drink."

Tracey clinks her glass and they each take a drink. Emma's comforted by the oaky taste of the wine and the company of her oldest friend.

"Trouble with the baseball coach?" Tracey asks. "I notice he's not around tonight."

"Well, yeah, among other things. Have you been paying attention to the news?"

"You mean the book ban?"

A neighbor's dog barks.

"Yeah, the book ban," Emma says. "But you're not going to believe this—the board president, the one who pushed it through, is the baseball coach's brother."

Tracey's eyes pop. "No way."

"Yup," Emma says, and takes a drink of wine, a bigger drink than she intended, and a droplet runs down her chin. She wipes it with the back of her hand.

"What are the chances?"

"In a town like this? There's a chance."

"So what does the baseball coach say about it?"

"Not much," Emma says. "He said he'd talk to his brother, but he didn't, blamed it on phone tag, and I haven't heard from him since yesterday morning."

"They'll talk about it, I'm sure."

"Yeah, maybe, but that's not exactly the point. I'm not even expecting that asshole board president to listen, but the point is—" She stops and stares toward the disappearing sun.

"What?"

Emma shakes her head, takes another drink of wine. "I don't know. I just know I felt like I got no support from him, and I needed some support."

Tracey nods sympathetically. The neighbor's dog barks again.

"Should we check on the kids?" Tracey asks.

"I'm sure they're fine."

"Katie's had a long day—gymnastics in the morning, then a friend's birthday party at a bowling alley in the afternoon. I'm not sure how much longer an eight-year-old like her can hold up."

Emma swigs her wine. "I hope she holds up. I need a wine-drinking friend tonight."

Tracey lets out a little giggle and says, "Ahh."

Emma holds up her glass, looks it over. Only a drink or two left.

"It's going down way too fast," she says.

"I better catch up," Tracey says, and takes a drink.

Emma sits up, looks out across the back yard, the high grass, the bushes turning thick and green. "I feel like I have no control over anything in my life," she says. "Things happen to me, and to Thomas, and I'm powerless to do anything. Now I feel like I'm just waiting for something else bad to happen, and that's such a horrible feeling."

"Are you sure proposing that book list was a good idea?"

"What do you mean?" She sits back.

"Well, first of all, look what it's doing to you. And secondly, are you sure it was a good idea?"

"I don't get what you're saying," Emma says, a little stiffly.

"We were talking about it today at the bowling alley—"

"I'm sure everyone around here is talking about it."

"Yeah, right," Tracey says, an apologetic quiver in her voice. "And don't get me wrong, I'm here to support you and everything, but we were talking about it, and we thought maybe it's the right thing to do, considering the circumstances and everything."

"You mean the ban is the right thing to do?"

"Well, yeah, I mean...I mean we talked a lot about parental rights, and how important they are, and how important it is that the school board look out for parental rights, and what a slippery slope it is with certain books."

Emma's floored. She feels suddenly numb. Another bad thing is happening to her, right here and now.

"Are you being serious?" Emma asks.

"I mean, yeah," Tracey says. "We have to be vigilant about what our kids are reading, just like we need parental controls on our televisions. We don't want porn in the libraries."

Emma does a double-take. "Porn?" she says, her voice rising.

"How can you equate books on diversity with porn?"

"I'm just saying. It's a slippery slope."

Emma stares at her, mouth agape. It's dawning on her: Her oldest friend has changed, too, just like her hometown. This friend she walked to grade school with, jumped rope with, double-dated with at drive-in movies, parked in the woods with as they made out with boys, stood at the alter with as members of each other's wedding party. Why didn't she realize it sooner? Tracey never left Cumberland. She stayed home after college, met an engineer, married and had kids, became a suburban stay-at-home mom who hangs out with other suburban stay-at-home moms, and the irascible conservative culture here is her culture. Tracey may look like the same girl—smooth-skinned and slim, with her gym membership and pricey face creams—but she's not the girl she used to be.

Emma slumps in her plastic chair. "So that's what people are saying," she says disbelievingly. "That's their twisted way of rationalizing hate—parental rights, slippery slopes, porn."

"It's not hate," Tracey says defensively.

Emma stares into her wine glass, shakes her head. "I have a nine-year-old boy in there with dark skin," she says, half-turning her head toward Tracey. "And you know him, your daughters love spending time with him, and you know he's a great kid, and somehow you see books that appeal to him as a slippery slope to porn? I don't know how you can make sense of that."

"I love Thomas."

"I hope so. He deserves to be loved."

Tracey tucks a loose lock of hair behind her ear. "I should check on the girls," she says. She sets her wine glass down on the porch, gets up and goes inside. A minute later, she half-opens the screen door and pokes her head out.

"Katie's wiped out," Tracey says. "So I think we better go."

TWENTY-SEVEN

THE DOORBELL is ringing. It wakes Emma, who fell asleep on the couch. The television is flickering in the darkness, and she sits up and tries to blink away the confusion—what time is it, and why is the doorbell ringing? It's late, that's for sure.

She lets out a groan as she hoists herself off the sofa. Her back aches and her head hurts—she downed two more glasses of wine after Tracey left, watching the end of the movie with Thomas and then dozing off during a sappy Netflix movie. She lumbers toward the door, stretching her neck and back along the way, flicks on the porch light, peeks out the window.

Myles is standing there. She cracks open the door.

"Hey," he says.

"Hey, what?"

"I came to see you." He's holding a gold box, tucked under one arm like a football. His other arm is pressed against the door jamb, as if he needs it for leverage. The smell of his whiskey breath wafts into the doorway.

"Yeah, I see that," Emma says.

"I'm thorry about everything."

"Thorry? Did you say thorry? You're drunk."

He scrunches his eyes shut, wiggles his head.

"It's pretty obvious," she says.

He opens his eyes, tilts his head. "I just wanted to see you."

"This isn't a good idea."

He holds out the gold box. They're chocolates. "I brought you this," he says.

She waves it off. "No, thank you."

"I couldn't get flowers this late at night."

"Where did you get those?"

"The drug store on Main Street."

"It doesn't matter," she says. "I don't want them."

"Can I just come in? Can we talk?"

"No."

"I have to pee, though. Can I come in and use your bathroom?"

"You're pathetic," she says, opening the door wider, motioning him inside. "But you can come in, because I don't want you peeing on my porch."

"Thank you." He offers her the chocolates again as he steps inside.

"Keep them," she says. "I told you I don't want them."

"The bathroom—it's upstairs, right?"

She nods, and he scoots upstairs.

"Please be quiet," she says. "Thomas is sleeping."

She pushes the door closed, leans her shoulder against it, closes her eyes. She stays there for a moment, lost in the dark and swirling moment. Doesn't feel like moving, doesn't want to deal with this.

When she hears a flush, she opens her eyes. Myles comes downstairs yawning, covers his mouth with an open hand. Doesn't have the chocolates. Must have forgotten them in the bathroom.

He drops himself into the sofa.

"This is so uncool," she says.

"Can I have a glass of water?"

She blows a loose strand of hair away from her eyes.

"Fine," she says.

Slowly, she walks into the kitchen, pulls a glass from the cabinet, pours the water, as she considers how to phrase this in a way a drunk guy will process it: I'm dealing with a lotta shit these days, and I had no idea I was falling for Ron Halprin's brother, and I don't know why it's been so hard for you to support me at a time like this, and it's the middle of the night, and I'd rather not see you right now, but we can talk later, when we're both rested and sober. Got it?

When she returns to the living room, glass in hand, his head is arched back on the top of the couch. His jaw hangs open.

"Myles?"

No response.

He's passed out.

She grabs his shoulder with her free hand, gives it a shake. "Wake up," she says. "You have to go."

"Huh?" he says, half out of it.

"You have to go."

"I love you," he says, a half-mumble.

"Oh, God, no." She puts the water glass on the coffee table. "This can't be happening."

He falls over, face down, into the arm of the couch, then rolls onto his side, curls up in the fetal position.

"You've got to be fucking kidding me," she says, but he doesn't hear her. He's out.

***

Emma's face-down in her pillow when Thomas wakes her up, tapping her shoulder. "Myles is downstairs," he says. "Sleeping on the couch."

She rolls onto her side, blinks the sleep out of her eyes, processes the hazy memory of Myles's middle-of-the-night visit. "I know, honey," she says. "What time is it?"

"Ten o'clock."

"Oh, God."

Bad mom. No doubt. A horrible parenting moment. But hey, how much of it is her fault? Gotta give some of the blame to that drunk boyfriend on the couch. Wait a second—boyfriend? Did she just think of him as her boyfriend?

"Oh, God," she says again, and sits up, throws her legs over the side of the bed. Her head throbs, her back is sore, and her eyes ache.

"Should I wake him up, too?" Thomas asks.

She rolls her head gently. "Sure, why not?" She stretches. "I'll be down in a minute."

On the stairway, she bumps into Myles—wrinkled clothes, knotty hair, bloodshot eyes, on his way up the stairs. "Good morning," Emma says coldly.

He rubs his eyes with the heels of his hands. "Yeah, look. I know this doesn't look good."

"Nope."

"Can I use the bathroom first?"

She steps aside. He smells bad, too, like boozy sweat.

In the kitchen, Thomas has helped himself to orange juice and a Pop-Tart. Emma pops two Advil, starts coffee. When Myles appears, his hair is damp and patted down, a hangdog look on his face. Emma has a big cup of coffee, and she and Thomas are seated at the little kitchen table.

"I can't stay long," Myles says. "I have to be at the field at eleven. One o'clock game."

"Can we go?" Thomas asks.

"No," Emma says.

"Why not?" Thomas asks.

She doesn't know, so she doesn't answer.

"Can I grab a cup of coffee?" Myles asks.

"Help yourself," Emma says.

Myles stops suddenly at the counter in front of the coffee machine. "Where are the cups?" he asks.

"In the cupboard on the right."

She rubs her temples with her fingertips while he pours his coffee.

"How's your tire?" Myles asks.

Oh, yeah, the tire. She hasn't even thought about it. "Good, I guess. I haven't checked it. I assumed it was fixed."

He covers his mouth, lets out a little burp, then softly says excuse me. "You should still check it after a repair job," he says. "I'll check it before I go."

"Thank you," she says. The little things, she reminds herself—it's just one of those little things, his specialty.

"How did you get here last night?" she asks.

"I drove."

"You shouldn't have been driving." As soon as she says it, she realizes she shouldn't have said that in front of Thomas.

"I know," Myles says guiltily.

"Thomas, honey, would you take your juice and Pop-Tart in the living room and watch some television? I want to talk to Myles about something."

Thomas picks up his cup and plate and asks, "Can we go to the game then?"

"No."

Thomas makes a face as he leaves the kitchen.

Myles takes his seat. "So you're mad at me because of my brother?" he says.

"No, I'm mad at you because you didn't support me. Did you talk to your brother yet?"

"Yes. Yesterday."

"And?"

He looks into his coffee cup. "And the same old thing. We can't talk politics, like I told you, which is why I avoid it."

"Exactly what did he say?"

"He told me he knew what he was doing, something about fighting to keep the wokeness out of the school district, and that if I wanted to get involved in district politics I should run for a school board seat."

Emma tilts her head, thinking.

"Maybe I'll go talk to him," she says. Not an idle threat; she means it. "But not today. I have some other things to do, and I'd need to collect myself first."

***

Sunday evening, and Gayle's kitchen is packed with people. It's much nicer than Emma's rental kitchen, big and airy with granite counters and frost-white cabinets, and there must be twenty people squeezed inside. Mostly women, a few men and teenage girls, but a mix of white, black, brown, yellow. Emma recognizes Grace Miller and Dennis Graham, exchanges waves with both of them. Trays of store-bought cookies are laid out on the center island, alongside a stack of printed agendas.

Emma was one of the last to arrive—she didn't know what to do with Thomas, because she wasn't comfortable calling Tracey, not after that distressing conversation on the back porch, so she finally called Myles, who eagerly offered to come over and take him to the batting cages. Though it felt awkward asking Myles for a favor, she's glad she did, now that she's here. There's energy in the room, a fierce and determined energy, and there's nowhere in the world she'd rather be.

She wiggles through the crowd to grab an agenda. It lists talking points, social media strategies, letters to the editor, fundraising for yard signs, support for the student walkouts, and candidate recruitment for next year's school board elections. Gayle must have worked on this all weekend.

Gayle and Clarissa are standing together in the middle of the kitchen, in front of the sink. "By now, you all know my daughter, I presume," Gayle tells the crowd as she starts the meeting. The kitchen fills with applause, plus a few hoots and hollers.

TWENTY-EIGHT

FIRST LUNCH PERIOD on Monday, and Eric Sounders peeks out his office window, which gives him an unobstructed view of the whole area in front of the school, the parking lot and the long, covered driveway, and he's relieved to see nothing out of the ordinary. No news vans, no protests, no pissed-off parents. An hour ago he received an email from the superintendent: There's a bigger media presence today at the high school, including a news van from CNN. Their school district is national news, and "under a spotlight," as the superintendent put it, so all administrators should be prepared.

Just what he needs.

So it's a lousy Monday, which followed a lousy, lonely weekend, which followed a lousy and stressful end to the previous week. He might not have to deal with any reporters, but he's dealing with a baffled staff and ornery parents, many more than usual. Which is worse? Parents have been bombarding him with emails, and since it wasn't his weekend to watch his troubled teenage son, according to the custody agreement with his ex-wife, he was alone at home and spent half of his sleep-deprived weekend answering those emails. They've ranged from the rational: ie, How will the school respond if my child asks for one of these books? To the ignorant: ie, Do you teach any books for white people? To the absurd: ie, Are my hard-earned tax dollars paying for copies of *Hustler* on those shelves? Meanwhile, teachers have also been pummeling him with questions: What if I've taught one of these books in the past? How should I handle my classroom discussion if a student asks about the ban? And the librarian: What are we supposed to do with these books?

This is perilous territory, especially now that national news outlets have picked up the story. That spotlight is bright, and the temperature surrounding the issue could crank up to white-hot. Who knows where this will lead, and who knows how the school board will react as the spotlight brightens? He's got to be careful every step of the way, answer every email and navigate every turn with deftness and diplomacy, especially with this school board. They're not educators, not a single one, and most of them aren't even civic-minded or student-centered. Most are either tax rebels or culture warriors, or some combination of both. He's afraid of this school board.

His secretary pokes her head in his office, says Mrs. Kovalchik is here. He's been expecting her. A stout, gray-haired woman who's been the grade-school librarian for thirty years, she waddles into his office pushing a cart full of books.

"Here they are," Mrs. Kovalchik says.

The banned books.

He shakes his head knowingly, lumbers across the room, looks over the cart.

"So what are we supposed to do with them?" she asks.

"I don't know," he says. "I'll have to get guidance from administration."

That's going to be his go-to line during this whole brouhaha—guidance from administration. No one can blame him for anything if it's guidance he gets from administration.

"You're lucky I'm a year away from retirement," she says. "Otherwise, I wouldn't be obeying this edict. It flies against everything I've committed my whole career to, but I can't afford to play the role of the protester at my age. Believe me, I've thought about it, but I can't put my pension and my health coverage at risk."

"I understand," he says.

"I'm so proud of those kids at the high school, organizing their own protest against it. I've been telling everyone that. I can't get in trouble for telling people I'm proud of kids."

"That's true."

"So what should we do with the books?"

He scratches his chin.

"Do you have any extra closet space in the library?" he asks.

"No."

He checks the clock on the wall.

"Leave them here for now," he says. "And I'll get guidance from administration later."

***

Emma collects another round of research papers at each of her classes at Penn-State Harrisburg on Monday. Thirty-six papers total. Four kids blew off class, so they'll probably bring their papers to class Wednesday along with some dubious explanation for why they missed class. What they won't realize is this: Emma's actually relieved she has four fewer papers to grade right now.

Not that she would grade them right away. She's tired. Seems like every day, so tired, and the challenge of getting through the day gets tougher. And besides, she still hasn't finished grading their last round of papers, though she made some progress over the weekend and during office hours today. When her students filed out of her classes today, only one stopped to ask if she'd finished grading their previous papers. Emma felt a pang of guilt, promised to have them next class.

So her teaching bag is overstuffed and heavy as she lugs it to the parking lot after her office hours. Six piles of papers in all, one for each of her classes at Cumberland and now two each for here. This can't be good for her back. But what's she going to do? Hire help? A caddy?

She opens the passenger door first, plops her bag on the seat, then her phone buzzes.

It's a New York number. Not one of her contacts, and she doesn't recognize it. Her mind flashes back to her previous life with Abid. Seems so long ago, but it could be important, something about her ex or her child support or her previous teaching jobs, and her phone hasn't labeled it as potential spam. She better answer it.

"Is this Emma Muller-Farooq?" asks the caller, a woman with a firm voice.

"Yes."

"This is Maggie Springer from *The New York Times*. I got your number from Gayle Brungard. I'm working on a story on the book ban in your school district. Do you have a few minutes to talk?"

Emma pushes the passenger door closed. "I have all the time you need," she says.

***

Norm Baker is in a tizzy. For the past hour, he's been up and down the stairs and in and out of just about every office at the *Telegraph*, searching for some sort of visual backdrop with the paper's logo on it. But he can't find one.

As far as anyone can remember, no one from the *Telegraph* has ever appeared on a national news show before—Norm and the other editors and their reporters often do the morning weekend shows on Harrisburg public television, but never a national program. So this is big-time, especially for Wanda. Twenty-six-year-old Wanda.

"I think we should just do it at my desk," Wanda tells Norm, after he returns glum-faced and empty-handed from advertising. "With my Zoom camera showing the newsroom in the background."

"I guess we don't have any choice," Norm says. He puffs out his cheeks, then exhales.

"It's a professional look," Wanda says. Yeah, she's a career woman now, for better or worse.

She's already texted her parents in Altoona and told them to tune to CNN at 6 p.m., because she's being interviewed by Wolf Blitzer about the big book-ban story she broke last week. She also texted three of her best friends—one from Altoona and two from Penn State—all of whom have been married or engaged in the past two years. Sending those texts felt particularly good, something for Wanda to brag about for a change. She also tweeted about it to her 1,456 followers.

"Now remember," Norm says, his demeanor modulating, from promoter to coach. "No editorializing. Stick to the facts. This story is too sensitive around here for us to be taking sides."

"No problem."

He does that puff-exhale thing again, and Wanda gets the impression he doesn't completely trust her. Sure, he's a small-time editor with a nervous nature as it is, a skinny, balding, baby boomer with wire-rim glasses, showing the wear and tear of his many losing battles with the paper's tight-fisted publisher. But still, she wishes he could show some faith in her. She's nervous, too, but she's trying her damndest not to show it.

She spins her desk chair to the left, bends down for her purse, sets it on her knees. She pulls out a tube of lipstick, berry blush, her go-to color, and a compact mirror. She wishes she had dressed nicer, but how was she supposed to predict this morning she'd get a call from CNN? So she's wearing a blue-checkered linen shirt over khaki pants, which is fine for Harrisburg newspapering; it's just going to have to do for CNN, too. And her hair—she'd have washed it if she'd known, but Monday's always a no-wash day for Wanda, so she has it pulled back in a clip, and it's going to have to do, too.

She touches up her lips while Norm turns and gives instructions to the rest of the newsroom—keep the volume down, avoid unnecessary movements in Wanda's background, remain professional.

Wanda logs onto the CNN Zoom link five minutes early, takes a series of deep breaths as she waits for the producer to connect. She checks her face in the compact mirror again, readjusts her hair clip. The producer appears on the screen, all business, a middle-aged woman whose brown hair is also back in a clip. In a rehearsed tone, she rattles off a list of instructions, and she must sense Wanda's jitters. "And just relax," the producer says, flashing a comforting little smile. "You'll do great."

When Wolf appears on her screen, the moment feels surreal, as if she's living outside it, watching down from someplace else. But then Wolf's first question comes at her—*Can you tell us about the school board meeting where the ban was approved?*—and she's back in the moment, explaining it as if she's talking to a neighbor. She stumbles over her words once, mistakenly says the vote was 18-1, but she corrects herself right away, 8-1, so no big deal. She fields the next few questions just as well, and she's sticking to the facts, feeling good about this, and then it's coming to an end, Wolf thanking her for her time, and she smiles into the screen, says thanks for having me, and she feels a glow inside.

As she clicks off the red Zoom button, Wanda can't remember the last time she's felt so good about herself.

From their cubes in the newsroom, her colleagues bark out congrats and compliments. A sportswriter jokes, "Can we start acting unprofessional now?" Norm comes over to Wanda's desk, gives her a little pat on the shoulder, says "great job." He seems both pleased and relieved.

Though her daily story is filed—about the ongoing fifth-period walkout, which on Monday had the same level of energy and same approximate number of participants as the first—Wanda lingers at her desk. She checks emails, responds to laudatory texts from her mom and friends who watched her on CNN. Before she goes home, she checks her Twitter feed, sees an unusual response to her earlier tweet from a strange account dubbed Stonewall X. Jackson, with a confederate flag as a profile picture.

Saw u on cnn, it reads, *with your fake news, stirring up trouble, but we won't let that go on. Be afraid little girl, be very afraid, we're coming for u.* It's accompanied by a GIF of a man in a skeleton mask firing a handgun straight at her.

TWENTY-NINE

A PICKUP TRUCK is riding Emma's tail. It's a big, black vehicle, shiny as a showroom model, the morning sun twinkling on its chrome bumper and grill.

Emma has just turned onto Main Street, cutting through town on her way to her first Tuesday class at Cumberland College, her usual route. The pickup jumped on her ass as soon as she made the turn.

At first, it didn't phase her. Just another local yokel, she figured, in too much of a hurry. But halfway down Main Street, with the heavy weekday traffic moving slowly through the lights, she starts to fret. The big pickup is still smack on her back bumper, and with that jacked-up view of the street, the driver has to see traffic creeping along, nothing Emma can do to speed it up.

It's almost as if the driver isn't out for faster-moving traffic as much as he's out for *her*.

Could it be? Just an hour ago, she read the story in the *Telegraph* about the death threat Wanda Nicholls received last night. It was a sidebar to Wanda's main story about the ongoing student walkout, and it was chilling. Now Emma feels another chill, as she peeks in her rearview while she's stopped at the third and last red light on Main Street, hoping to get a glimpse of whoever is driving the pickup. But she can't—the truck is too close, and all she can see is the shiny chrome grill and the front of its black hood.

Maybe her imagination is just running wild: envisioning this guy as more than a local yokel, a culture warrior who tracked her down after seeing her own quotes last week in the *Telegraph* or today in the *The New York Times*, and decided to put the fear of God in her. If that's the case, it's working. But how to know?

The light turns green, and she taps the accelerator through the intersection, nearing College Avenue, where she normally turns left. But this time, a block before College, she turns left onto a residential side street, hoping the pickup stays on Main. But no, the pickup follows her.

Oh God, oh God, oh God. What to do now?

She's wigging out, her fingers clamped to the steering wheel, her brain doing shimmies and shakes. Now what? Just drive to campus, call security. They'll be there in a heartbeat because they have nothing else to do. That is, unless they're investigating a missing toilet.

So at the next intersection she makes the turn toward College Avenue, but the pickup doesn't. It speeds past her as it continues down the side street, engine roaring.

She heaves a sigh of relief. Stops at the stop sign at the intersection with College. Stays there for a moment to collect herself. More deep breaths escape her. A car horn interrupts the moment. Her eyes shoot back up to the rearview mirror, but it's not the pickup; it's a sedan whose driver apparently wants through the intersection.

She pulls forward, then onto campus, parks in the faculty lot, still unnerved. No reason to call security now, but she feels a need to call Myles—he's likely somewhere on campus, entertaining a recruit or sitting through an Athletic Department meeting, and he'd surely be there in a flash. She decides against it, though, as much as she'd like the reassurance of a big, athletic guy who cares about her escorting her around campus today. The pickup driver's gone, hopefully forever, and things are just too complicated with Myles right now.

Before she gets out of her car, Emma empties half of her teaching bag, leaving all of her papers from Penn State-Harrisburg on the passenger seat, to lighten her load. A stiff spring breeze whips across campus, and the manure smell is strong this morning, one of the worst she's experienced. When she gets inside her classroom building, the smell lingers inside her nose. When she gets to her classroom, the first student she encounters is Madeline Garvanitis, who recently changed her pink streaks to blue. She approaches Emma at her desk.

"Did you grade our last papers yet?" Madeline asks.

"Sorry," Emma says. "Still working on them."

Madeline frowns. "Okay."

"Something unexpected came up," Emma says.

"Do you know when you'll have them?"

"As soon as unexpected things stop coming up."

Madeline looks confused.

"Hopefully next class," Emma adds, and that seems to satisfy her.

***

Wanda's dad is not very handy. If he took on a project at home—a new light fixture or faucet repair—it would take him the better part of a Saturday or Sunday, and he'd grow increasingly frustrated as the day went along, grumbling and cursing, and half the time he'd end up calling a friend or neighbor for help, and it wouldn't get completed until late in the day or even the following weekend.

A longtime high school football coach and phys ed teacher, he's a motivator, not a doer, with his thick neck, big forehead, and burly frame. Wanda knows she inherited more from her mother—her slim frame and her creative capacity—than from him. But she loves him just as dearly. He's devoted and dependable, and he immediately offered to make the two-hour drive to Harrisburg and sleep on Wanda's couch after she called home with news of her death threat.

So when he returns from the hardware and sporting goods stores on Tuesday, and unpacks the door-cam and pepper spray, Wanda knows the door-cam is going to be a major undertaking.

Wanda has the day off. Norm gave her a comp day, told her to stay in touch, take what she needed. She slept surprisingly well, maybe because her dad was on the couch, or maybe because the exhaustion finally caught up with her at midnight. It's almost noon, and she's still wearing her pink pajama pants and baggy gray Penn State T-shirt.

Her dad unpacks the parts and instructions for the door-cam, lays them out on the coffee table. "I want you to think about something," he says.

"What?" She's across the room, in the kitchen area, loading their coffee cups into the dishwasher.

"Buying a handgun."

"No," she says reflexively.

"Just for protection," he says.

"No." She bangs the dishwasher closed.

"Why not?" He pushes the door-cam instructions aside, leans back and crosses his arms. "I'd like to talk about this."

"I don't," she says. "Are you hungry? Do you want some lunch?" She opens the refrigerator door, not much inside. She twists her face.

"I wish you wouldn't change the subject," he says.

"Dad, please," she says. "I'm just not comfortable with it."

"I'll go with you. We can rent one first, and we can practice together at the shooting range. I'll help you get comfortable with it."

She closes the refrigerator, checks in the cabinet. "I don't have much to eat," she says.

"That's okay. We can go out for lunch. My treat."

"But I don't want to talk about buying a gun." She turns to face him, throws one hand on her hips.

"Okay, but just promise me you'll think about it."

"Maybe I will, maybe I won't."

She's not expecting much to come from the police investigation. She knows these things rarely go anywhere, and the cop who came to the newspaper office was not at all reassuring. He was young, kind of cute, but he didn't say anything that led Wanda to believe they'd be able to nab Stonewall X. Jackson. He took a report, promised to have a patrol car drive by her apartment every couple of hours, said a new county-federal task force on terroristic threats would pick up with the investigation, but it can be hard to prove that the threat was made with the actual intent to follow through. Too often, the cop said, these nutcases are deemed "a howler," meaning they're just spouting off, versus "a hunter," who intends to track down their prey.

So maybe she will think about it—buying a gun—but probably not. Either way, she doesn't want to think about it now. It's been a helluva twenty-four hours since Stonewall appeared in her Twitter feed, and right now she just wants some normalcy in her life, starting with a good hot shower and some food in her stomach and her refrigerator. Tomorrow, she'll go back to work.

She grabs her purse from its place on a hook by the door, carries it over to the coffee table where her dad is struggling with the door-cam, picks up the pepper spray and drops it in her purse. "I'll keep this stuff in here," she promises her dad. "Okay?"

He nods, but he doesn't seem satisfied.

***

Emma brings a pack of papers to the Little League field. She's determined to knock out a big chuck of her ungraded papers today, even if she has to sit in the stands, pen in hand, and grade throughout the Astros game. The semester is almost over, and if she doesn't return them soon, her students will skewer her on their course evaluations or complain to the department chair, or both, and Emma can't afford either.

The morning wind has died down, and the sun is hanging in the westward sky, a nice spring afternoon, the smell of cut grass and pollen in the air. Emma finds a spot on the bleachers, Astros side, end of the second row. Thomas is a sub again today, so she has little to pay attention to for a couple of innings. The first few papers she grades are typical, grammar errors and filler, and the game starts out as usual, the mighty Astros grabbing a 6-0 lead over the Dodgers. Emma senses some catty stares from the other moms—*Why isn't that woman watching our kids?*—but she ignores them, refuses to let them rattle her. She keeps her head down, peeking up only occasionally for the score and for Thomas's first appearance, keeps her purple pen moving over page after page of uninspired student writing. A mom beside her keeps sneezing, and after saying "Bless you" once, Emma ignores her, too.

When Emma gets to Madeline Garvanitis's paper, she considers putting it back in the pile to read later. She's making too much progress to deal with Madeline right now. But grudgingly, she reads it, and it's good, not great, has a few grammar errors and wordy spots. Not quite an A paper. More like an A-, or maybe even a B+, but God forbid that should happen again to Madeline. Emma dreads the inevitable after-class drama if she assigns another B+, and even an A-feels like a risk. It's just not worth it. So she marks the paper with an A, moves on to the next one.

Thomas comes up to bat in the bottom of the third, and Emma puts down her pen and papers, stretches out her back, which is starting to bother her. Maybe it's time to see a chiropractor—yeah, but when? How to squeeze those appointments in right now?

She watches Thomas with a mix of parental interest and pessimism—after all, he's only had two hits all season. He takes the first pitch for a ball, then drives the next pitch for a single over the shortstop's head, and a runner on third darts home. Emma slams down her papers, hops up and claps, shouting, "Wow! Go Thomas!"

Okay, so she's cheering only for her own kid. Big deal. Who else roots for hers?

Next inning, Thomas comes up to bat again, Astros leading 9-1. Again, he takes the first pitch for a ball, then fouls off the second. Parental anxiety replaces Emma's simple parental interest—he's got to be feeling good about himself after that first hit, got to be feeling like he can do this again, and oh how wonderful it would be if he could rack up a second hit today. Another foul ball. Emma can feel herself breathing. She thinks maybe she should temper her suddenly higher expectations; maybe two hits is just too much to ask for.

The mom beside her blows her nose loudly into a tissue, just as Thomas drives another ball to the outfield, a one-hop single between the first and second basemen.

Emma is up and clapping her hands above her head: "Way to go, Thomas!"

After the game, a 12-2 Astros victory, Thomas is the first kid out of the dugout, black bat bag strapped across his back, a little bounce in his step as he strides through the gate to the field.

"You had a fantastic game," Emma says, bending down for a quick hug.

Thomas takes a half-step back, embarrassed by the hug.

"I kept my nose on the ball," he says.

Emma straightens up, casts a quizzical look at him. "What?"

"It's what Myles told me to do when we came to the batting cages—keep your nose on the ball."

"It doesn't make sense."

"Makes sense to me."

"But how do you do that? The ball's moving."

"It's pretend," Thomas says. "As the ball comes in, keep your nose down, so you see it better."

"Ah, I see."

"I wanna tell Myles I had two hits," Thomas says.

"Certainly," Emma says, though she's in no hurry to talk to Myles about anything right now, and doesn't even know where she wants that relationship to go, if anywhere.

More Astros file through the gate—some of them stop to meet smiling parents, some head straight to the concession stand. Behind them, an auburn sun is setting in the west.

"And can we go to the concessions stand?" Thomas asks.

"Yes, of course." No reason to leave this moment behind. She wants to sit down on an aging wooden picnic table on this splendid spring evening and enjoy a hot dog and a Coke with her son, revel in the moment and learn more about the art of keeping your nose on the ball. She has ground beef for tacos in the fridge at home, but no reason Taco Tuesday can't become Taco Wednesday.

There's a long line at the concession stand, but it doesn't bother Emma. She stretches out her back while they wait. In front of her are two Dodgers with their moms, and the moms are talking about vacations spots at the Jersey Shore. Both of the moms are wearing sporty pullovers and black Spandex pants; one is tall and dirty-blonde, the other short with curly black hair and a Botox face. Emma and Thomas decide what they want—two hot dogs, two Cokes, an order of nachos to split between them.

The line is moving slowly. The Dodger moms change topics—the last month of school. And then the book ban comes up.

They're all for it.

"I don't want some teacher with a liberal agenda teaching my kids about books," says one of the moms.

"I hear you," concurs the other mom. "It's indoctrination."

Emma inhales suddenly, but says nothing.

When the line moves forward, Emma stays right where she is, feet planted. The extra space feels like a good idea, even if it's just a few feet. She's fighting back the urge to respond to these moms. Oh, how she wants to respond. But she also doesn't want to cause a scene, not here, not after everything Thomas has been through at this damned baseball field, and in this damned town of theirs, not in the midst of an otherwise momentous moment for him. He doesn't enjoy many of those.

So she locks her lips, keeps that extra few feet of space between them as she nears the window to the concession stand.

When they sit down with their food, Emma and Thomas are two tables away from the Dodger moms. Emma tries to shake off their comments, but she can't. She can feel the tension in her jaw as she chews her hot dog. When the Dodger moms ball up their napkins and strap their purses across their shoulders, apparently ready to leave, Emma tells Thomas she's getting up for napkins.

Thomas points to the two unused napkins on the table between them. "We have some," he says.

"I want some more," she says.

The Dodger moms turn their back on the concession stand and stroll toward the parking lot. Emma walks up behind them.

"Excuse me," Emma says. They turn and look at her, sociably.

"I just want you to know," Emma says, "if you don't trust teachers to teach your kids about books, then I don't know who you would trust."

She turns sharply on her heels and struts back to sit with her son.

THIRTY

GAYLE FINALLY makes a big dinner again on Wednesday night: chicken marsala, snap peas, and red potatoes. The past several nights she relied on delivery or something easy, tacos or Sloppy Joes, so a nice family dinner is overdue. The whole family is there and everything gets devoured, the marsala and the sides. Gayle's glad to see it. Now, if only they would talk like a normal family again.

Her husband still hasn't acknowledged their daughter's coming out. Doug and Clarissa have talked, though. Just nothing important. All small talk: Don't stay out too late, please pass the hot sauce. At least he gave her extra gas and burrito money on Sunday without complaining.

After dinner, Doug disappears to the basement, their son bolts up to his room, and Clarissa hangs around the kitchen, helps her mom with the dishes. Gayle rinses, Clarissa loads them into the dishwasher. It's a rainy night, the prattle of raindrops against the window above the sink.

"The printer called this afternoon," Gayle says. "The signs are in."

"Cool. What do they look like?" Clarissa asks, stuffing a handful of silverware into their basket.

"Yellow with black letters," Gayle says, handing off the potato dish. "The lettering says 'Reverse the book ban.' Nice and simple."

"Why yellow?" Clarissa rearranges the plates on the bottom rack so she can squeeze in the potato dish.

"It pops, and it's the color of sunshine."

"Cool," Clarissa says, nodding agreeably. "When are we going to put them up?"

"Tomorrow afternoon." Gayle hands off two water glasses. "I sent out an email for volunteers, and I've already heard back from several."

"I can get more from school. No problem."

"Bring them here at four o'clock. We're meeting in our driveway. I'm picking the signs up in the morning."

"Easy peasy."

Clarissa says she has homework, so when the dishwasher is loaded she too disappears to her room upstairs. Gayle brews a cup of tea, sits down at the island, looks out the rain-sopped window. After five minutes and a few sips of tea, she's ready to tread downstairs and broach another difficult topic with her husband.

The smell of his cigar hits her as soon as she steps onto the stairwell, and she's reminded this is his turf. She always feels like a visitor in part of her own home when she ventures down here, but tonight she's undaunted. If he's determined to follow through with a Senate campaign, this conversation is a must, and a rainy weeknight is as good a time as any to get it out of the way.

He's reclined on his La-Z-Boy, tapping his cigar into the ashtray on the little table beside him. A car commercial is on the big screen. Gayle sits down in the wingback chair on the other side of the little table, teacup in hand. She asks the score. Sixers are winning by eight, so that's good, might help with his mood. He's also not drinking tonight, another reason this is a good time to tackle this discussion.

"Anything developing on the Senate front?" she asks.

"I heard Mike Carlson is interested," he says. "But I'm not surprised. The local House member usually steps up when there's a Senate vacancy, but he has no chance of getting Ted's endorsement. Ted can't stand him."

"You sure?"

"Most definitely."

"I want to ask you something else about the Senate campaign," she says in a soft, guarded tone, the exact tone she had planned to convey. "And if you haven't thought about it yet, I want you to. It's a serious question, and I want to be helpful, so don't get upset."

He looks at her warily. "What?"

"Have you thought about how you'll respond to questions about the book ban if you become a candidate?"

He rubs his forehead, doesn't like the question. "Seriously?"

"Yes, seriously," she says gently. "I told you it's a serious question, one you'll have to deal with. This book ban is a big deal here right now, and the school board race will also be on the ballot next year. We're recruiting candidates for it, and we have a lot of interest."

He puffs on his cigar, blows the smoke away from her. "You realize I'll have to first win a Republican primary, right? So if I don't win that, there won't be a general election."

"Of course I realize that."

"Did Clarissa put you up to this?"

"No, she didn't."

He looks at the big screen. The Sixers surrender a three-pointer, which cuts their lead to three. He makes a disgusted face, but it's hard to know if that's because of her question or the score. Probably both.

"How do *you* feel about the book ban? I don't mean Doug Brungard the candidate. I mean Doug Brungard the person?"

He gives a dismissive shrug of his shoulder, takes another puff of his cigar.

"Well?" she asks.

"It's one of those cultural issues," he says. "I don't like to get too involved in cultural issues. I'd rather focus on taxes, the economy, things like that."

"That's a candidate answer."

"Well, Doug Brungard the person is preparing to be Doug Brungard the candidate, so that's my answer. We're one and the same right now."

She wraps both hands around her teacup, stares into it.

"I was hoping for better from you," she says, and she gets up and leaves.

***

Myles is out of town with the baseball team Friday night, has a Saturday doubleheader up at Ithaca College, his last games of the season, and Emma's glad. She needs some time and space, needs to figure out if he's the kind of guy she wants to stick with. One day she thinks no, the next day she thinks maybe. But two words keep coming back to her: life partner. It's a high bar, sure, but she's thirty-eight years old, not getting any younger, and she can't ignore the question: Is Myles a life partner?

No baseball for Thomas on Friday either. He also has a Saturday game, and they practiced on Thursday. Emma caught up on her grading Friday afternoon, sat down and plowed through twenty-some papers, so she's finished with grading until final papers roll in next week. So for Friday night...what to do?

She might not have a date, and she might not have her best friend, which is really bothering her, because the thought of losing a friend, especially such an old and close friend, is too much right now, but she still has a guy in her life, her little guy.

"Let's get out and do something tonight," she suggests to Thomas.

He's on the floor in front of the television, immersed in a video game. "Like what?" he asks, his attention stuck on the game.

"How about a movie?" She grabs her phone, googles movies in the area, and the only kid's movie is *Puss In Boots*. Thomas turns his nose up at it.

"Hmm," Emma says, recalculating. "How about the Java Hut? I hear they have a great guitar player and great milkshakes."

It's kind of an adult thing to do, but he's a mature little guy, has already shot down *Puss in Boots*. He contemplates it.

"Okay," he says.

She won't tell Thomas this, but there's another reason she'd like to visit the Java Hut tonight—Sounders. He was the one who told her about the acoustic guitarist, in that awkward moment in the parking lot after their first coffee meeting with Gayle. She had the impression it was his hangout. She had no desire to see him then, but now? Not for a date. Certainly not. But for the company, adult company, a guy other than Myles, someone she can talk to about something of substance. Their campaign against the book ban, for example. So yeah, as surprising as it might seem, it would be nice to bump into Sounders tonight.

They drive to the Java Hut in the half-light of dusk, and the yellow signs are out. They dot the yards on Cedar Street and the storefronts on Main Street—at least one on every block. It's comforting to know there are people here who care, people she otherwise might not have recognized as people who care, and she adores those signs—the color yellow was her idea, the color of sunshine, perfect for a campaign to brighten the lives of children. The average person wouldn't notice the symbolism, but even at this hour, with daylight fading, those signs are hard to miss.

The Java Hut is crowded, every booth and table full, small groups of college kids and middle-aged couples out for a cool date night, the mellow strums of acoustic guitar and the low hum of pleasant chatter drifting through the place. The lights are dim. The guitarist is a twenty-something bearded guy with a scratchy voice, seated behind a microphone in the back corner in a denim shirt and work boots. As Emma and Thomas stroll up to the counter, the guitarist finishes one song and introduces his next, a Bob Dylan tune.

Sure enough, Sounders is there. He's sitting alone in a booth near the back, wearing a khaki baseball cap, jeans and sneakers, tapping his foot slowly to the tune: *Buckets of Rain.*

There's a line at the counter, two teenage baristas, one girl and one guy, hustling to fill each order. When Emma steps up and orders coffee and a chocolate milkshake, the girl barista blows her cheeks out, a miffed face; the shake apparently takes extra effort. While Emma and Thomas wait at the side of the counter, Emma tries to make eye contact with Sounders, but no luck. He's locked in on the guitar player, oblivious to everything else around him. Emma feels sorry for him, a guy with no real personal life to speak of, and then it dawns on her—maybe people feel the same way toward her.

She gives the barista a good tip when their coffee and shake come, suggests to Thomas that they say hello to Mr. Sounders in the back. He nods agreeably, takes a spoonful of shake.

Sounders looks dog-tired. Emma sees it when she gets to his booth and sees him up close—his face looks worn, his eyes cheerless, his shoulders slooped.

"Want some company?" she asks.

For a split-second, he looks at her blankly, as if he doesn't recognize her, then he snaps into the moment.

"Yes, of course," he says, sitting up straight. "Please."

Emma and Thomas slide into the opposite side of his booth.

"I remember you mentioning this guitar player to me earlier," Emma says.

"Yeah, he's great, isn't he?" Sounders says.

Thomas looks up at Emma and asks, "Can I take guitar lessons?"

Emma smiles at him. "Maybe," she says. "Are you really interested?"

"Yeah." He scoops a spoonful of shake.

"We can talk about it," she says. "But you have to stay interested."

"I would," Thomas promises, slurping at his spoon.

"Have you seen the signs?" Emma asks Sounders.

"Yes, they look great."

"I was surprised to see as many as I did," she says. "Pleasantly surprised."

He lifts his cap, scratches his head. "Our school district gets a bad rap sometimes," he says. "But there are a lot of good people here. They might not show up at the school board meetings, but they're here."

She takes a sip of coffee. "Do you think it will make any difference, the signs and everything else?"

Sounders tilts his head, thoughtfully. "The high school kids are still walking out," he says. "And then there's all the media attention. You should see my emails. Parents are really worked up about it, asking all sorts of questions about how it's supposed to work and what we're doing at the school. I'm sure board members are getting just as many emails. And you should see the district's Facebook page—I'd hate to be our communications director—it's full of bitter arguments. The ban is topic number one around here right now."

"I don't do social media," Emma says. "I have enough problems without having to navigate that world, too."

"Wise choice," Sounders says. "But to answer your question, I don't know. I just don't know. Our board can be very stubborn."

"Bastards," Emma says. She shakes her head gloomily.

"Richard Weaver called me today," Sounders says. "He asked me to sit in on a meeting with the student protest leaders on Monday, said they might listen to me because I'm on the Diversity Committee. He wants to convince them to get back in the classroom, end their walkout, try another strategy for protesting the ban."

"Are you going to?"

"Of course. It's part of my job. I feel like it is."

"What are you going to say to them?"

"I haven't decided yet."

Emma sips her coffee. "It seems like you're in a difficult position. Stuck in the middle of all of this."

He rubs his chin with his fingertips. "It's my job. I signed up for it. But it's not about me. It's about the kids, always about the kids."

"That's admirable," she says.

Sounders looks at Thomas, who's immersed in his shake, which is already half gone. "I often have to remind myself that, about the kids, because it's not always easy."

"Understandable," she says.

His gaze is still fixed on Thomas, fondness in his eyes, and Emma's reminded about the rumors about his family, a broken marriage and a boy who's often in trouble, expelled and stuck in cyber school. She's saddened by the irony—a man whose life is devoted to the kids but can't hold his own family together. He's a good man; she can tell. He deserves better, but life dumps those damned buckets of rain whether we deserve it or not. She knows that as well as anyone. At least he's hanging in there—or he seems to be. Kind of like her.

The guitarist introduces a John Prine tune.

"So Thomas," Sounders asks, "what are your summer plans?"

"We're going to the beach," Thomas says.

"Really?" Emma says. "Who told you that?"

"Myles."

"Oh, did he?"

"Yeah."

"I'm not so sure about that," Emma says.

"Who's Myles?" Sounders asks.

Emma feels herself blushing. "A guy," she says. "We've been seeing each other—well, yeah, been seeing each other, that's accurate. But we're not going to the beach. It's not that serious, not really. Thomas must have misunderstood."

"Then why did he say it?" Thomas asks.

"I don't know, honey." She tries to smile, but she can only muster an embarrassed half-smile. "Maybe because it came up in conversation one night, but that's all. We made no plans."

The guitarist croons a little louder, his voice scratchy and pained, a song about coming home.

Sounders lifts his coffee mug, stares into it, finally takes a sip, then flashes an icky face. "Coffee's cold," he explains. He says it in a flat, matter-of-fact tone, and that distasteful look on his face has disappeared—he'll deal with it, just like everything else.

THIRTY-ONE

"I'll be home in a couple hours," Myles texts. "OK if I stop over?"

Emma is drinking alone, just a glass of chardonnay, out back on the porch in her bare feet, gray T-shirt and her comfiest jean shorts. It's late afternoon on Saturday, the sun sliding into the westward sky, the heat from a summer-like day tapering off, and she just felt like a glass of wine and some peace and quiet, that's all, nothing wrong with that, right?

She stares at the text, unsure how to respond. Takes a drink of wine, sets the glass down on the porch, then types her response: "I'm pretty tired, so sorry, not tonight."

His reply comes immediately: "No problem." He must be on the bus, nothing to do but keep an eye on his phone.

She doesn't want to be too rude, though. "How did the games go?" she asks.

"Awful, lost them both. Glad this season is finally over. Worst season I've ever had."

"Better luck next year."

"Can't get much worse."

"Don't be so sure," she types. "You never know."

"Your wise beyond you're years." Two grammar mistakes in one text. She shakes her head but decides against correcting him—what's the point? She doesn't reply at all.

A minute later he texts back: "What did you do last night?"

She picks up her wine glass, takes another drink. She holds onto the glass while she considers how to respond. What the hell, she decides, tell him the damn truth. No reason to dither or dally with him. She sets her glass back down.

"Thomas and I went to the Java Hut," she types. "We saw an acoustic guitarist and hung out with the principal at Thomas's school."

No immediate response. It dawns on her that Myles probably doesn't know the principal, might not know if it's a he, she, or they. Myles probably assumes it's a he, because that's how guys are, always assuming someone in a position of authority is a male. Still, she's tempted to clarify, so she does: "He's a very nice guy."

A minute ticks by, then another, still no response. But he must have seen it, must be on the bus, eyes on his phone. Now she has qualms about sending that last text—a minute ago she didn't want to be too rude, but maybe now she's being cruel.

She watches a squirrel scurry across the yard.

The screen door opens, and Thomas pokes his head out.

"Tracey's here," he says.

"What? Where?"

"At the front door," he says.

"Oh."

Emma wasn't expecting this. Hadn't heard from Tracey since a week ago, that unsettling conversation about the book ban right here on this very porch. She's not sure she's ready for this, not sure she's ready for more conflict, or to confront an old friend who might not be the person Emma thought she was. Regardless, she stands up, takes a deep breath, sticks her phone in her back pocket, heads inside.

The walk from back door to front door is a long one, a minute that feels like thirty. Emma knows she's been putting this off, practically repressing it. She's already lost her mother, lost her husband, and she feels herself losing her father and her new boyfriend, and now her best friend? And to what? To the times, to their own hometown, what it's become, and what it does to those who let it define them.

Tracey's standing on the rug at the door, like a visitor who hasn't been welcomed inside. She's holding a bottle of white wine in one hand and a gift bag in the other. Her face is plaintive, her eyes wide with contrition. She holds out the wine and gift bag, a peace offering.

Emma's shoulders fall and she feels herself melting away. Her eyes well up.

"Ah, Emma," Tracey says in a lullaby tone. She leans into Emma, wraps both arms around her, the wine and gift bag resting against Emma's back. "I'm so sorry—sorry about everything I said."

"Thank you."

"I've been a wreck for the past week," Tracey says.

"Welcome to my world," Emma says. "I'm a wreck all the time."

Emma steps back, out of the hug, waves Tracey inside, wipes her eyes with the back of her wrist.

"The wine is cold," Tracey says with a waggle of the bottle.

"Perfect," Emma says. "I already have a glass on the back porch, but I'll take some more."

Thomas is on the floor in front of the television, playing his video game, paying them no attention.

In the kitchen, Emma grabs a wine glass from the cupboard. Tracey hands the gift bag to Emma. It's a scented candle, coconut, one of Emma's favorites. She takes the lid off and smells it.

"Thank you," Emma says. "I can't imagine losing you as a friend."

"I feel the exact same way," Tracey says. She opens the wine bottle, pours herself a glass.

"We've been friends since what—first grade?" Emma says.

"Yeah, first grade. I remember your mom walking us to school on our first day. I was so nervous, and I was so glad she was there."

"I miss her so much." Emma closes her eyes, lets the memory of her mom wash over her—the nurse, who, it often seemed, could cure anything, any ailment or negative emotion, just by being there. If only she were still here. If only.

"I'm sure," Tracey says knowingly. "Also, I feel like I owe you an explanation."

Emma opens her eyes. Time to face reality: A lifelong friendship is at stake here, and she feels a responsibility to it. She wants to hear this. "Let's go out back," she says.

As they each pull up one of the plastic chairs, the late-day sunshine angling onto the edge of the porch, Emma's phone pings with a text. She yanks her phone from her back pocket before she sits down. It's Myles.

Emma huffs. "I'm going to ignore this, for now at least."

"Let me guess—the baseball coach?" Tracey sets her bottle of wine on the floor between them.

"Yes, and it's complicated," Emma says. "I'm not sure where things can go with him."

"But he's cute, and he seems like a nice guy."

Emma pauses, looks down at her wine glass. How to explain that nice guy's flaws to her?

"Well, yeah," Emma says, "but there has to be more. Do you know what I mean? I need someone who shares my values, too."

"I think I know what you mean," Tracey says.

But does she? Or is she just trying to be agreeable? What is that explanation she's promised?

There's a pause between them. Emma twists in her plastic chair, her back tightening up.

Tracey takes a healthy swig of wine. "So I guess I should explain myself," she says.

"I didn't think the things you said where the kind of things my oldest friend would say," Emma says.

"They're not," Tracey says, and her face opens up, plaintively. "I wasn't thinking. I mean, I wasn't thinking at all. About you and Thomas, especially. I should have known better."

"It takes a big person to admit that," Emma says.

"It's hard, though. For me, at least," Tracey says. "I need to be a bigger person, I really do. Because when other people say things like that, like those other women at the birthday party, it's hard to know everything about what they're saying. I don't follow the news all that much. I know—I should, but I don't. So it's easier to just go along. Especially when you're at a little girl's birthday party. You don't want to argue, so you go along."

Emma breathes in the spring air, laced with lilac and pollen. She sneezes. Tracey says, "Bless you."

"So are you just going along with me right now?" Emma asks.

"No, no." She shakes her head. "God, no. This has been torturing me all week. Believe me."

"It is hard. I know," Emma says. She's reminded of Myles, wonders if he's been tortured all week. Even if he has been, does he really understand why he upset her so much? Is he a big enough person to admit it—admit that he should have known better? Even if he did, would he mean it? Really mean it?

They each take a drink of wine. It's going down easy.

"I can't imagine everything you're dealing with right now," Tracey says.

Emma twists in her chair again. "And on top of it all, my back is bothering me. I need to see a chiropractor. Or maybe I need to get a breast reduction. I don't know."

Tracey finishes off her wine. "In that case," she says, hoisting her empty glass, "more wine?"

"Yes. More wine."

They finish the bottle, as the sun dips behind the mountains to the west and the grayness of dusk settles in.

***

That last text from Myles is still waiting for her. Tracey's gone, Thomas is in bed, and her phone battery is almost dead. She plugs the phone into the charger on her bedside table, sits down on the edge of the bed, taps his text.

"I'd like to see you."

She's glad she didn't see this earlier, glad she didn't respond, because he's probably home by now, so he probably got the message— she doesn't want to see him right now. Not tonight, at least. She just hopes he doesn't show up drunk with a box of drug-store chocolates.

Maybe she should tell him that—please do not come to my house drunk tonight. No, no. Just leave it as is for now, let it be, no reply.

What does she owe him, though? Eventually, a reply, at the least. She looks up at her bare bedroom wall, vanilla paint which could use a fresh coat. Moments like these, she wishes she had prints hanging on her walls, but that's another consequence of her bad marriage. Abid was a minimalist, liked the "clean" look, maybe because his personal behavior was anything but, and she went along. Now, she wishes she had prints to look at—mountains, beaches, city skylines or cobblestone streets, anything really. But since moving here and getting Thomas enrolled in school and lining up work at two colleges, she had yet to get around to it. When she moved in last year, she was just glad to get all of those damned boxes unpacked.

She falls back onto her bed, tosses her phone aside. Doesn't want to see it, doesn't want to deal with it right now. She's tired but she knows she can't sleep, and she's a little drunk. She's lying square on her back, looking straight up at the ceiling, and she realizes it needs painted, too.

Her mind thrums with difficult questions, over herself, her son, her life, over this confusing moment in time, and what's going to happen next, what should happen next. Questions about what happens to women like her, a single mom, divorced, late thirties. Troubling questions: Are her standards too high, and will she never find someone who meets them? Is she unlovable? A lost cause?

It won't be long before she'll be expected to settle for someone she's not really in love with, someone flawed, because you know, at some point you just have to settle. If not, she's a lost cause. Will she be okay with that, with settling? She inhales deeply, slowly releases her breath.

Why did she seek out Sounders at the coffee shop? Was it really only for adult companionship, or was it because she senses something more, something deeper, underneath his bad hair and baggy sweaters? Even if she did, could she get past the bad hair and bad clothes and his awkwardness? Probably not. She feels no romantic pull toward him, nothing that makes her heart pound. It's a purely practical attraction, if you can even call it that. Which means she shouldn't have done anything to lead him on. But did she? As far as he knows, it was purely a coincidental meet-up, and she doesn't have to explain anything else to him.

She thinks about Tracey, their reconciliation. Why does reconciling with Myles feel so different? Maybe because, with Tracey, a lifelong friendship is at stake, and that brings with it that extra responsibility, or is it loyalty? A willingness to work on it. Emma doesn't feel that same sense of responsibility toward Myles. Guys come and go, even if she wishes one could stay.

Emma didn't expect Tracey to be so remorseful—which is so rare to see, and commendable—but maybe she should have, considering what was at stake. Besides a friendship, Tracey's own sense of herself was at stake; she surely didn't want to move forward in life with someone who knows her so well realizing that her human decency has slipped away. Still, the terms of their friendship have probably changed, even if the friendship will survive. For a while, at least, Emma will have to be careful about what topics she brings up in Tracey's company. So she will. People do that all the time. But with Myles, different story. How do you change the terms of a relationship with someone who wants you to completely turn over your heart to them?

***

When she wakes up Sunday morning, streaks of pale daylight peeking through the blinds, that last text from Myles pops into her head before she even sits up in bed. She decides she doesn't want to put it off any longer. Yes, she owes him a reply, also doesn't want it weighing on her, yet doesn't want to lie to him about anything. So she'll text a casual apology and some basic facts about her night. Yes, that'll do. She reaches for her phone and thumbs it: "Sorry I didn't reply sooner. Tracey came over last night and we had a lot to talk about."

Good. Non-committal, accurate and polite enough.

She rubs her eyes hard, hears Thomas's footsteps pattering toward the bathroom.

Maybe it's not so good, her text to Myles. She didn't really address his last text, his plea to see her, so maybe it was too evasive. He won't give up so easily.

What to do, what to do? She studies the text she just sent, which is labeled delivered. That doesn't mean he saw it, though. He might have been drinking last night, probably was, in fact, even if he wasn't drunk enough to show up here with drug-store candy, so he might not be awake yet. But when he does see it, he'll follow up, no doubt.

She hears the toilet flush. Thomas's footsteps patter back to his room.

What to do? She can feel her hair flat against her head, so maybe a shower and breakfast first. Thomas will want breakfast, too.

But why wait, why put this off any longer? Why not give Myles one more chance? That's probably where this is going anyway, so stop dithering and dallying already. Try working on it. See if he shows up with the appropriate level of contriteness, see if she can get past his complicated family ties, if she can look deeper and see something more in him, if it exists. Who knows when another guy will come along?

Give him that one more chance, and stop overthinking it. Just send the damned text. What's the worst that can happen?

"Let's do dinner next weekend," she texts. "I'll cook."

THIRTY-TWO

MONDAY MORNING, and Sounders still doesn't know what he's going to say. Doesn't know what he wants to say. He drives to the high school in his ten-year-old Toyota, reciting certain lines in his head, but they all sound like principal-speak, so they all sound fake: *You've raised enough awareness already; you don't want to jeopardize your schoolwork; sometimes you can take something too far.* These kids will see right through every one of them, and besides, he's not sure he believes any of them himself.

It's an 11 a.m. meeting, and Sounders is five minutes early. He checks in with Weaver's secretary, who shows him to a conference room, says Weaver's running a few minutes late, but the students should be in soon. The room has old green carpet and eight chairs around a boat-shaped conference table. The fluorescent bulbs in the ceiling put off a yellowish light.

Sounders takes a seat, checks his messages on his phone, responds to one from a long-term sub who started that morning. A minute later the students arrive, four of them in a group, eyeing Sounders suspiciously. Sounders puts his phone face-down on the table, stands up and introduces himself, notes his membership on the Diversity Committee, says Principal Weaver should be here soon.

"I'm Clarissa Brungard." Sounders knows who she is. Everybody knows who she is by now.

"I'm Amelia Phillips." A white girl with short reddish hair.

"I'm Kylee Miller." A skinny black girl wearing distressed jeans. Grace's daughter.

"I'm Chad Hoffner." A soft-faced white guy in a black T-shirt that reads *I Woke Up Gay Again Today.*

They stand together across the table from Sounders, and he has to tell them to take a seat. Clarissa sits down first, then the others.

"I don't know why we're here," Clarissa says.

"Principal Weaver wants to discuss the walkout with you," Sounders says.

"I know but I don't know what he wants from us," Clarissa says.

"Are we in trouble?" Chad asks.

"No," Sounders says. "You're not in trouble. As I understand it, he wants to have a constructive dialogue with you."

Clarissa and Amelia exchange a look from the corners of their eyes. Kylee makes a confused face. Chad picks at a scab on his arm.

"What do you mean by constructive?" Kylee asks.

"Why don't we let him take the lead," Sounders says.

"Why are you here?" Amelia asks.

"I'm on the Diversity Committee. We put together the list."

"So you're on our side?" Chad asks.

Sounders folds his hands together on the table. "I don't want to say that I'm picking sides," he says. "But I'm supportive of diverse resources for our students."

"That's weak," Clarissa says. "It's time to pick sides here, if you want to be part of the solution. If not, you're part of the problem."

Sounders unfolds his hands, scratches the side of his face. "I understand why you might believe that," he says.

"Am I wrong?" Clarissa asks.

"I think it's more complicated than that," Sounders says.

Weaver arrives, apologizing for his lateness, says something unexpected came up. He's wearing a crisp white shirt and burgundy tie, has a little hunch in his gait, the only sign in his appearance that the years are taking their toll. He sits beside Sounders, across from the students, thanks everyone for coming.

"Did I miss anything?" Weaver says.

"We were just getting to know each other a little," Sounders says. "But I told them I wanted to wait for you to take the lead."

"Yes, very good, thank you," Weaver says, and his tone carries the force of a man who, after two decades as principal, is accustomed to being listened to. "So—"

Clarissa and Amelia trade another look from the corners of their eyes.

Weaver straightens his tie. "I understand why you felt the need to organize the walkout," he says. "But it's been ten days since it began, six class days so far, and today will be the seventh. I'm concerned about all of the class time you're missing, and I want to talk to you about that. I think it's time to think about getting back into the classroom during fifth period."

"I have a study period," Chad says.

"Regardless," Weaver says. "A lot of you are missing a lot of class time, and that's concerning."

"So what are you saying?" Clarissa asks.

"I think it's time to get back to class," Weaver says. "Consider other ways to continue protesting."

"Like what?" Amelia asks.

"What about a petition?" Weaver says. "Or an afterschool protest?"

"They won't have the same impact," Clarissa says.

Weaver rakes his hand through his silver hair. "How do you know?"

Clarissa spits out a *pfft* sound. Weaver looks to Sounders, eyebrows raised, as if he expects him to join the conversation now.

"I think," Sounders says, "that Mr. Weaver's suggestion is worth thinking about." Weaver sends him a look that says, *That's the best you can do?*

"Don't we have rights?" Amelia asks. "First Amendment rights?"

"Of course," Weaver says diplomatically. "Nobody is trying to deny your rights. We're suggesting you consider other ways to exercise them, so that you can exercise your rights and get back to class."

Clarissa blinks rapidly in succession. "We're thinking globally but acting locally," she says. "Isn't that what our teachers encourage us to do?"

"You can still do that and get back to class," Weaver says.

Clarissa looks down the table at her fellow students. "I say no way," she says.

"No way," Amelia concurs, and Kylee and Chad nod along.

Weaver breathes heavily through his nose, looks back at Sounders, who shrugs helplessly. He doesn't want to say this in front of Weaver, or even in front of the kids, but he thinks they're doing the right thing.

***

After the meeting breaks up, Weaver tells Sounders why he was late: He received a call from a school board member, Robert Lingenfelter, who is planning to visit the school today. Lingenfelter wants to see the walkout and discuss it with Weaver.

"You're welcome to stay and join our discussion," Weaver says, though he sounds like he doesn't completely mean it. "I told Mr. Lingenfelter you were here."

Sounders thumbs his phone, says he needs to check messages first. A minute later, he says, "Yes, I'll stay."

***

White-haired and ruddy-faced, Lingenfelter shows up wearing a blue blazer over an open-collared pink shirt. He's a retired banker who has the look of a retired banker. He's also a lifelong Cumberland resident, and at age 76, the longest-tenured member of the Cumberland Area School Board. He was also the board member who ten days ago seconded Ron Halprin's proposal that set all of this in motion.

Weaver and Sounders are standing outside the front entrance with a school security guard when he arrives. He's holding a white handkerchief and wiping his nose. The sun is out, warmth and pollen and tension in the air.

"Damn allergies," Lingenfelter says, sniffling, as he steps up to the principals. They don't shake hands. Instead they exchange nods and hellos and form a semi-circle, facing the long driveway in front of the school, where only one local news van is parked today. There's also a photographer and the young reporter from the *Telegraph*.

"How many days?" Lingenfelter asks.

"Seven," Weaver says. "Today will be the seventh day of the walkout."

"Why is this still news?" Lingenfelter says, shaking his head at the small media presence.

"We must be selling a lot of papers," Weaver says.

"Subscriptions," Sounders says. "They sell online subscriptions now, not papers."

The doors swing open, and out comes the crowd of kids, marching under the concrete canopy and down the long driveway in front of the lone news van and the *Telegraph* reporter. Their ranks may have dwindled a little over the past seven walkouts, but only a little, and more of them tote homemade signs: *Reverse The Ban, Diverse Books Matter, Education Is Not Indoctrination, I Hate Hate.*

Lingenfelter wipes his nose with his handkerchief. "My granddaughter is in that crowd," he says. "She hasn't talked to me about this. Not a word. And she just saw me standing here. I could tell by the look on her face when she came out. But nothing, no acknowledgement whatsoever that I'm here."

"I'm sorry," Weaver says.

Sounders toes the sidewalk.

"I have to wonder," Lingenfelter says, "how far do we want to take this fight?"

They watch as Clarissa peels off from the crowd and draws the attention of the two reporters. She has something to say, and the reporters are listening. The cameraman turns away from the crowd, squeezes between the two reporters and points his camera at her. The *Telegraph* reporter starts taking notes.

"Looks like our little meeting today is going to be the next headline," Sounders says.

"I just hope she portrays it accurately," Weaver says.

"I'm convinced we have to get these kids back in the classroom," Lingenfelter says. "I'm also convinced this thing is tearing this community apart. My wife urged me to come here today, and she wants me to go talk to Ron. She's nervous about going anywhere. In the grocery store the other day, a woman pushed her cart past her and mumbled, 'Racist.' It upset her very much. She's afraid to go out to eat now, afraid the staff will recognize us and spit in our food."

"These kids are determined," Sounders says. "They're not quitting."

"I see that," Lingenfelter says. "I voted for this because I'm concerned about how the movie and publishing industries push their liberal agendas, and Ron was very persuasive, very passionate about it, but now I'm having second thoughts. I didn't expect it to play out like this, and this isn't good."

"Are you going to talk to Ron," Weaver asks.

"I think so," Lingenfelter says, wiping his nose again. "But I have to think about what to say. He's not going to be an easy sell."

***

Eric Sounders is calling. It's Monday evening, late for a principal to be calling a parent, but let's face it, their relationship is more than principal-parent, even if it's nowhere close to anything romantic, at least as far as she's concerned, so Emma answers.

"It was good seeing you on Friday," he says.

"You too," she says, and she decides she'll be completely frank— why not? "I really needed a night out, and some adult company, and you were right, the guitarist there is great."

"He'll be back this Friday, in case you want to—"

"I can't," she says. "I have plans this Friday."

"Right, I'm sure." A hint of bruising in his voice. "Anyway, I called to report some news, about the ban."

"What is it?"

"Robert Lingenfelter came to the high school today. He said he's having second thoughts about voting for the ban, because he sees it tearing the community apart and he wants the kids back in the classroom. He's thinking about talking to Ron Halprin about it."

"What a coincidence," Emma says. "So am I."

THIRTY-THREE

MYLES SHOWS UP five minutes early, wearing dark jeans and a parka over a sky-blue Polo shirt, with a bottle of red wine and a bundle of fresh-cut tulips in a green paper wrapper. It's been a rainy day, and there's still a mist in the air, and the grayness lingers.

"That's nice of you," Emma says, waving him inside, accepting the bundle of tulips. She's wearing a sleeveless beige crewneck sweater. "Much nicer than drug-store candy."

He nods knowingly, guiltily.

She takes his parka, shakes it with one hand and hangs it. On the coffee table, a candle burns, and a coconut scent mixes with the faint smell of garlic from the kitchen. She puts the tulips on the coffee table.

"I have a vase somewhere," she says. "But I don't know where, so let's just put these here for now."

She takes the bottle of wine from him. "I have beer, too, if you'd like a beer," she says.

"What's for dinner?"

"A rigatoni dish. With chicken and tomatoes."

"Is that your mom's recipe?"

"So you remember that from last time?" She blows a loose strand of hair away from her eyes. "No, this time I googled easy yummy pasta dishes."

He chuckles. "Still sounds good," he says. "I think I'll have red wine."

"Let me get an opener."

Emma leads him into the kitchen. A large covered skillet simmers on the stovetop.

"Where's Thomas?" he asks.

"My friend Tracey is watching him tonight."

She opens one drawer, doesn't see the bottle opener. Tries another drawer, finds it.

"How's baseball going for him?" Myles asks.

"Believe it or not—good," she says, twisting the opener into the bottle. "He has his nose on the ball."

"Fundamentals," he says with a nod of confidence. "They go a long way."

"Apparently." The cork comes out. "He wants you to know, by the way, that he's been hitting much better."

She pours two glasses of red. He leans against the laminate countertop, and she leans against the front of the sink. They sip their wine, and there's a pause between them. He looks past her shoulder, toward the windows, the grayness outside.

"Shall we talk about the weather?" he says, quip-like.

"Hah," she snickers.

"It was nice of you to have me over," he says.

"It was nice of you to do so much for Thomas. And to take care of my tire, too."

"So does that qualify me as a nice guy?" He tilts his head, raises his eyebrows.

"You certainly are a nice guy." She looks him straight in the eye. "I've never said otherwise."

"But—"

"I didn't say 'but.'"

"But you were about to."

"You think?" Her eyes widen, wittingly.

"I think."

Emma lifts her wine glass for a nip. "So how about that weather?"

He smiles at her. "Yeah, how about it."

She turns to the stove, lifts the cover off the skillet, stirs the chicken and tomatoes with a wooden spoon. Takes a bigger drink of wine.

"Seriously, though," he says. "I'm really glad you invited me over."

"Are you glad your baseball season is over?" she asks, covering the skillet.

He blows out a puff of air. "You have no idea. Worst losing streak of my life."

"It happens to all of us, right? At some point?"

"When was your big losing streak?" he asks.

She cackles. "I think I'm still on it."

"Don't say that." He takes a drink of wine.

She shrugs. "Let me ask you a question," she says. "Have you ever broken up with a girl via text message?"

A quizzical look crosses his face. "I don't think so."

"But you're not sure?"

"I can't remember doing it, not off the top of my head."

"Have there been that many women?"

"No, that's not what I mean. What I mean is, I just don't remember doing it, so I guess not."

"That's how my husband—or my ex-husband—ended our marriage."

"Wow."

"That's the best you can do—wow?"

"I mean, I'm sorry. That's terrible."

"Yeah, well." She wraps both hands around her wine glass. "I've been trying my best to forget about it, but that was the beginning of my losing streak."

"I hope it ends soon," he says. "But things could be worse."

She winces. "Ugh," she says. "I hate it when people say that—it could be worse. Why do people say things like that? It's a breezy platitude, and it completely disregards how we feel about things. Sure, things could be worse, but things could also be better—should be better, in fact."

He nods slowly, pensively. "I didn't mean it that way."

She purses her lips. "It's okay."

He takes a drink of wine. "Back to the weather?"

The outline of a smile tugs at her lips. "Been such a rainy spring," she says, playing along.

Emma reaches into the cupboard above the stove, pulls out a box of rigatoni, sets it on the counter, returns to the spot in front of the sink, facing Myles. "What about the bloody sock guy?" she asks. "The pitcher you told Thomas and me about. That story was such a profile in courage."

"What about him?"

"I don't know. I loved that story, and I thought it inspired you in some way."

He shrugs, as if he hasn't thought much about it. "It did, I guess."

"You should keep that story in mind," she says. "I mean, I did, and I'm not even a baseball person."

"I can't confuse myself with guys like that," he says. "He was an elite pitcher, the best of the best."

"So?"

He blinks, then blinks again, gives another shrug. "I was a minor leaguer."

"Don't think like that. We can't think like that." She turns back to the stove, stirs the chicken and tomatoes again.

"What do you mean?"

"I mean," she says, tapping the wooden spoon on the edge of the skillet, then turning to look at him, "we're all important. Whether we're elite athletes or small college baseball coaches, world-renowned scholars or adjunct professors, we're all important. Look, nobody feels more beaten down than me sometimes, believe me, because I'm a single mom on a losing streak, with a little boy who looks different than all the other little boys around here. Some days I feel completely hollow inside, like the world around me has completely hollowed me out. But I get up every morning and I do what I have to do, and every little bit of inspiration helps. Every bloody sock."

He sips his wine as if he doesn't even taste it, stares across the room. She stretches her back.

***

Emma opens the fridge, pulls out a bowl of greens and a bottle of her favorite light Italian dressing. She dishes the salad onto two small plates, hands one to Myles, grabs napkins from a small basket on the counter. She turns to the stove, boils a pot of water, opens the box of rigatoni. They pull up chairs at the little kitchen table, and they both fork their salads.

Emma feels a wine buzz, and she eats fast. Halfway through her salad, she asks, "Will you tell me about your family?"

"Water's boiling," Myles says, pointing his fork at a puff of steam above the stovetop.

"Shit, I forgot." Emma hops off her chair, whips the lid off the pot, dumps in the pasta. "Caught it just in time," she says. "Now, where were we? I hope you didn't think I'd forget about my question."

"My family?"

"Yes, I want to know more." She sits down, settles into her chair.

He puts down his fork, wipes the corner of his lips with a napkin. "About my brother, or my family?"

She stabs a bite of salad. "I know about your brother."

He picks up his fork, holds it above his plate. "I realize that."

"So?"

"So we grew up in Camp Hill, on the south side, not the ritzy side. Still, it was a nice neighborhood. We could walk to school, walk to the baseball field. My dad was an accountant and my mom worked for the state, thirty years at the Department of Agriculture. They sold our house five years ago, bought two condos, one in the township and one down in Florida."

He digs back into his salad.

"Happy childhood?"

"Pretty much, I guess."

She picks up her napkin. "It seems like you don't like to talk about it."

He chews, thinking. She wipes her mouth.

"I mean," he says, "it wasn't perfect. We had some problems. My folks separated for a little while, six months or so. My dad moved out. He had a girlfriend, but it didn't last. Mom and dad reconciled, and he moved back in. I was pretty young then, only about five, so I don't remember much. He was my first Little League coach, too, but he was too intense, lost his temper too easily at the games. I remember that stuff better. When I was ten, my mom insisted he had to quit."

"Did he?"

"Yup. He listened to her."

"What was their relationship like after that?"

He forks the last of his salad. "They were mom and dad, at least to me. They got along on the surface, mostly. If there was tension, they didn't let it show."

"Repressed emotions," she says.

He finishes chewing his salad. "Yeah, maybe."

She drops her napkin beside her plate, gets up and checks the pasta. "That wasn't so hard, was it?"

"What?"

"Telling me some details about your family."

He takes a swallow of wine. "I guess not."

"And Ron's your only sibling, right?"

"Right."

She stirs the pasta. "I'm going to talk to him," she says, her gaze on the swirling rigatoni.

"You're kidding, right?"

She taps the wooden spoon on the lip of the pot. "No."

"He's a hard guy to talk to." He finishes off his wine.

"I know. You told me. You don't talk politics."

He gets up, pours himself another glass of wine. "I can't give you any advice," he says. "I wish I could."

She opens a cabinet, pulls out a strainer. "It's okay. I'm a big girl."

She takes his salad plate, scrapes the remainder of hers into the trash. She drains the pasta, stirs it into the pan with the chicken and tomatoes. Myles wanders over to the sink, the window. The mist has turned to rain, the sky a deeper shade of gray. A wind gust catches the limbs of the tree between the houses.

"I hope you like this," Emma says, dishing out two plates of pasta.

"Smells great. I'm sure I will."

"I'm not a great cook," she says. "But there are certain dishes I feel like I can handle—that is, besides tacos and Hamburger Helper."

She eats fast, he eats slowly, regular sips of wine in between bites. He compliments her cooking. Emma offers him a second plate, but he declines, says he'd rather have another glass of wine, pours it himself, plus a refill for her.

"After dinner, do you want to stay and watch a movie?" Emma asks. "Thomas and I are big movie watchers, but I'd love to see something other than Willy Wonka."

"Sure," he says, tilts his head toward the window. "This is a perfect movie night, as they say."

"I need a comedy, though. Nothing heavy."

"What kind of comedy?" he asks. "Something clever or something wacky—Will Ferrell?"

"Definitely not Will Ferrell."

"What about rom-com? Reese Witherspoon? Or a nineties version—Meg Ryan?"

She shakes him off.

"Older and wacky? Chevy Chase?"

"No."

"Ferris Bueller?"

She makes a cringey face. "Please, God—no."

"I had a feeling you wouldn't like that one."

"What about Albert Brooks?" she asks. "Do you know his stuff?"

"Maybe I'd recognize him if I saw him."

"Nobody watches Albert Brooks anymore," she says with a little pout. "And it's a damn shame."

"Sorry," he says.

"So you never saw *Broadcast News*?" she asks. "*Lost in America*?"

He shakes his head no.

"Let's watch *Lost in America*," she says. "The main character loses his job and decides to live in an RV on the road. I haven't seen it in ages."

"Fine by me," Myles says.

She loads the dishwasher, and he offers to help, but she tells him it's not that much, she can handle it. He takes his wine into the living room, waits for her on the sofa, tries to click on the television, but can't figure out her remote.

"Which button is it?" he asks.

She joins him on the sofa, takes the remote from him. "Guys are never as smart as they think they are," she says.

***

After the movie, Myles goes upstairs to the bathroom. When he comes back, the television is off, and the only light in the room comes from the coconut-scented candle on the coffee table. Emma is still on the sofa, gazing toward the rainy darkness outside the front windows. Myles sits down beside her.

"What's on your mind?" he asks.

"That movie, that whole idea that they tried to drop out of society. It's been a while since I saw that movie, and I never thought about it like that before. And I know it was comedy, but still. You just can't drop out of society. It doesn't work that way."

"I guess not."

She turns to face him. Their eyes lock. He leans into her for a kiss. Her neck stiffens; she seems nervous, hesitant, but she doesn't resist. It's a light kiss.

"It's okay," she whispers.

"I don't want this to end," he says. "What we have."

She pulls back, just slightly. Her eyes soften.

"I don't know if I want it to end," she says. "But I want to give it a chance."

His lip curls into a smile. He leans in again. Another light kiss. Then she stands up, blows out the candle. She takes his hand, leads him upstairs to her bedroom.

The foreplay is slow, considerate, surprisingly intense. So is the sex. When they finish, she calls Tracey, makes sure it's okay if Thomas stays the night. Then she and Myles lay on their backs, naked and quiet, an affectionate quietness. They can hear each other breathe, and they can hear the pitter-patter of the rain, and they sense the torrent of everything that has happened between them, and what remains.

THIRTY-FOUR

MYLES IS UP FIRST, early the next morning, his mouth a stale garlic funk. He climbs out of bed, stretches his back with a soft groan, steps into his boxer shorts. A shank of hair is sticking up on the side of his head. He peeks out the window. The sky is dismal, clouds dark and thick, a mist hanging over the street, large puddles leaning against the sidewalks.

Emma wakes up, her face wan in the gray morning light. She blinks the sleep out of her eyes, runs her tongue over her teeth.

"What's it look like out there?" she asks.

"Ugly. Does Thomas have a game today?"

"He's supposed to."

"Don't count on it."

She gets up, pulls on gym shorts and a T-shirt, steps into the bathroom. When she comes back to the bedroom she says, "I left my toothbrush on the sink for you. That rigatoni dish makes for bad morning breath."

"Is this progress," he asks, "if we're sharing toothbrushes?"

"Hard to say."

Downstairs, she starts coffee in the kitchen. Drops two English muffins in the toaster. Wipes down the table, sets out cream cheese, butter knives, and napkins. Wipes down the counters, too. She's in a mood to get things done.

"So how was my toothbrush?" she asks when he comes downstairs.

"I'm not a fan of the hard bristles," he says. He's wearing his jeans and sky-blue-Polo, but still in bare feet. His hair is wet and patted down.

"I must be a hard-bristled girl."

"Guess so." He takes a seat at the table, the same spot he ate last night.

"At least the bed was more comfortable than the couch?" she quips.

"Guess so," he repeats. "Though I don't really remember sleeping on the couch."

The muffins pop up. Their toasty smell fills the kitchen.

"Coffee? Muffin?" She pulls two small plates and two coffee cups from the cupboard.

"Both, please. Do you have butter?"

She lets out a low growl. "I'd have to dig around in the fridge," she says. "I'm not the buttery type. Can I sell you on cream cheese?"

"Can I sell you on another dinner tonight?" he asks. "My treat this time."

She stops what she was doing—opening the refrigerator door. Her head jerks his way. "I don't know."

"Thomas can come," he says. "I imagine it'll be hard to find someone to watch him again."

"It's going to be a busy day," she says. She opens the refrigerator door wide, sticks her head inside, poking around.

"But his game will rain out."

"I know," she says, emerging from the fridge with butter in hand. "But I still have to drop off care packages for my dad, and I want to take Thomas to the bookstore in Harrisburg. They're doing a thing for our district. They have a special table set up with our banned books, with fifty percent off today for Cumberland students."

"Anything else?" he asks, suspiciously.

She plops the tub of butter on the table, lets out a little huff. "I haven't decided yet."

She pours both cups of coffee. Fast, aggressive pours. One cup overflows onto the counter. "Damnit."

"I'll get a paper towel," he offers, popping up to rip one from the roll on the counter. He wipes up the spill.

"Here's your coffee," she says, handing him the cup that spilled. "You might wanna wipe down the sides of the cup, too."

He nods and wipes it down with another paper towel.

She plates both muffins, hands him one, grabs her coffee and sits down across from him, jabs a butter knife into the tub of cream cheese. "I want to know more about what happened with your brother," she says. "When you talked to him about our book ban."

He bites into his muffin, chews slowly. "We didn't really talk that much," he says.

"What do you mean?"

He stops chewing. "I mean, it was a pretty short conversation."

"Tell me the details."

He nods as he finishes his bite of muffin, takes a sip of coffee. "Okay, so we played phone tag for a few days—"

"Why is that?" she interrupts. "Why is it so hard to connect with your own brother, who lives right here in town?"

He stares into his coffee mug. "I don't know."

"You weren't eager to talk about this with him, were you?"

"I told you," he says, "it's not easy to talk to him about things."

"But I told you how important it was to me. That's what I'm really struggling with here." She chomps into her muffin, and a smudge of cream cheese blots her lip.

He looks up at her, points at his own lip. "Right here," he instructs her. "You have cream cheese on your lip."

She wipes it quickly with the back of her hand. "Thank you."

"So where does that leave us?" he asks.

"Tell me the rest," she says. "What happened when you finally did talk to him?"

He clears his throat. "I know this isn't going to make you happy, but it was probably a two-minute conversation. Small world, I told him, because I'm dating the woman who was at the school board meeting advocating for the books, and you apparently had an exchange with her, and she's really upset about what happened."

He pauses for a sip of coffee. "He basically cut me off," he continues, "told me he's the school board president, not me, and he's the one who knows what's really going on, something about out-of-control wokeness, and he'll fight it tooth and nail in his daughters' school district. 'If you wanna do something about it,' he told me, 'then study these issues and run for school board yourself.'"

"And how did you respond?"

"There was no point," he says. "I've been trying to tell you that."

"You're right," she says. "That doesn't make me happy."

***

Third Street Books sits on the corner of Third and Charles streets, a converted lumber and textile mill on the edge of midtown Harrisburg. The sidewalk out front is lined with metal carts of used books, hardbacks and paperbacks, many with worn spines and scuffed dust jackets, a buck a book. The space inside is vast, two stories, with a coffee bar and little round tables and comfy reading chairs in the back of the first floor, the roasty smell of coffee wafting throughout. Greeting customers at the very front of the store on this drizzly Saturday is a large table of books underneath a sign that reads: *Books Banned by the Cumberland Area School District, 50% of with CASD I.D.*

It's an impressive collection on the table: *I Am Rosa Parks* by Brad Meltzer, *All Are Welcome* by Alexandra Penfold, *Under My Hijab* by Hena Kahn, *Mixed Me* by Taye Digs, *The Colors of Us* by Karen Katz, *Same, Same But Different* by Jenny Sue Kostecki-Shaw, *Pink Is For Boys* by Robb Pearlman, *Skin Like Mine* by Latashia M. Perry, *Jack (Not Jackie)* by Erica Silverman, *I Am Enough* by Grace Beyers, *The Story of Ruby Bridges* by Robert Coles, *The Undefeated* by Kwame Alexander, *Harriet Tubman: The Road To Freedom* by Catherine Clinton, *More Than A Dream* by Yohuru Williams and Michael G. Long, *How To Be An Antiracist* by Ibram X. Kendi, *Thurgood Marshall: American Revolutionary* by Juan Williams, *The Mayor of Castro Street: The Life and Times of Harvey Milk* by Randy Shilts, *Between The World and Me* by Ta-Nehisi Coates, and three James Baldwin books—*The Fire Next Time, Giovanni's Room,* and *If Beale Street Could Talk.*

"Incredible," Emma says, scanning the table. "This is so incredible."

"I don't see any about Jackie Robinson," Thomas says, perusing the table alongside her.

"It's okay," Emma says. She picks up *The Undefeated*, hands it to him. "Here's one you haven't read yet, and it's your reading level. I think you'll like it."

Thomas looks it over, nods his approval. Emma grabs a copy of *Giovanni's Room* for herself, looks up and takes in the rest of the store. This is her first time here; it opened shortly after she married Abid. She spots Gayle sitting alone at one of the coffee tables in the back.

"Come with me," she says to Thomas. "I want to introduce you to someone."

Gayle looks tired. She has a mug of coffee in front of her and she's leafing through *The Fire Next Time*. She seems happy to see them, very happy to meet Thomas.

They sit down with Gayle, and Emma points at the book she's been leafing through. "Have you ever read Baldwin?"

"I have to confess—no," Gayle says. "That's why I'm getting this."

"It's powerful," Emma says.

"A *USA Today* reporter was here," Gayle says. "Ten minutes ago. She saw me reading this and stopped to interview me. She sat right there, where Thomas is sitting now."

"No kidding?" Emma says.

"She said she's doing a story on a town fighting back," Gayle says. "She said that when she learned about what the bookstore is doing here, she wanted to come down and talk to people about what's going on."

"That's awesome," Emma says.

Gayle gives a somber nod, sips her coffee. "Yeah, but will it all make a difference?"

Thomas asks for a soda, and Emma reaches in her purse, hands him a ten-dollar bill. He gets up and starts toward the counter. "Hey," Emma says, "bring me the change."

"I will," he promises.

Emma sits up straight, squares her shoulders toward Gayle. "I've made up my mind," Emma says. "I'm going to talk to Ron Halprin."

"He's a hard-head," Gayle says, another nip of coffee. "Like talking to a brick wall."

"I don't care," Emma says. "We have a personal connection—I've been dating his brother. And if I don't try, I'll never forgive myself."

"You're dating his brother?"

"Well, sort of," Emma says. "We've been dating, but I don't think it's going to work out."

"How did you meet him?"

"On campus. At Cumberland College. He's the baseball coach."

Gayle gives a not-so-surprised look. "Is he anything like his brother?"

"Not really, but—" What else to say? Too complicated to explain right now.

Gayle raises an open hand, waves it apologetically. "I hope I'm not prying."

"No, it's okay."

"Let me change the subject," Gayle says, wrapping both hands around her coffee mug. "You'll want to hear this—I got a call yesterday from a group in Washington, D.C. A big free-expression group. They've filed a couple of lawsuits against book bans like ours, ones that involve books about race and identity, and they're interested in our case."

"That's great."

"I'm zooming with one of their lawyers on Monday," Gayle says. "And we'll go from there. If you do follow through with your plan to talk to Ron, tell him that."

"Are you sure? Do we want to tip our hand like that?"

"I'd rather not be a party to suing my own school district," Gayle says. "So yes. Use it as leverage."

Emma turns, checks on Thomas. He's at the counter, front of the line, ordering. She turns back toward Gayle. "So you sound a little skeptical that I'll follow through," she says.

"And talk to Ron?"

"Right."

"Not necessarily."

"I'm not afraid of him," Emma says.

Gayle nods appreciatively. "He's not afraid of you, either. Believe me."

***

"So what happened last night, between you and me?" That's Myles's text. It comes Saturday just before dinner time.

Emma and Thomas have just returned from the grocery store, and the groceries are stocked in the cabinets and fridge. She doesn't feel like dealing with this right now, doesn't know exactly how to break it to him. And maybe she shouldn't, at least not right now. She can put it off, right? He would.

THIRTY-FIVE

SUNDAY AFTERNOON, and Thomas has a game, a rain makeup. Emma drops him off at the field, wishes him luck with a kiss on the forehead, sucks back her regret over not staying to watch, because he's been playing better than ever lately and she still doesn't trust that damned coach and his kid. But she has to do this.

She pulls up at the Halprins', a two-story gray Colonial on a cul-de-sac just outside of town, newly sided, nicely landscaped, a modern-black aluminum fence wrapping around the back yard. The front door is an unusual color, something purplish—boysenberry, would you call it? The sun is out but the air is heavy, humid. Her chest is pounding.

She stops on the front stoop, catches her breath. *Okay*, she thinks, *okay*. She presses the doorbell. A woman answers. Forty-something, thick frame but friendly face.

Emma introduces herself by name, adds "a constituent."

"Is he expecting you?" the woman asks.

"No."

The woman peers over Emma's shoulder, suspiciously, as if trying to determine if she's alone. "I'm not sure he deals with constituents at home like this," she says.

"I've been dating his brother, too. Myles."

"Oh," the woman says, a note of pleasantness entering her tone. "Emma, is it?"

"Why don't you wait here. I'll see if he's available."

The woman returns a minute later, and the boysenberry door opens wide. "Yes, come in. He's out back," she says. "And I'm Jen, by the way."

"Thank you," Emma says and steps inside. She can't help but notice the ring on Jen's left hand. A rock the size of a swollen knuckle.

The house is cool and smells vaguely sweet, and Jen leads Emma through a lime-green hallway to a sliding screen door that opens onto the back patio. When they step outside, Ron Halprin gets up from a cushioned patio chair, pale-green drink in hand, a constipated smile on his face. He's barefoot, wearing khaki cargo shorts and a brown V-neck T-shirt, loose and untucked. Music is playing from a small device on the covered fire pit at the center of the patio chairs; something country, but Emma doesn't know the artist, a guy singing about wanting to be back in his hometown. Ron's phone sits beside the music device.

Emma's reminded how little Ron looks like his brother, because up close, he looks even less like Myles. And it's not just because of his thinning hair. His fleshy skin isn't even the same tone as Myles—it's pasty and dry. And his teeth are so perfectly white and straight. He must pump a fortune into those teeth.

"So you're the English professor," Ron says. "We've encountered each other before, haven't we?"

He offers a limp handshake. Jen disappears back inside the house.

"Yes," Emma says. "And yes."

He waves toward the chairs around the covered fire pit. "Have a seat," he says. "Can I pour you a margarita?"

"No, thank you."

"Are you sure? I have Jimmy Buffet make them—his machine, you know."

"I'm sure." She settles into the cushion on the chair closest to the sliding patio door.

"This isn't a social visit, is it?" Ron says as he sits down across from her. He crosses his legs at the ankles.

"Afraid not." She feels the heat and humidity; she's lightheaded.

"I don't usually talk to constituents at home like this," he says. "Actually, none have ever come to my house. I usually get emails and phone calls. Lots of them, particularly emails, but considering your relationship with my little brother, I thought I should."

"Thank you," she says, and she finds it odd the way he describes Myles, who's so much taller, as his little brother.

"Robert Lingenfelter came over yesterday," he says. "He's a school board member—do you know him? You guys are really turning up the pressure. You've converted him."

"I don't know him," she says.

"But you want to talk about the Diversity Committee's list, too."

"The ban."

"It's not a ban," he says reflexively. "It's a review. The media is miscasting it as a ban, but that's how the media works."

"I think a ban is an accurate way of describing it," Emma says.

"I'm sure you do." He picks up his phone, peeks at the screen.

She adjusts her butt in the chair cushion. The pounding in her chest has stopped, her lightheadedness has vanished.

"What are you afraid of?" she asks. It's not a question she intended to ask, but one that just dawned on her, and it suddenly seems like a question that goes right to the heart of the matter.

"Afraid?"

"Yeah." Her eyes bore into him. "I'd like to know."

"I'm not sure what you mean."

"You must be afraid of something."

"I think you're missing the point."

"What is the point?" She tilts her head slightly.

"Okay," he says, "the point. Let's talk about the point. Parents need control over their kids' education. And I'm just a parent, really, with two daughters in the district, and I'm standing up for other parents, too."

She straightens her head. "You're not standing up for me. And not for my son. That's for sure."

"Well." He shrugs.

"Let me tell you about my son," she says. "He's nine years old, in fourth grade, and he's very bright, by the way. His name is Thomas, and he's Pakistani. That's right—Pakistani. You didn't expect to hear that, did you? He's Pakistani because his father is Pakistani. We're divorced, and his father is no longer part of his life. But in a way he is, because Thomas's dark skin and Pakistani heritage make his life harder here. He doesn't always fit in, because he's Pakistani. That's it. Simply because he's Pakistani. Can you imagine? Can you? Really?"

Ron hardly reacts, just a little curve of one corner of his lips.

"And I worry about him terribly, and constantly," she says. "So when you banned these books—and yes, it's a ban, no matter how you try to spin it—you sent the message to everyone in this school district that kids like my son don't matter, that their experiences don't matter and their need to connect with the stories about similar experiences don't matter. You sent the message that it's okay if they don't fit in. And I'm going to worry even more about what someone is going to do to him next."

She intended to say that, and it came out just as she'd planned, word for word, practically.

"But the white kids matter, too," Ron says. "That's what you people keep forgetting."

Emma sits back hard. "Us people, huh?"

"Yeah." He takes a drink of margarita.

She looks around the yard. The grass is freshly cut; Ron must have mowed it this morning. The bushes are neatly trimmed. She feels so out of place here—her bushes are so thick and raggedy, and her yard could go another week before the landlord mows it.

She's reminded of what Gayle told her: the lawsuit. Leverage. She looks back at Ron, leans into what she's about to say. "I saw Gayle Brungard yesterday, and she told me to tell you something."

He re-crosses his feet at the ankles. "What's that?"

"She's been in touch with a group from D.C., a free-expression group, and they're interested in suing the district over the ban. Apparently they've filed similar suits in other places. Gayle is zooming with their lawyer on Monday to get the ball rolling here."

He traces his jawline with his fingertips, thinking. Finally he says, "Boy, you guys are pulling out all the stops."

"What did you expect?"

Emma hears the sliding door open behind her. She turns, and Jen steps onto the patio, margarita in hand. "Did he offer you a drink?" she asks Emma.

"Yes, thank you," Emma says.

"How about a soda or a water?" Jen asks.

"I'm good, thanks."

"I won't stay long," Jen says, still standing in front of the sliding door. "I just wanted to check on you guys."

"They're gonna sue the district now," Ron tells his wife. "They have a D.C. group backing them. Do you believe that?"

Jen's eyebrows pop up and back down. "Maybe you should talk to Robert Lingenfelter about that," she says. "Get his take on it."

Ron shakes his head, disgusted. "He's just going to repeat what he told me yesterday, that it's time to undo it."

"It's time to undo it," Emma says.

"I know you think that," Ron says.

"Gayle told me that she doesn't want to sue, by the way," Emma says. "She'd much rather you undo it."

"Well, sure," Ron says. "The legal costs."

Gayle was right—leverage. It matters. She wants more, what else?

"One more thing," Emma says. "Next year's board elections. They're going to be heated. Really heated. We're lining up candidates, and some are going to be formidable—Grace Miller, for instance."

Ron flashes a thin, tight smile, his polished enamel sending out the message—you're not going to beat me that easily. "I heard that," he says. "Robert and I talked about it yesterday."

"Are you thinking about running?" Jen asks Emma.

It never really occurred to her. Not seriously, anyway: a single mom, adjunct at two colleges, with a dad in a city encampment. No, a school board race and the responsibilities of the position would be demanding; she wishes she could, but she also knows to leave some things to the people who can do it better. But—leverage.

"Not right now," Emma says. "But it's early, and I have plenty of time to get in it if I want to."

Ron finishes off his margarita, smacks his lips. "So how serious are things with you and my little brother?" he asks. "Do I have to worry about what holiday conversations are going to be like around here?"

Emma lets her eyes wander across the yard again. No reason to look his way, no reason to stay any longer.

"Don't worry," Emma says, gazing off in the distance now. "We're not that serious."

THIRTY-SIX

BEFORE THE JUNIOR PROM, Clarissa and Amelia have planned photos on the steps in front of the state Capitol. Clarissa drives her own car into Harrisburg, and Gayle follows in the family SUV, because the plan is to let Clarissa drive to the prom. They park on State Street and meet Amelia and her parents at the bottom of the Capitol steps—both of Amelia's parents. Gayle's alone.

A swath of late-day sunlight covers the Capitol grounds, and the building's green-and-gold dome shimmers above them. Clarissa's wearing a strapless burgundy mermaid-style dress, gripping the edges of the train to keep it off the ground. Amelia's wearing a tight green sequin dress with spaghetti straps. It's short, way short, but Gayle knows girls dress like that today, so she's not too bothered. She's relieved they didn't choose anything radical—no tuxedos or pantsuits—because this is hard enough as it is. And they look stunning, they really do.

Amelia's parents look mismatched: her mom tall and heavyset with frizzy hair, her dad short and slim with receding hair and a pencil-thin mustache. They make small talk—the weather and the beauty of the Capitol backdrop—as the kids amble up and down the steps. Amelia's dad looks uncomfortable, looking away, shading his eyes from the sun, and saying little, but good for him, at least he's here.

Other kids are here, too, about a dozen of them, most from Clarissa's friend group, and a smattering of their parents. A black couple, guy and girl, and another couple of white girls, one in a gray tux with black Chuck Taylors. Two guys are together, both in pink tuxes, though different shades of pink. The kids are grinning and giggling, and Clarissa drops her train, enjoying herself as they strike a variety of poses—arm in arm, hand in hand, and the goofy variety, making faces or sticking out their tongues.

Clarissa points out the engraved inscription on one of the white stone benches on the side of the steps. It's a quote from Muhlenberg: "There is a time to pray and a time to fight." She wants a picture there with her and Amelia. Clarissa sits on one side of the inscription, Amelia on the other. Gayle has to take a few steps back, but is finally able to fit them both into the frame.

Gayle feels like the scene is unfolding before her in slow motion. Even her own movements—lifting her phone to snap a pic—feels listless. The sun warms the back of her neck, moist with sweat.

Clarissa and Amelia abandon the bench and saunter back to the middle of the Capitol steps. They strike a sideways pose, the dome as backdrop, arms wrapped around each other's waist, and they gaze into each other's eyes. Gayle obliges, snaps a pic. And then they lean into each other for a kiss.

Gayle freezes; her thumb won't move. She's not sure she wants it to move. She's dealt with Clarissa's sexuality as best she can, but she's never seen the girls kiss before. Yet alongside her discomfort, she's able to read her daughter's mind: Clarissa knows she's pushing a boundary, wants her mom to take this particular picture, will give her hell later if she doesn't, and moreover, she wants her dad to see it.

The other kids see the kiss and send up a cheer. The girls pull back, smiling warmly at each other, reveling in the moment, which passes without being captured by a picture.

The other gay couples kiss, too. First the guys in pink tuxes, then the girls. Their friends hoot and holler.

Gayle rubs at the moistness on the back of her neck.

When she gets home, Gayle needs a glass of wine. Doug isn't there yet. Her son is upstairs practicing his drums. Gayle reaches for a bottle of white in the fridge, then stops herself. What she needs is a drink, a real drink. Gin and tonic. She goes downstairs to Doug's liquor cart, makes herself a stiff one.

The pounding of the drums is faint down here, so she decides to stay. Doesn't want a migraine, and with so many things compounding today, the drums could be the last straw. She reclines in Doug's La-Z-

Boy, clicks on the big-screen television. Doesn't know what she wants to watch, so she surfs the channels, taking frequent nips of her drink. It's going down easily, too easily. And the chair is too comfortable; no wonder Doug spends half his life in it.

She stops clicking on a cable show about house hunting. A young black couple is looking for a starter home somewhere down south. At least it looks like a southern city, with Lowcountry-style homes on sun-drenched streets, and a river winding through it. Gayle envies them. They're both chubby, but they're affable and they're cute together, and they seem so hopeful as they wander in and out of different homes with their realtor in tow.

Gayle drains her gin and tonic, makes another, just as stiff as the first. Then back into Doug's recliner. Where the hell is Doug?

She knew he wouldn't go to photos with her. He still hasn't acknowledged Clarissa's sexuality, and said he was golfing after work. But he should have been back by now.

She left her phone upstairs in the kitchen, so she can't text him from down here. And besides, she doesn't want to. She'd rather watch the chubby black couple make an offer on a home. The one they choose is white with tall black shutters, a breezy front veranda, and large screened-in back porch, at the very top of their price range. Her second gin and tonic goes down easily, too.

Another episode, same cable show. This time a middle-age couple is moving from New York City to the country. Gayle doesn't find them as likable as the young black couple, but she watches nonetheless, finishes her second drink. She makes another, lighter on the gin this time. It's going to her head. And that's okay—better than a migraine.

Footsteps upstairs. The drums are still drumming, so the footsteps must be Doug's. Besides, they sound like Doug's footsteps, heavy and plodding. The thought that she knows her husband's footsteps is dispiriting—just one more thing about him that she finds unappealing. She takes a pull of gin and tonic.

She decides not to go up to greet him. Just stay right here, sipping her drink, enjoying this comfy chair of his for a change. Let him come find her. And the truth of the matter is, she has absolutely no desire to see him right now.

The footsteps ascend the stairwell to the second floor. The drums pause. Then they start up again, and the footsteps descend the stairwell.

She hears the door at the top of the basement stairs open—the hinges could use a squirt of WD-40, one of those little household chores Doug never bothers with.

"Gayle?"

"Yes."

He's still at the top of the stairs, hasn't bothered walking down. "What are you doing down there?"

"Having a drink, watching television."

A pause. The footsteps come down the basement stairs. She turns to look at him, and he's standing on the bottom step, one hand on the railing, as if he's not sure he wants to completely enter the room, not sure why his wife is in his chair watching his television drinking his booze. His eyes are glassy, his red golf shirt untucked. He's been drinking. He left the door at the top of the stairs open, so the drums are louder. She takes a drink of her gin and tonic.

"Where were you?" she asks, an edge in her voice, intentional.

"A late round of golf."

"That's all?"

"And a few drinks afterward."

She turns her attention to the television, a Toyota commercial. A perky woman in tight black pants is waving at cars in a showroom, and the woman's perkiness annoys her. Still, she'd rather not look at her husband as she tells him, "You missed photos."

"Oh, yeah?"

"Yeah."

"The girls looked beautiful," she says. The plural—girls—is deliberate.

"Uh, huh." He turns to head back upstairs. "I'm gonna grab something to eat."

She whips her head around. "Don't you want to see the pictures?"

He climbs the stairs, back turned, pretending he didn't hear her. She pops out of his chair, drink in hand, follows him.

"Don't you want to see the pictures?" she repeats.

She catches up to him in the kitchen. He's holding the refrigerator door open, head poked inside. She sets her drink on the counter.

"God damn you," she says. "She's your daughter. Your daughter!"

He pulls out a dish of leftover lasagna, covered in foil, sets it on the counter. "I know she's my daughter," he says. "I was there when she was born, remember?"

She steps toward him, close enough to smell the bourbon on his breath. "You're not there for her now."

He peels back the foil, opens a drawer for a fork. "What am I supposed to be there for?"

"Her," she says. "Her! You bastard."

He forks a big bite of lasagna out of the dish, stuffs it in his mouth.

"Does she have a roof over her head?" he says, his mouth half-full. "What about that car she took to that damn prom? What about that college education that I'm about to pay for? I'm there for her."

"That's a really shitty way of looking at fatherhood."

He finishes chewing, stabs another bite.

"I provide for her. She should be grateful," he says.

"You've turned your back on her," she says. "You should be ashamed."

She takes her drink, turns her back on him, stomps back to the basement, slamming the door behind her.

***

The gun counter is on the second floor of Jake's Sporting Goods, alongside the hunting gear section. Jake's is the megastore that anchors the Harrisburg Mall, and after Wanda enters, a zit-faced teenager in a green collared Jake's shirt points her toward the escalator, says that's the best way to get to the second floor.

The gun counter is a long, glass counter with at least a hundred handguns in it; Wanda's surprised how many handguns there are. Hunting rifles are lined up on a shelf behind the counter, each one standing on its butt. At least fifty hunting rifles. A yellow rope separates the counter from the aisle, and a sign at the end of the rope reads, "Enter Here." Two clerks in green collared shirts are helping customers at the counter. One customer is a scruffy twenty-something guy in a red hockey jersey, the other is an Amish guy with his family in tow, his wife and two kids. The clerks have laptops.

Before she stands in line, Wanda decides to peruse the handgun selection from behind the rope. They're expensive—most are in the range of seven hundred, eight hundred, nine hundred dollars. She didn't expect them to be so expensive. A couple of Berettas sell for over fifteen hundred. Some of them have menacing names: Black Gorilla and Hellcat. There are also a few that look like Wild West pistols, which are cheaper, two or three hundred dollars, with names like The Rough Rider and The Barkeep.

Wanda's dad doesn't know she's here, but she remembers his reasoning, his exact words: Just for protection. She's still not sure she's comfortable with it, but those three words sound so reasonable, at least on the surface, and yes, she'd like some protection, and she sure can't count on her dad for that every single day of her life. Especially not these days.

She's scared.

And she's tired, hardly slept last night.

So she's here.

Yesterday she heard from an agent on the county-federal task force, who told her they'd tracked down Stonewall X. Jackson. He lives in Michigan, and agents pored over his history and went to his home to interview him. No significant criminal history—just a couple of bad checks. He's never been to Pennsylvania, never made any plans to travel here. After interviewing him, they determined he wasn't a real threat to her. They believe he's a "howler," not a "hunter." So she should be okay; that's what they said. But they'll keep him on their radar. And if anything suspicious happens, she should contact them right away.

But she's still scared.

He's out there. As are other people like him.

Maybe it's just her imagination running wild.

Or maybe not.

Who the hell knows.

Her dad can't protect her forever. He still doesn't know what the agent told her yesterday, because she hasn't told him. She doesn't know how. She doesn't know how he'll react. Will he offer to drive here and sleep on her couch again for a few days? Okay, fine, but then what? Sure, she has the door-cam, which is working fine, because her dad finally figured it out, and the pepper spray in her purse. But they only do so much.

So here she is.

The Amish guy finishes his transaction, and his family follows him away from the counter. Their clerk closes his laptop and waves Wanda up to the counter.

She's in a haze as she lumbers up. Not only operating on little sleep, but she's in a different world, too. This is not her element. She never thought she'd find herself in a place like this: all these guns and ammo, the aura of malevolence, fear, and testosterone.

"Help you?" the clerk says. He has oily brown hair and a lazy eye that leans up against his pupil.

"Yeah, um—" She can't break out of that haze.

"What are you looking for?" he asks.

So many guns. She looks up and down the long counter, up and down again. "A handgun, I guess. Just for protection."

He sticks his finger in his ear, scratches around. "This your first time buying a gun?" he asks.

"Yes."

He taps the top of his laptop. "We'll have to do a background check, and there's a twenty-dollar fee for that, and I'll need a driver's license. You're over twenty-one, right?"

"Yes."

"Before we do that," he says. "I can suggest some models and show you some. Do you have any training?"

"No." She looks up at him, tries to avoid staring at his lazy eye. "Do I need it?"

"We'll start slow," he says.

"Okay."

"Do you know anything about caliber? Or magazine capacity? Which one you'd prefer?"

"I don't know." She feels overwhelmed, and a little freaked out. His lazy eye isn't helping. Maybe this is a bad idea. Does she really want to do this?

"What about price point?" he asks.

"Um, yeah." She looks up and down the counter again. "They're more expensive than I thought."

"How much did you want to spend?"

"I don't know. A couple hundred dollars? But I don't want one of those Wild West guns."

"Right, they're not what you want," he says, nodding. "Not for protection."

She tugs at her earring. Why did she even bother with earrings today? Is she thinking straight?

He steps to his right, reaches into the counter, takes out a handgun.

"Here's one for three hundred," he says. He holds it up and shows it to her. It has a matted black barrel, a military-green grip, and a metallic-gray trigger. "It's a twenty-two gauge, semi-automatic. It's good for what you're looking for."

She stares at it.

"Do you want to try holding it?" the clerk asks.

"Um, okay, I guess."

He holds it out. "Just keep your finger off the trigger," he says. "That's a safety precaution."

She takes it. It's heavy, heavier than it looks. And cold. She puts it down on the counter, steps back away from it. She's not thinking straight, and she knows it.

"I can't do this," she says, and turns and leaves.

THIRTY-SEVEN

"I'll believe it when I see it," Gayle says.

She's huddling at the back of the Educational Service Center with other members of the Diversity Committee, and tonight all of the original committee members have turned out—Eric Sounders, Grace Miller, Dennis Graham, Emily Satchell, and Anna Heffner. Emma isn't here yet, but Gayle expects her any minute. The May school board meeting starts in five minutes.

Robert Lingenfelter has told Gayle that he has the votes to overturn the ban, but there's one holdout: Ron Halprin. Even so, board policy allows any member to make a motion. When Lingenfelter called Gayle last night, he told her he'd rather have Ron on board, but he'll do what he has to do.

"If Lingenfelter calls the vote, are there procedural mechanisms that allow Ron to block it?" asks Grace. "I mean, are we looking at a long, drawn-out procedural battle here?"

"He can muck it up with amendments," Gayle says. "It could be a long night, and I suspect our solicitor is going to earn his pay here tonight."

Emma arrives, sees their huddle and joins it. She's out of breath. "Sorry if I'm late," she says.

"No problem," Gayle says, and then she briefly repeats for Emma the main points she just laid out for everyone else.

"What about adopting our resource guide?" Emma asks. "Is that going to happen? I mean, that's what the Diversity Committee was all about. That's why we started this whole thing."

"Not yet," Gayle says. "I talked to Robert about it, and he's amenable, but he wants the repeal out of the way first. I think we can approve the list when the board comes back in the fall."

"Don't let the perfect interfere with the good," Sounders says.

"Exactly," Gayle says.

"Okay," Emma says. "One thing at a time, I guess."

The room is packed. Outside is a student protest, about fifteen students with signs opposing the ban; Clarissa organized them. One security guard mans the parking lot and one is stationed inside the doorway. A Cumberland Borough police car is also parked outside, as are vans from all the local news stations.

"Try to hold your emotions in check," Gayle says, training her eyes on Emma. "We're too close to let our emotions hurt our case."

"I'll try my best," Emma says.

"Either way," Grace says, reaching out and rubbing Emma's back, "we still love you."

"I'm not sure I can hold my emotions in check," Dennis says.

"You're a teacher in the district," Sounders tells him. "So do your very best."

"I'll keep reminding myself," Dennis says.

Dennis saved seats for the committee members in the front row, and Emma sits between him and Grace. She feels the brightness from the fluorescent lights in the ceiling. The board members take their seats amidst a hum of chatter, and Ron calls the meeting to order.

The public comment period drags on for over an hour, despite the five-minute limit for each speaker. Emma decides against speaking; she doesn't want to lose it, and she's already said what she wants to say to Ron at his house. Twenty-three people speak, and Emma keeps track of where they stand. Eleven speak against the ban, ten speak in favor of it, one speaks against kitty litter in the bathrooms (the same woman from the last meeting), and one warns everyone in attendance about a social media post she saw recently about the FBI investigating conservative parents who attend school board meetings. The board members sit poker-faced; they respond to none of the commenters.

The agenda is full. A lot of new hires to be considered, but the board approves all of the administration's recommended hires swiftly and unanimously, no debate there. A bid for laundry services for sports uniforms sparks a ten-minute discussion, but it wins approval unanimously, and everything else moves quickly.

The room is still packed, the crowd captive. A few people have gotten up from their seats to make a call or go to the bathroom, but they returned after a few minutes. Whispers have ebbed and flowed throughout the evening. The room is a bubble of tension straining not to burst.

Emma throws her shoulders behind her, stretching her back. She twirls her neck, stretching that, too.

"I have a motion," Lingenfelter says.

"You have the floor," Ron Halprin says reluctantly.

Lingenfelter adjusts his microphone, clears his throat. He's looking squarely at no one in particular.

"This past month," he begins, "has been the most difficult month I've witnessed in all of my years on this board. I've seen our district torn apart like never before, and I want to say publicly that I regret my part in it. I supported a motion last month which I thought was a good way to limit liberal indoctrination of our students, but upon reflection I don't think it was well thought out."

He wipes his forehead. "Therefore," he continues, "I move to repeal the previously approved motion which prevents the teaching of books and resources proposed by the Diversity Committee."

The crowd reacts with a mix of applause, hoots, groans, and boos.

"I have an amendment," Ron says.

"Can I say something?" Gayle interrupts. She's sitting upright, all business.

"Can I propose my amendment first?" Ron asks.

"I'd like to comment on the amendment process," Gayle says.

"What about the amendment process?" Ron says. "Any motion can be amended. I think we all know that."

Dennis leans toward Emma and whispers, "Nothing's ever easy."

"Welcome to my world," Emma says.

Dennis chuckles.

Gayle remains upright in her seat. "I have concerns," she says. "And I think it's best for everyone if we address them up front."

Ron huffs. "Go ahead," he says.

"Mr. Lingenfelter's motion is very straightforward," Gayle says. "It's a simple repeal, and I'm afraid that the only reason for amendments is to muddle up the voting process. In other words, they're an attempt to kill it, not to amend it. As Mr. Lingenfelter said, our district has been through a lot in the past month, and we don't need a string of unnecessary amendments on top of everything else. But I can assure you, those of us who are committed to reversing this ban are also committed to sitting here all night long if we have to."

"Okay, fine," Ron says. "Now, I have an amendment."

"We can sit here all night," Gayle says, staring lasers at him.

Ron throws up his hands.

"Fine," he says, spitting out his words. "I can read the writing on the wall here. I withdraw my amendment."

"In that case," Lingenfelter says, "we have a motion on the floor. Is there a second?"

"Second," Gayle says eagerly.

After each board member announces their vote—yea or nay—the crowd responds with a mix of applause, hoots, groans, and boos. The repeal passes by a vote of 8-1. Ron Halprin is the only nay vote.

When it's over, some people leave, some stay. They congregate in the aisles, or form little huddles in the back of the room, some gloating, some grumbling. Reporters descend on the board members for interviews. Ron departs quickly, no interviews.

Emma remains in her seat. "Someone tell me that what I just saw was real," she says. "I'm not dreaming, am I?"

"You're not dreaming," Grace says. "It was real."

Clarissa comes inside, surveys the room, ignoring the people brushing by her on the way out. Her mom is being interviewed by a reporter, so she stops at the front row where Grace and Dennis are standing in the aisle, Emma still in her seat. Clarissa's hair is damp, her skin glazed with a light sweat from the warm evening sun.

"Did they really do it?" Clarissa asks. "Did they really repeal it?"

"Yes, they really did it," Dennis says, smiling broadly.

"So we did it," Clarissa says, and she thrusts her two fists above her head. "We beat the ban!"

"That's right," Emma says, and it's sunk in, so she finally stands up, pumps her own fists above her head. "We friggin' did it!"

THIRTY-EIGHT

MYLES HAS A NOON BEER BUZZ. He downed two light beers without eating any breakfast, and now he's at the track. No live racing here at this hour, but the simulcast room is open, so he can bet races that are streamed onto television screens from up and down the East Coast. It's a long, narrow room on the third floor of the grandstand, the row of big-screens on the wall showing five different tracks, opposite large windows that look out on the empty, sun-struck racetrack. The room is half-full of gamblers, old dudes mostly, lumbering up to the betting window or sitting at square little tables and poring over their programs, with a concession stand at the far side. Myles buys a draft beer, saunters back to the big-screens to check the odds on the first races of the day.

He's already decided: He doesn't need a program. He's betting all the favorites, five bucks a pop, despite the low payoff. Doesn't matter if he doesn't win big. He just wants to win something today, maybe go home with a few bucks in his pocket. More than anything, he wants to feel like a winner, for a change.

Last night, Emma dumped him. She did it in a phone call. He'd been pestering her with texts, asking to see her and pressing her about that rainy night when he'd slept over after dinner—he kept asking, *What was that about?* But she'd been avoiding him. Finally she called and explained everything, said that rainy sleepover was a nice night, and at that moment in time she just wanted a nice night, also wanted that night to happen because she didn't want to give up too soon on them, and by the way she was really grateful for the way he interacted with Thomas. Then she said, "I'm looking for something different."

Looking up at the big-screens, Myles notes several favorites in his head, then steps up to the betting window, pulls a twenty from his wallet. Five bucks on Number Four at Pimlico, five on Number Two at Gulfstream, five on Number Five at Belmont, five on Number One at Saratoga. He sits down, sips at his beer, watches two of his horses lose, then Number Two at Gulfstream wins by a neck.

A win. There's something different.

He pockets his winning ticket, which will only pay him seven bucks on his five-dollar bet, then watches Number One at Saratoga come in fourth. He steps back up to the betting window, bets all the favorites in the next race at each track.

The next few hours: same routine. And after a whole afternoon of betting the favorites and drinking light beer and filling his belly with cardboard-tasting pizza from the concession stand, Myles has lost fifty bucks and feels sluggish. He decides he needs a jolt. So he gives up on the ponies, chucks his beer cup and the last of his balled-up betting slips into the trash, and moseys over to the adjacent casino. He bellies up to the bar on the casino floor, the pings and dings of the slot machines ringing through the purified air.

"Give me a shot of your cheapest tequila," he tells the bartender. "I need some fire in my belly."

After slamming the shot, he's off to the roulette tables. He'd rather play poker, but that's a thinking game, and he's too drunk for that. Roulette is easier—pick your numbers and stick with them, be nice to the croupiers, tip them well, and they'll give you a little leeway if you get a little sloppy. At least he's sober enough to realize he's too drunk to play a thinking game. Right? Does that even make sense?

He plays for a while, loses a hundred bucks, then bellies up to the bar again, orders a light beer. The casino has filled up, the Saturday-night gamblers out in force. After finishing his beer, he hits the ATM machine for another two hundred. He has no idea what time it is.

Back at the roulette table, a different one this time, because he's trying desperately to change his luck, he slides onto a seat between a fat guy in an untucked shirt and a bleached blonde with pouchy eyes who's drinking something with a lime. Myles plunks his two-hundred bucks on the felt.

First spin: 29. A win for Myles. The fat guy and the blonde immediately seem impressed.

"Mr. Lucky," the fat guy crows.

"Where have you been all my life?" the blonde asks. Her voice is low and raspy.

Myles smiles and nods, plays the same numbers the next spin.

"I'm riding this horse," the fat guy says. He reaches across Myles to drop two chips on 29.

"I'm in, too," the blonde says. Another chip on 29.

It's 16. The blonde lets out a little groan and says, "Damnit." For the next spin, Myles sticks with his numbers, 29 included, while the other two abandon 29, spread their chips elsewhere.

It's 29.

"Fuck me," the fat guy whines.

This time the blonde says nothing, just nips at her drink, sends a look at Myles. The look is hard to read—could be anything from resentment to attraction. Now Myles can't help but steal extra looks at her. She has slight creases of age in her face, ruby red lipstick that matches her little purse. Late 30s, probably, a stunner ten years ago. No wedding ring.

"Tell me something," the blonde asks Myles. "What's with 29?"

"It was my jersey number when I played baseball. Still is, in fact."

"Don't they call it softball at your age?"

"Very funny. I'm a baseball coach. At Cumberland College."

"No shit," the fat guys says, as if Myles's job marked some great coincidence. "I deliver there. I drive a truck for Pepsi."

The blonde shoots the fat guy a who-the-hell-cares look.

Next spin: 10. It's another one of Myles's numbers—his birthday, November 10th. The croupier slides thirty-five more winning chips in front of Myles, and Myles only.

"So you're living the dream?" the blonde says to Myles in a backhanded tone.

"That's one way of looking at it. What do you do?"

She sips her drink, smacks her lips together. "Whatever I want."

"Hmm," Myles says. "That means daddy's girl, or wait, don't tell me—aspiring actress, but waiting tables just for now."

"Tending bar—just for now."

"Shouldn't you be working?" Myles asks. "On Saturday night?"

"I called in sick," she says, reaching into her purse for more cash. "A girl's gotta enjoy life sometimes." She slaps $100 on the table, and the croupier slides her five more piles of chips.

"Just stick with your numbers," Myles says instructively. "This game is about discipline and patience. That's why the casino wins—most people don't have enough of either."

She sucks on her cigarette in an elaborate pucker, rankles her eyebrows. This woman knows sexy—how to show it, how to be it. Moreover, she has the kind of body language that tells Myles she doesn't give a flying fuck about discipline and patience.

"Is your baseball team this good?" the blonde asks, nodding toward Myles's big pile of chips as the ball clanks in and out of 22.

It lands on 34. Only the fat guy wins.

"First of all," Myles says, answering the blonde, "I'm not this good most nights. This is a nice lucky streak. And my baseball team isn't this good either. Most years we play .500 ball, but this year we were terrible. I try not to get too emotionally involved in wins or losses."

"Hmm," she says. "Maybe you should."

It's a piercing comment, one that cuts right through his beer-and-tequila buzz, freezes him as he's spreading his ten chips around the table for the next spin. How can a blonde bartender-gambler, who's probably half-drunk and doesn't even know his name, sense enough about him after sitting with him at a roulette table to suggest that he's guilty of some sort of character flaw? And what might that flaw be? The same thing Emma saw?

He tells the croupier to cash him in and announces to the entire table that he's going to the bar to get a beer.

"With all those winnings," the blonde says, "I suppose you'll be able to buy a girl a drink?"

"You're a pip," Myles says flatly.

"That's what my ex-husband used to say," the blonde says as she signals the croupier to cash in her chips, "before I caught him in bed with my girlfriend."

They discuss the ignoble details of their lives as they sit at the bar, a game between the Phillies and Cubs on the big-screens. She's drinking vodka tonic; he has another light beer. Her name is Carly, and she works at a bar in downtown Harrisburg, has an apartment downtown, too. And yes, she really did catch her husband screwing her friend, so they've been divorced three years. No kids. Her ex makes a killing in software sales, so she took him all the way to the bank with the settlement.

Myles admits that he's had one marriage break up and recently another relationship. He confesses that the marriage was his fault, which elicits a knowing nod from Carly, but he doesn't say any more about the recent relationship. She doesn't ask.

"So," she says, finishing off her vodka tonic. "Are you ready to disappear?"

"What does that mean?"

She tilts her head at him. "Are you kidding me?"

He gives her a blank stare as he envisions her whipping a sparkly little wand out of her purse.

She clarifies: "Disappear to my room."

"Oh," he says, taken aback by this extra level of directness.

"Don't tell me you're not interested," she says.

"Sure, sure, I'm interested," he stutters. Then he collects himself and asks, "I thought you lived around here? Why'd you get a room?"

"I already have one DUI," she explains, pulling a pack of cigarettes from her purse. "I can't afford another."

Her room is at the Comfort Inn next door to the casino. Sometime in the middle of the night, Myles wakes up naked with a full bladder and a headache, but she's not there. He sits up and scans the darkened room, blinking the haziness out of his eyes, but no sign of her. Did she go home or back to the casino? Does it matter?

***

The restaurant is a trendy, small-plate place on State Street, just down from the state Capitol. Restored brick walls, high ceilings, a small bar, soft jazz on the stereo system. Sounders arrives early, wants to get acquainted with the place before his date arrives. She suggested it, and he agreed, even though he never feels comfortable in the city.

They met on Bumble; Sounders opened an account as soon as the school year ended. Her name is Teresa. She's a lawyer, handles employment and labor law. Divorced with a 13-year-old daughter.

Sounders is dressed like a principal, because it's his look and might make him feel a little more comfortable: tan chinos and Navy tie under a gray sweater. He takes a seat at the bar, orders a water. Doesn't want Teresa to think he needed a drink before he met her.

"We have an excellent wine menu," the bartender says.

"I don't mind looking at it," Sounders says. "I'm meeting someone for dinner."

He takes the menu from the bartender, glances at it, then turns his attention to the crowded restaurant and the front door. He wiggles on his bar stool, trying to get acclimated.

Teresa arrives early. He recognizes her from her photo. She has a pretty, angular face, dark hair and thick hips, and she's wearing white jeans and a pale-blue funnel turtleneck. Sounders slides his water glass back toward the bartender, meets her at the hostess stand.

He extends a hand, says, "Hi. Teresa?"

She looks at his hand strangely, agrees to shake with—is that a smirk on her face? "Yes," she says. "Eric?"

"Yes." He's embarrassed already. How should he have approached her? Certainly not with a hug. Maybe no physical contact at first. Oh, well, try to forget about it; what's done is done.

They get a window table which looks out onto State Street. The waiter brings menus, asks what they want to drink, and Teresa orders cabernet, as does Sounders.

Teresa has a heavy Philly accent, from South Philly, she explains. She's Italian-Irish, though she still has her ex-husband's last name, Carrington, which she hates. So British and pretentious.

"Where do you teach?" she asks.

"I don't teach," he says, looking up from the menu. "I'm a principal."

"That's right. Sorry, you told me that. Where?"

"Buchanan Elementary in Cumberland."

She squints suspiciously. "Cumberland? Isn't that the district that banned the books?"

"Yes, that was us."

"That was all over the news," she says. "National news, too."

"I'm aware."

Their wine comes. Teresa asks the waiter for another minute to peruse the menu.

"If you're going to get to know me," Teresa says, "you should understand that I tend to be very direct. It's a South Philly thing, so I don't make any apologies. And I think only a bunch of racist bastards would ban books like that."

Sounders sips his wine. "I was upset about it, too," he says. "I was on the Diversity Committee that proposed the list, but as an administrator, I was in a tough position when the board voted to ban the list."

"Yeah, I'm sure," she concedes.

"I was relieved when they rescinded the ban," Sounders says.

"Well, yeah, they should have. Still, it left a black eye on that school district, on all of central Pennsylvania, too."

He nods agreeably.

"We moved here fifteen years ago," she says, "when my husband—sorry, ex-husband—was offered a job as a lobbyist, one of the big firms, so he couldn't turn it down. And I'll never forget what my friends said to me: What's in Harrisburg? Isn't that the sticks? You'll be surrounded by dumb rednecks. And sometimes I think, yeah, they were right. Dumb rednecks."

"I grew up in Cumberland," Sounders says. "It's my hometown."

She takes a swallow of wine. "I didn't mean to suggest that you're a dumb redneck," she says. "I was just speaking generally."

They turn their attention to their menus, a welcome distraction. "What looks good?" she asks. "Have you ever been here before?"

"No," he says. "Us dumb rednecks don't make it into the city much."

***

June 30, and Wanda gets called into Norm Baker's office. A Thursday, the last day of the quarter, and Wanda has just arrived at the newsroom with a large cup of Starbucks. She's immediately suspicious. Panicked, really. Rumors have been circulating for weeks. She stands up in her cube, feels a brick slide down to her stomach. She leaves her coffee on her desk, then straightens her shoulders, sets her jaw, and feels the curious eyes of her colleagues on her as she strides across the newsroom. Feels like she's moving in slow motion.

The first thing Wanda notices in Norm's office is the morning sunshine. It bursts into the office through the open blinds on the large corner windows behind the desk, and it doesn't make sense. This isn't a sunny moment, so how can this be a sunny place?

"Have a seat," Norm says, motioning to the matching set of armless chairs in front of his desk. This is only the third time Wanda has been in this office; the other two were the day she was interviewed and the day she received the threat.

She sits down, cautiously.

"Oops," Norm says, hopping out of his chair. "I should close the door."

That brick in her stomach, heavier now.

The door closed, he sits back down at his desk, lets a moment pass, scratches the side of his face.

"The first thing I want to tell you," he says, "is how much I admired your work on the book ban. Really, top-notch stuff."

"Thank you," she says timidly.

"But," he says.

She feels a tear forming in the corner of her eye.

"Things aren't good here," he says. "Financially, I mean."

She fights back the tear with a double-blink, doesn't want to appear frail. She's a career woman.

He explains that the paper is making significant cutbacks, fifteen percent of staff, and will no longer publish a print edition seven days a week. Only three days of print—Tuesday, Thursday, Sunday—with a daily online edition. That's where the industry is headed. He explains that the quality of her work and the importance of her beat, education, weren't enough to save her job during such a major reorganization;

she just doesn't have enough tenure. There's a small severance and a paper to sign for it. He promises to write her a "five-star" letter of recommendation. He's confident she'll land on her feet somewhere. He tells her to take the rest of the day to clean out her desk and get her things in order, and take Friday off; it won't affect her final weekly paycheck.

The walk back to her desk feels like wading through a fog. Her thoughts come in fragments. My first big job. Couldn't keep it. Happens, though. Not my fault. Land on my feet. Somewhere.

Land on my feet, land on my feet. But how? Where? Doesn't feel possible right now.

She calls her parents, and her mom answers, puts her on speaker. Dad offers to drive down and spend the night with her.

"No, Dad," Wanda says. "But thanks. I'll be okay—I think."

"Let us come down and take you to dinner, at least," her mom says. "We won't stay over."

"We'll drive home afterward," Dad adds.

"Okay, yeah," Wanda says. "That's nice of you."

When she ends the call, Wanda whips off her glasses, drops them on her desk. She pinches her eyes, trying to control the moistness. She's not going to cry. Not here. Thoughts keep coming in fragments. Clean out desk. Get things in order. Things. Apartment lease. Resume. But, but, but. Not much of a career woman. Not really.

Land on my feet, land on my feet.

***

The church smells like wax and must. Gayle dips her fingers in the holy water, crosses herself, kneels down in a pew in the back. A Wednesday afternoon in early July, and the church is empty. The confessional curtain is pulled shut, though, so someone must be in there.

It's been a while since Gayle has been here, and the guilt tugs at her conscience. She feels like a bad Catholic, but that can happen when you marry a Lutheran. She doesn't even know who the priest is these days.

She says a prayer for herself, her son, her daughter, her husband. An extra one for her husband. Finally, one for her entire community.

The confessional curtain opens, and a gray-haired woman shuffles out, nods a hello at Gayle. Gayle smiles and nods back.

Gayle crosses herself again, stands up and steps into the booth, pulls the curtain shut. Kneels down and kneads her hands together, tightly.

The screen cover slides open.

"Good afternoon," the priest says. His voice is monotone. She can hear him breathing lazily after he speaks.

"Bless me father, for I have sinned," Gayle says.

"When was your last confession?"

"I'm so sorry, but it's been a while. I don't remember, exactly, but it's been years."

"It doesn't matter," the priest says. "God is still glad you're here."

"Thank you," Gayle says.

"Do you have sins to confess?"

"Yes," she says. "I've taken the Lord's name in vain, and I haven't been to mass regularly."

She pauses, hears his breathing.

"God can forgive you for those," the priest says. "Do you have something else to confess?"

"Yes," Gayle says, but she doesn't know how to say it. She squeezes her eyes closed, sucks in her breath, lets it out slowly. "I've condoned a same-sex relationship, and I still condone it, because it's my daughter, and I love her dearly, but that's not all."

"Take your time," the priest says.

"I went to see a lawyer recently."

"That's not a sin," he says.

"It was a divorce lawyer," she says. "I'm asking my husband for a divorce."

THIRTY-NINE

A LATE-JULY HEAT WAVE: six consecutive days of ninety-plus heat combined with thick humidity. The late-morning sun already baking the small riverside city. Foul air at the encampment, a blend of garbage and stale food and body odor, flies circling in squadrons. Emma's standing beside her car, which is parked at the curb with her weekly care packages, an extra case of bottled water with this delivery. But her dad's not answering his phone, and when another guy straggles by, unshaven and shirtless, obviously leaving his own tent, Emma asks him to check on her dad, because she still can't muster the courage to see the way he lives.

"His phone's probably dead," she tells the guy.

She's not choked up this morning, for a change. Instead she's in a hurry, eager to get home so she can get back to work. She recently started a part-time online job with an advocacy group based in Washington D.C. which works to overturn book bans nationwide. The director of the program contacted Emma after seeing her quoted in *The New York Times* story about the reversal of Cumberland's ban, urging Emma to apply. The extra income isn't much, but it's helpful, and the extra screen time means relying on more eye drops to offset the soreness, but more than anything, the work is rewarding, a daily reminder that her life is worthwhile.

And soon, her efforts might be trained back on her very own school district again: A rumor has been circulating that Ron Halprin is planning to introduce a new policy this fall that would ban certain books for content deemed sexually explicit, and he has a small team of parent allies poring over books this summer to identify which ones to target.

The shirtless guy comes out waving his arms and yelling for an ambulance.

Emma calls 911, and the ambulance arrives in a matter of minutes, pulls over the curb and stops abruptly in a small clearing at the edge of the camp; they've done this before. When they carry his lifeless body out, moving much slower than when they went in, navigating the aluminum gurney patiently down the hard-dirt path, because they know this drill and it's obvious there's nothing they can do, Emma knows what they're about to tell her. She doesn't cry, and she feels guilty about that. At least Thomas wasn't with her, so he didn't have to experience the scene. She had just dropped him off at his summer baseball camp.

The next day, she has to figure out if her dad still had life insurance. He had it at one point, but she can't remember the name of the insurance company, and even if she could, she's afraid he stopped paying on it, just like the house, and let it lapse. Tracey agrees to go to the encampment with her to root through his belongings in his tent, see if they can find any insurance papers.

"I can't do this," Emma says, choking up, when they pull up at the curb. They're in Tracey's maroon SUV, Emma in the passenger seat with a bottled water between her legs, one of the bottles that was intended for her dad yesterday. She rakes her hands through her hair.

"I can go," Tracey says. "I'll do it."

Emma explains which tent is her dad's, the blue one on the left beside the slab of old concrete, and Tracey ventures in alone.

It's another steamy day, no relief from the heat. Emma takes a gulp of water, stares straight through the windshield, sees a dead groundhog, fat and sprawled on its belly, beside the curb ten yards ahead. It's all alone, so that's probably how it died. Just like her dad. The thought hits Emma like a two-ton truck, and she starts bawling.

She's still crying, wiping tears from her cheek, when Tracey returns to the car.

"Are you okay?" Tracey asks.

"No, not really."

"Ah, honey."

"Did you find anything?" Emma asks.

"No papers. No papers at all. Just a lot of trash and junk." She holds out a small Swiss Army knife, red and white.

"What's this?" Emma asks.

"I found it in his tent. I thought Thomas might want it, so he has something from his grandfather."

Emma rubs her eyes with her knuckles. "I don't know. He's kind of young for something like that."

"Then hang onto it until he's older," Tracey says. "It's something from his grandfather."

"Okay, thanks." She takes it, stuffs it in the pocket of her shorts, and sniffles.

***

Emma calls the county coroner's office the next day to tell them she doubts he had life insurance, can't find any papers, and ask what her options are. She's told that the county has a funeral home under contract to handle the cremation of the unhoused, and relatives can obtain the remains for a $250 fee. The remains will come in a cardboard box. Otherwise, the county-contracted funeral home will bury the remains in a plot beside other indigent deceased people. Emma says thank you, she'll think about it.

That night she dreams she's standing alone in front of her dad's open coffin. He's a young man, though, lean and sturdy, a firm jaw, a full head of hair. He opens his eyes. Emma steps back from the coffin. He climbs out, pats himself down, looks Emma over, but apparently doesn't recognize her. "Excuse me," he says, and walks away.

The next day, Emma drives to the county office while Thomas is at baseball camp, pays the fee to obtain her dad's remains in the cardboard box, puts the charge on her credit card. When she gets home, she takes the box down to the basement, puts it on a dusty shelf in the back corner.

Emma wants a service, though, wants to pray for her dad's soul, and she wants Thomas to be there, wants him to learn respect for the dead, to witness something more dignified than a cardboard box in a basement.

Even her mom, during those horrible early days of the pandemic, received a funeral service, though it was restricted to immediate family, no more than ten people. The only people who attended were Emma, with six-year-old Thomas, and her dad, all in masks, sitting six feet apart.

That afternoon, Emma drops Thomas off at Tracey's and drives to the rectory, right next door to the Catholic church. She hasn't been to mass since she was a girl, lost touch with the church when she was a teenager, as did her dad, but she's hopeful the priest will understand. Her mom never lost touch—she kept coming to mass regularly, and alone, until the day she died. Her pandemic funeral service was at this church, April 19, 2020. Hard to forget that date.

The priest answers the door. He's the same priest who presided over her mom's funeral, but he wasn't the parish priest when Emma was a girl. He's about her age, with wire-rim glasses and a fleshy face—a friendly face, which doesn't seem to match his monotone voice. Still, he remembers her.

He leads Emma to his small office on the first floor, and there are two chairs in front of his desk; she's reminded of that damned second chair in Sounders' office, reminded that she has to do this alone again. She chokes up. He tells her to be patient. She takes a big swallow and apologizes for getting emotional, then apologizes for her years-long absence at church, as well as her dad's, then explains the situation. Yes, he says, he can conduct a funeral mass, but he suggests Emma come in for confession first, as she nods in agreement, then he asks where the remains are.

"I have them," Emma says.

"All of them?" he asks.

"Yes."

Good, he says. The Catholic Church requires they not be separated, and then be buried. We'll need to have arrangements for burying the remains, he says. When Emma leaves the rectory, she drives to the cemetery on the edge of town where her mom is buried. She makes arrangements for an adjacent plot for her dad's remains, puts it on her credit card, maxing it out.

Emma decides on a private mass, family only, small as it is. And the only other family is her Uncle Dan, her dad's younger brother, who lives in North Carolina now, and his wife Sheila. Emma hasn't seen Dan in thirty years. When she was little, he lived a half-hour away, down in York, worked for Caterpillar, making industrial equipment, but he lost his job in a wave of layoffs 1996 and moved down to Winston-Salem, found a job in a furniture factory. Emma tracks down her Uncle Dan and calls him, invites him to the service. Dan takes the news of his brother's death as if it's nothing more significant than a change in the weather. Dan and his brother hadn't kept in touch regularly, so Dan didn't know he was living at the encampment, though he did wonder why he hadn't heard from his brother lately.

"I can make it up," Dan says.

"I'm glad."

"We have two cousins out in Dayton, you know," Dan says. "They might want to come, too. I haven't seen them in a zillion years, and I'm guessing the same goes for your old man."

"In that case," Emma says slowly, wary about the relationships her dad had with various distant relatives, "let's keep it to close relatives only. I want to keep it small."

"Your call," Dan says agreeably.

The service is on a sunny Saturday morning, the first Saturday in August, the heat subsiding, the sky cloudless and tender. The only people coming are Emma and Thomas, Uncle Dan and Aunt Sheila. They meet in the vestibule.

Dan has a ham-like face under a full gray beard, and he walks as if every step is too much effort. He must be three hundred pounds. He's wearing a black sports jacket with white open-collar shirt over blue jeans. Sheila looks better, and younger, a small woman with sun-spotted skin and salt-and-pepper hair. She's wearing a knee-length black dress and has a large seahorse tattoo on her calf.

As they chat in the vestibule, Dan tells Emma and Thomas about his motorcycle accident five years ago, a bad one, lucky he lived to tell about it. He hasn't worked since. He's on Social Security now. Sheila still works, manages a Dunkin'.

All four sit in the front pew. Emma's back feels surprisingly good against the straight back of the hard wooden pew. Sunlight filters in through stained glass windows. Organ music drones. There are no remains—Emma didn't want a cardboard box at the service, so it's at the cemetery.

The priest begins the mass—*In the name of the Father, the Son, and the Holy Spirit*—and Emma closes her eyes, thinks of home, thirty years earlier, the smell of garlic and oregano wafting through the kitchen, her mom busy at the stove in her apron. Her mom was always busy.

Then her dad. There aren't memories like that, none that she can pull up simply by closing her eyes and wishing for them. It's one of the reasons she agreed so readily to go to confession yesterday—she wanted to let it all out, to someone, even a young priest she hardly knows who's behind a screen in a darkened box. After she confessed that she hasn't been to mass in many years, she confessed that she feels no love for her very own father, and when life dealt its harshest blows and left them alone together, she did what she could, but she couldn't take him back into her life, except for that one morning a week. Care packages, that's all.

He was hard to love, closed-minded and crude. But she wants to feel something for him, even if it's not love. He was a working-class guy who had a hard life, endured the daily drudgery of driving a beer truck, lost touch with his only sibling, lost his wife too soon and his mind along with her. Emma wishes he'd had a better life—that's what she told the priest in the confessional, really wishes he'd had a better life. Maybe then he'd been a better person.

"That's empathy," the priest said. "You feel empathy for him."

"Yes," Emma said, and she found it consoling to hear someone like him articulate it. "I suppose I do."

When the mass is over—*Go in peace, and glorify the Lord by our life*—Emma walks out into the Pennsylvania sunshine holding Thomas's hand. They drive to the cemetery, just the four of them, Emma and Thomas and her aunt and uncle, plus the priest, for a brief burial service. Emma's eyes are dry and clear, but her Aunt Sheila tears up.

Afterward, Uncle Dan says he and Sheila are hitting the road, driving back to North Carolina. He hugs Emma, gives Thomas a fist-bump. Stay in touch, he says.

***

"Can we stop for ice cream?" Thomas asks on the drive home.

Emma's first instinct is to say no, it's not appropriate right now, but she quickly reconsiders. Why not? After all, Thomas was a perfect little gentleman throughout the services, and in the absence of a wake, they should at least get the chance to sit down together over some ice cream, mother and son.

"Yes," she says. "I think that's a splendid idea."

She knows where he wants to go, because they're about to drive by it: Strawbaker's, a family-owned staple of Cumberland's Main Street since the 1960s. They've been there twice recently, so Thomas knows it by now.

She parks and they stroll inside. The place looks much like it did when Emma was a girl, with a Formica countertop and Pepsi-Cola sign above the counter listing the flavors, and two teenagers scooping ice cream from round containers. Thomas chooses a waffle cone with chocolate chip and sprinkles; Emma chooses a dish with butter pecan.

They sit out front at one of the sidewalk tables underneath an umbrella. It's nice here, a shady spot on a clear and windless day, and as she digs into her butter pecan with her spoon, Emma recognizes the tastes and smells of her girlhood. Remembers coming here as a little girl with her mom, then as a teenager after high school football games. She's glad to be here, glad this place has endured. Throughout the decades, as various ice cream chains have sprung up in the shopping centers of outlying townships, they've managed to stay.

Emma's staying, too, with her son. She knows that now: This place where she was born and raised, where she brought her son when she had nowhere else to go. Her present and her past and all of her promise may have collided here in these few difficult months, but it's okay. She's doing the best she can, fighting the battles she has to fight, and figuring things out, who she is and who she wants her son to be.

She's an advocate, a teacher, a mother, an only child raising an only child, and they're in this alone, the smallest of families. He's a remarkable boy, smart and personable and resilient, and she has reason to believe he'll grow into a remarkable man. She must be doing something right. Maybe she doesn't fit here perfectly, but she fits in her own way. It's not a perfect place, but she's part of it, and she's doing her small part to make this little corner or the world a better place, and besides, where is there a perfect place? Especially in a world that's been rocked by a cacophony of ignorance, coarseness, hostility, paranoia, and polarization. And now, even if this place is strained by the tension between the old and the new, the good and the bad, she wants to be part of the good and the new.

Sunlight reflects off the windows of the hardware store across the street. That store has endured, too, been there for decades, battling the big-box stores. It's not easy, Emma knows, enduring like that. She might not be a businesswoman, but yeah, she knows.

She licks the last of her butter pecan off her plastic spoon, stares pensively down Main Street, where not all of the businesses have hung on. There are vacant storefronts between the pizza place and the nail salon, between the law office and the Army-Navy store, between the dry cleaner and the newly opened Thai restaurant.

"Are you sad?" Thomas asks.

"Yes, it's a sad day," she says, yet she's impressed by his insight. She manages a smile and says, "But I'm really glad I have you."

He bites into his cone, and a smudge of ice cream lingers below his lip.

"I'm really glad I have you, too," he says.

Her smile broadens, because she knows those words will stick with her for the rest of her life.

ABOUT THE AUTHOR

Richard Fellinger is an award-winning author, former journalist, and longtime college writing instructor. He is the author of two previous novels *Summer of '85* and *Made To Break Your Heart* and a story collection *They Hover Over Us*. He is the winner of the Serena McDonald Kennedy Award and the Thomas E. Kennedy Novel Award. He's also a Pushcart Prize nominee and winner of the Flash Fiction Contest at *Red Cedar Review*. Fellinger lives with his wife in Harrisburg, PA.

www.ingramcontent.com/pod-product-compliance
Lightning Source LLC
Chambersburg PA
CBHW061754190726
48289CB00007B/1945